Dead Easy

Also by E. S. Russell

She Should Have Cried on Monday
Nice Enough to Murder
The Fortunate Island
Death of a Cloudwalker

Dead Easy

E. S. Russell

Walker and Company
New York

Except for Sarah M. Smith, Clerk of Land Evidence, Wakefield Town Hall, Wakefield, Rhode Island, who finds herself temporarily in my home state, the characters in this book are fictitious. Well, Ben F. Louis may or may not be. The returns are not all in yet.

First published in the United States of America in 1992
by Walker Publishing Company, Inc.

Published simultaneously in Canada by Thomas Allen & Son
Canada, Limited, Markham, Ontario

Library of Congress Cataloging-in-Publication Data
Russell, E. S. (Enid S.).
Dead Easy / E. S. Russell.
p. cm.
ISBN 0-8027-3214-3
I. Title.
PS3568.U766D38 1992
813'.54—dc20 91-46498
CIP

Printed in the United States of America
2 4 6 8 10 9 7 5 3 1

For Stan—B.A., M.A., Ed.D., master teacher, counselor, school superintendent, and so much more—of course, and now more than ever.

Part I
Ben

▽

ONE

THE LATE AFTERNOON SUN lay like a friendly arm across Ben Louis's shoulders, but he paid it no heed. (Mistake, Jane would have said. A high school principal needs all the help he can get.)

He stared at the two letters on his desk, once again considered the problems implicit in them, hissed angrily through his teeth, and swiveled around to face the parking lot, possibly in the hope of seeing at least one solution there. But there was only his ancient Ford, alone and stubbornly dull in the sunlight. Annoyed afresh, he whirled around again and gingerly picked up one letter as if it were infected.

It was a mess of inkstains and bad grammar, but its import was clear enough to cost a good man like Merran Shaw his job and his career, and the Manton Public School System its first and perhaps its last school psychologist. Any more letters like it, and the entire guidance program, that most vulnerable department of public schools, could go down the drain.

The sun slipped off Ben's back like a scarf that someone had tweaked away. He shivered and threw down the letter. Like so many that had reached his office over the years, it was unsigned. Unlike them, its errors seemed deliberate.

I wouldn't go so far as to make book on it, he thought, his fine brown eyes narrowing in concentration, but it smacks of disaffected parents who don't like Merran but aren't decent enough to come right out and say so—literately. Now, who . . . ? Any particular family he's been having trouble with?

Another, if understandable, mistake. Whenever a member of his staff was being gunned down, Ben naturally assumed, as would every other school administrator, that a furious parent had his finger on the trigger. He would have had to be a very different sort of person to suspect that the attack was a red herring of a sort—and, accidentally, a prelude to arson, murder, more murder, and more arson.

He sighed and for the tenth time that day picked up the second letter. Just then the phone rang. He wasn't in the mood to talk to anyone, and he wouldn't have had to if the office staff hadn't scooted out at four. (Some people know when to quit, Jane would have said.)

"*What?*" he barked into the speaker.

"Is that your final answer or would you like more time to think it over?" Mack Post said, laughing.

Mack Post and Ben had been friends since college; Mack's consulting firm was handling the Manton School Committee's search for a new superintendent; and Alfred Elderkin, a former U.S. commissioner of education, presently professor emeritus of education at Boston University, and once Ben and Mack's department chairman, had proposed Ben's name as a candidate for Manton's top school post. These facts were overwhelmingly significant to Mack. He laughed happily.

"Think what over?" Ben said sourly.

"You didn't get my letter? Gee whiz, it went out a week ago."

"Oh, I got it." It was, in fact, in his hand.

"Well?"

"I don't know, Mack. It's tough enough being a high school principal in a town like this. Why would I want to be a superintendent—here or anyplace else? Not that I haven't thought of it now and then. Wish Elderkin had kept his mouth shut. He's complicating my life."

"Don't tell me you're offended because he thinks well of you. Or is ambition for or in a good man a criminal trait?"

"Well, I wouldn't go that far—"

"That's something, anyway. Look. We've finally got a short list of four candidates. I can't tell you who they are, but I can say you're the best of the lot, by very far. That should help you make up your mind one way or the other. And the School Committee's getting antsy, Ben. A word to the wise. Talk to you later."

Ben locked up his office and headed for his car. I'll decide over the weekend, he thought. Depends on what Jane thinks, as much as anything. And I'll talk to Merran. Whatever's going on with him, I'm sure it can be straightened out.

He was wrong. (And not for the last time, Jane would have said, had she known anything about it.)

▽

TWO

IN THE STILL AIR of early morning the flag on the town hall common drooped at half-staff, mourning as well as announcing the newly deceased.

Ben paused to wonder what town VIP had kicked the bucket this time, there having been four such punters in the last six months. Pity having to go now, when the Norway maples circling the common glowed scarlet, and a giant purple beech, like a very king attended by his ministers, spread and spread its royal robes.

Next Ben considered the small stubby-nosed cannons (said to have been with Israel Putnam's command in Cambridge in 1775) which, with their pyramids of rough black balls, flanked and guarded the flagstaff.

Then he admired, as he never failed to do when in the neighborhood, the antique building beyond the flagstaff. Had he not been a New Englander by birth and breeding, he would assuredly have been one by conviction—his undergraduate and doctoral majors encompassing American history from 1600 to 1880—and he loved the structure that stood so proud and self-contained in its white clapboards, its landscaping a skirt of swept cobbles instead of unkempt shrubbery, its narrow steeple not (in his wry view) so much aspiring to Heaven as sternly challenging it in typically uncompromising Yankee fashion to deliver the goods.

He laughed softly to himself over the unintentional play on words, acknowledged the unwisdom of trying its lovely subtlety on Jane, and walked on, but slowly, doubtful of the benefit of swimming for exercise before school or at any other time. Which doubt explained why Merran Shaw and Rebecca—Becca—Holdridge, the high school music teacher, his close friends as well as his colleagues, who had urged him to swim daily for his life, had not called for him on their way to swim for theirs. (Unless you get out of the ed biz, why bother? Jane would have said.) Rounding a bend in the road, he saw them now and hurried to catch up.

The two younger people were next-door neighbors who had grown up together in Manton's small, beautiful historic district. Except for their university years and the odd vacation, they were as much town fixtures as the cannons on the town hall grass. The disadvantages of such status were sometimes weighty, but to choose to exchange them for others elsewhere would be viewed as disloyal and therefore well-deserving of the pain of departure. And there would be pain: something comparable to amputation without anesthesia. (Whereas Ben and Jane Louis, after twenty years in Manton, had not been, and never would be, granted full citizenship, having come *from away*: *away* being a town immediately east of Manton on the Boston Post Road.)

"Who's the flag for this time?" Ben said, joining them. "You hear anything?"

Becca said, "No, Ben, I haven't." Her voice was rough and deep, a "whiskey" voice that had ruled out a singing career. It was, she had thought at sixteen, like being born with one foot and then finding that to live is to dance. Now a fine pianist and an exceptional teacher, she put aside the second serious disappointment in her life as resolutely and as privately as she had the other, sixteen years before, and got on with it. After all, a man was free to love whom *he* chose.

"Wouldn't be surprised if it were the Superintendent,"

Merran said glumly. "He didn't look too swift last time I saw him. I hear you're bucking for his job, Ben. Why? A superintendency's a killer, strictly a no-win situation in any town, even for a man who likes a challenge."

Ben was annoyed but not surprised. Except for the maintenance staff, he had been alone in the school yesterday afternoon when Mack Post called; in the privacy of his study Jane had unenthusiastically typed his formal letter of application to Mack the Headhunter; and like a thief he had slipped out under the stars to put the long white envelope into the letterbox in front of his house. But the bush telegraph is no less lively in Massachusetts than in the wilds of Africa, and he knew that speculation about his chances, and the merits and demerits thereof, was all over town, like an epidemic.

"Something just occurred to me," he said, sidestepping Merran's question, which Merran had answered to his own satisfaction anyway. "The flag'll dip for you two some day. But why the Cemetery Board? Why not the Conservation Commission? Or the Arts Council? I've never understood this."

Becca laughed. "Too serious for me, those people."

Merran said, "I was dragooned. Made the mistake of going to the memorial service for an old family friend who'd been on the board with Guy McKay and Bec. They needed a third body, as it were, to take his place, so they filed nomination papers on me and got me elected before I'd dried my eyes. Modern press gang's what they are."

There being no sidewalks in Manton's historic district, or indeed in much of the town, he scuffed along moodily in the road, kicking up geysers of dusty leaves. Ben and Becca walked more comfortably on the grass, under a canopy of maples.

Ben laughed. "Yes, well, I hear you three knock back plenty of Martell at your meetings. Which must ease the pain. Speaking of pain reminds me, Merran. I've had a letter—"

Before he could say more about the hate mail or ask

Merran why he seemed so depressed, Everett Upham, who had recently settled in Manton, fell into step with them. Lunging boisterously, his ninety-five-pound boxer Gifford knocked Merran down onto a bed of leaves and held him there with one huge paw, grinning like a triumphant gladiator.

"Jesus Christ, Giff! Not now!" Merran shoved him away and got up painfully. "What the hell! I'm supposed to go to work in these clothes! For godsake, Ev!"

Everett Upham had his own preoccupation. "A nice thing to do, I always think, Merran? Ben?" he said, characteristically half-asking, pointing to the flag. "A pleasant gesture. They'll lower the flag for you someday, Merran. And you too, Ben, if you get the superintendency? My word! I expect you're looking forward to running the whole ship, eh? I can appreciate that. Nothing in the world like being at the top, busy all day and all night and people at you constantly. Absolutely nothing!"

Ben grunted noncommittally. He was thinking smugly that Fee, a much bigger dog than Gifford, had long ago decided for himself that such behavior was lowering. Then he wondered why Everett had for the second time pointedly ignored Becca.

Still irritably occupied with brushing himself off, Merran made no answer.

"My goodness," Everett said. "Don't you want to be remembered? I want people to make a fuss about me when I pass away. A retirement dinner and a set of golf clubs aren't in the same league, believe me. In that connection, Merran," as they came to the cemetery, "about my burial—when the time comes—"

"With public mechanical tears?" Merran interrupted crankily. "And the campaign for a special election already going on before you're cold in your grave? Well, if that's what you want, Ev, you'll have to get into office first."

They walked, silenced by his crankiness, along the cemetery's low drywall. Beyond it, under May-green grass and new-fallen oak leaves as warm and puffy as a copper-colored quilt, slept Manton's dead. Near the rusted open gates stood a little building of quarried granite where funeral parties gathered and where Merran, Becca, and Guy McKay met on cemetery business. The ground rolled gently uphill and as gently down the other side to another perfect drywall and the soft folds of the country club golf course beyond.

They approached a vacant and valuable acre that abutted the cemetery. Merran eyed it hungrily.

"Merran, I want to talk with you about my burial plot," Everett said. "I'm the last of my line, you know, and I'd like to be with all the rest—you know, when the time comes?"

"I think your family plots are filled, Ev. In fact we've only got about twenty double lots—all reserved—left in the whole place. One of my several problems."

It should be your worst, Ben thought, and couldn't have known that it wasn't.

"But if the town buys this acre—" Everett said.

"Ev, get real. The town voted twice against buying it, and now some private party has a lock on it, I'm not sure who. Haven't been able to pry any information out of anybody. All I can say is, if it's still available by the next town meeting, which is doubtful, and if the Fin Com torpedoes it a third time, which is not, they can string your name in neon lights all over that flag when you kick the bucket but you'll have to be buried someplace else even if you're senior selectman by then. Okay, let's get with it. I should've been halfway through my laps by now."

Everett whistled, Gifford heeled, and the five crossed the road to a brick-ender (home of Dr. Josiah Bennett, 1740) facing the empty acre. To the town's intense chagrin, this fine residence now housed a business devoted to swimming and sports gear. In back of it was a cinderblock building containing a big swimming pool. Not that you can see how ugly it is, the Historical Society said, what with the landscaping John Chester did—we'll give him credit for that—but still, sneaking it in the way he did just before the town got a planning and zoning commission—!

"If I really thought there was a chance of that," Everett said, "of not being in my proper place, I mean, I think I'd—I'd—well, I don't know what I'd do!" He turned for another look at the empty lot, which was scattered with oaks and boulders and purple asters. "Maybe whoever does buy it will sell me just enough to let me in. Up there," pointing. "Then . . . then we'll all be together."

Everett's monomania, his inexplicable snubbing of Becca Holdridge, and Merran's uncharacteristic surliness were spoiling Ben's bid for mental and physical health. Sorry that he had bothered coming, he followed them around the old house to the pool building: John Chester, understandably, didn't like people trooping through his shop unless they bought something.

Blair Bush, a town selectman and an insurance agent with a big Boston firm, followed Ben into the men's dressing room, tiptoeing to avoid getting his trouser cuffs wet. Totally involved with himself, he undressed standing on a bench, hung his silver-gray suit, broadcloth shirt, and Harvard tie on fine hangers, covered his lean loins with a pink and blue bikini, adjusted his goggles on his little white cap, showered, and, still on tiptoe (an eighteenth-century dandy could have used those calves of his, Ben thought) went out to the pool before Ben had shucked his underwear.

The shower drain was stopped up, and scummy water stood inches deep on the stall floor. Opposite, over a thimble-size sink, was a mirror as big as a postage stamp. On the wall between sink and shower was an electrical outlet, the only one in the room.

"Cheeseparing fool, that John Chester," Everett grumbled, putting a reluctant foot into the shower. "It's unbelievable—such a magnificent pool, and this inadequate room! He should have put that outlet far away from water. It's dangerous. And this shower—incredibly unhygienic!"

"So tell him," Merran said.

"I have! He brushed me off. Well, I'm going to tell him again, right now, and if he isn't in the office, I'll wait. God knows I've got the time. We pay enough not to have to put up with this." He draped a towel over his shoulders and flip-flapped out in his sandals, then came back. "Oh, Merran, in case I don't see you before you leave, are we still on for this afternoon? I've really been looking forward to it—got a new mashie I'd like to try out."

"Don't think I can, Ev. Not today. I just don't feel up for it. And I've got a load of reports to write."

Everett nodded shortly and went out.

Merran said, "I'm not sure running for office would be the best solution for what ails him. And he'll lose John's vote if he drips on his floor."

Ben regarded the shower with disfavor. "What does ail him? I don't know him as well as you do."

"Oh . . . displacement, for one thing. Retirement, for another, which is probably responsible for the displacement. He's a nice guy. Well-spoken, well-dressed, well-heeled, loves this town—knows more about it than people who haven't been away in thirty years. But there's something off-putting about him, Ben. Can't put my finger on it. All I know is, he hasn't a hope of getting elected to anything. People just don't cotton to him. You know this town—practically the same people in the same offices, year after election year. People who are *known*. But he told me he and his mother moved out almost sixty years ago, when he was about ten, and his collateral relatives are all gone. Nobody's around who knows anything about him or them anymore. That wouldn't matter so much if he could connect with people on his own, but he can't, and beefing up his Boston Brahmin accent won't do it, either. Notice how it got more pronounced just now? Too bad he doesn't have a wife or even a cousin to make connections for him."

"You're doing a pretty good job."

"Believe me, I didn't volunteer for that, either. You'd think I didn't have anything else to do but play golf with him every day. He says he knew Dad when they were kids. Since he's been back, he's presumed upon the fact."

"Ah. Good man. You've been reading Dickens."

"*Nicholas Nickleby.* How'd you know? Whenever I want to get my head straight, I read Dickens."

Blair Bush had not closed the door to the pool, and through it now came the cool reedy sound of a recorder playing a sinuous Oriental melody. Merran uttered something unprintable and flung his clothes into a locker.

Dickens doesn't seem to be helping, Ben thought, and when the recordist switched to "Bring On the Clowns," maliciously keeping time with Merran's every step out of the dressing room and accompanying his hasty dive into the water with a descending *glissande,* Ben began to worry anew about his school psychologist (and then about himself: almost the very worst thing that can happen to a school administrator is to lose, for any reason, a valued staffer).

The musician was Val Elliot, who not only had figured prominently in Merran's life for the past few months but also worked for the local paper and covered the schools like a tent. She came lithely out of the lotus position and made for Ben, a sea sprite in her green bikini, her pale hair foaming around her narrow elegant face like the edge of a wave.

Even for Val this is going too far, Ben thought, struggling with the cap, which was old and sticky and wouldn't open. "I'm off duty, Val," he said, backing up to the edge of the pool.

She laughed. "Here or in your office, what's the difference? And don't fall in without a cap on, or you'll hear from John. Tell me, how long have you had your eye on the top spot? Have you and the Superintendent talked about your taking over? What changes do you have in mind? How would you resolve the growing opposition to Merran Shaw? Don't you agree that this poses a threat to the whole guidance program? Does the Moral Majority know about Merran and me?"

She laughed again as the cap tore in Ben's hands.

"Sorry, Val," he said, "time presses," and ran like a rabbit to the shop door, conscious of her mocking eyes on his all too rapidly aging body.

Expecting to see Everett having it out with John, he walked

instead into an ear-scorching argument between John and someone whose voice he recognized but whom he couldn't see. "Sorry, John—just need a cap—get it myself—pay later—"

Val was back on the bench playing her recorder, which sounded indescribably dreadful in the huge tiled space, and Merran's attack on the water was murderous.

Talk about displacement, Ben thought, pulling and stretching the cap, which John Chester, missing not a step in his argument, had told him to pay for on his way home. Obedient to one rule, he put it on, then broke another by diving in without checking the traffic. He slammed into someone, and his weight sent them both to the bottom.

It was Becca, generous and pink and without vanity in a flea-market bathing suit. She blinked and coughed, and Tah-rah-rah-BOOM-dee-ay issued from the recorder. "Did I—did I—hurt you, Ben? I'm so sorry—" she spluttered.

"My fault entirely, Bec. Guess I didn't look where I was going."

After a quarter-mile of surprisingly competent lapping, he heaved himself up the ladder and headed panting for the dressing room, thinking to preserve his hard-won sense of well-being by dressing as fast as possible and leaving behind Merran's moodiness, Val's nastiness, Everett's monomania, and John Chester's parsimony. Anyway, because of the cap business he was already late for school—a second reason to eschew another shower. All the same, he sat down on a bench—not, he told himself, to rest and get his breath but to dry his feet.

From where he sat he could not see that water was covering the floor between shower and sink and that Blair Bush, dressed now except for his jacket, was standing in it, trouser cuffs turned up, and artfully drying his long thick hair with a professional electric dryer and a special brush.

A commotion of barking and shouting outside brought Ben to his feet to see what was happening. Bush smiled faintly at his reflection in the tiny mirror as he swept the brush through his thick waves.

Gifford the boxer bounded in, joyous and soaking wet. Seeing Bush first, he cannoned into him, knocking him out of his trance. Bush staggered backward and fell over the high lip of the shower stall, landing solidly on his behind, still holding the brush and the dryer, his hands and feet up in the air.

Gifford danced from sink to shower and back again, barking in delight, and then Bush put both hands down in the water to right himself, and Ben saw the well-dressed body stiffen and convulse and flop about and then lie still while the pants darkened steadily around the waist and down the legs and the long hair floated lazily on the scummy wavelets and the expression of angry astonishment froze in the open eyes.

And Ben thought idiotically, They can't lower the flag for him, it's already down for somebody else.

▽

THREE

"HE DAMN NEAR KNOCKED me down," John Chester kept saying. "Went right by me when I opened the side door. It wasn't my fault. God. God. Just roared right past me and bang in the pool and then in the dressing room. Never saw anything like it, way he flew out of that pool. Goddam dog just went right by me."

He paced back and forth, slightly bent at the waist, wringing his hands, his gait heavy for so small a man, his flat feet wide apart as if he were straddling something; or as if, Ben thought, there were something nasty between his legs.

The body had been removed, the police and everyone else had gone, the pool and shop were closed, Gifford was tied up outside, and Ben, Merran, and Everett remained immobilized in John's office, chewing the matter over and over.

"It's possible I didn't close the door all the way, but the dog isn't liable, for godsake," Ben said for the last time, preparing to get up and leave. "Everett may be."

John gave Everett a cold bitter look. "Damn right he is. You're responsible for him, you should leave him home where he belongs, big dog like him. I don't drag my dog around, I keep him home where a dog should be, tied up. A dog should be treated like a dog."

"I agree," Everett said. "A dog *should* be treated like a dog, not an object that lives on the end of a chain. Dogs need space, they need company and a change of scene, like all intelligent—"

"Then tie that monster up when you take him here!"

"I don't have to tie him. He's almost five years old. When I tell him to stay, he'll stay if the house is burning down around his head."

"You're telling me I'm a liar, is that it?"

"I'm telling you I know my dog."

Ben said, "You're both responsible. Everett, either leave Gifford home or tie him at least for his own safety when you leave him alone anywhere. He may be well-trained, but he's still too young to be trusted as entirely as you do. As for you, John, no wiring inspector would okay the arrangement in that dressing room and you know it, and I wonder how you got away with it—and who did such a job for you. You have the wrong type of outlet so close to a sink. It wants a ground and its own fuse—"

"That's what I told him," Everett interrupted angrily. "If he'd listened to me the first time I mentioned it, none of this would have happened even if a herd of elephants had come in there." To Ben he seemed upset more because his advice had been ignored than by the tragic, useless, stupid death he had missed witnessing. "Someday, John, you're going to save one penny too much. I wouldn't be surprised if it's the one you keep in your fuse box!"

Ben said, "You can be sued, John, do you realize that? You stand to lose everything you've got if the Bush family takes you to court. I hope they do."

John looked scared. "No one's ever said anything about the setup in there."

"Christ! Is that a reason?" All at once Ben had had enough of them and of this place. Exercise was all very well in its way, but if he ever did any more swimming, it wouldn't be here. He picked up his things and left without another word, nor did he acknowledge Merran, who roused himself from his sullen silence and followed.

They found Becca Holdridge leaning sadly against the door, her curly wet hair combed for the first and last time that day. "I simply didn't want to be in there. I thought you'd never come out." The tears in her dark blue eyes gleamed in the sun. "Blair was a distant cousin of mine, did you know? It's somewhere on our family tree. I haven't looked at it since Mother and Dad died. Now I—I have to bring it up to date again," she said heartbrokenly.

Ben put an arm around her ample shoulders, thinking how right it was that her generous spirit was expressed in every part of her. "He was lucky in the connection. And in addition to that, a nice guy and a good selectman. I'm sorry, Bec." He bent and kissed her cheek, her skin white as paper with a red patch in the middle, like rouge inexpertly applied.

She sighed. "School's been open since eight, and we're just standing here."

"I called in," Merran said. "Nobody's expecting us. How about we get some meatball subs and go to the beach—or go to the sanctuary and watch the geese practice for the big push. We're entitled. All that trauma. How about it?"

"Mm," Ben said vaguely.

"Fine models you make for the young," Becca said, half smiling.

Merran said fiercely, "They'll survive. Wish I were as sure I would. I'll be damned if I go to school today. Waiting for me there are a broken home, a cerebral palsy, and a common-law marriage-cum-illegitimacy. Plus an afternoon and evening in my office of plenty more. But I have had a sufficiency lately of anger, bitterness, guilt, grief, unrequited love, and all the rest of it, and I am dealing myself out for now. I don't care what happens to any of them, and even if I did, what does life hold for them? What future can they carve out for themselves with their damaged hands and broken hearts? To hell with it. I'm going for a walk." He looked up at the bright blue sky, which was rapidly becoming smeared with clouds. "Besides, we ought to take advantage. There's going to be weather tomorrow. If you're coming, come. If not, not."

Becca sighed again. "Better not. The idea fills me with such joy that right away I know it's wrong." But she did not hurry her step.

Ben laughed gently. "Bec, you have the nicest superego in the world." His own could bear monitoring, he thought, recalling how he had hastened out of the dressing room as much to get away from the man who had died virtually at his feet as to discharge telephonically his civic and professional duties. There had been a certain bleak satisfaction in dripping all over John's immaculate floors.

They crossed the road, walked by the empty acre, and went along the cemetery wall. Dry leaves floated over it and crunched satisfyingly under their feet.

Of one accord they turned in at the gatehouse and wandered among the nearest plots. These were almost three hundred years old, older than the town itself. The velvety slates and chalky marbles, even the iron or other metal blackened by time, seemed to have melted, and many names and dates, death's heads and inscriptions were almost illegible. Too many markers were tiny and blank.

"Infants died so easily in those parlous days, it wasn't worth the bother to record their names," said Ben the historian. "If they'd been given any."

Becca's forebears: Holdridge. Ames. Merchant. Tower. Angell. "As often as I come here," she said, her deep rasp softened, "I still wonder about them. My blood relatives, poor forgotten mites. There are more of us farther up."

The roads in this part of the cemetery described a capital A with a square top and two crossbars. They walked slowly up one leg of the A.

Bush. Platt. Furneaux. Thorne. Gilbert.

"Blair'll be here," Becca said. "Between the Bushes and the Platts. There's plenty of room. Poor Blair, he was only fifty. He said only the other day that he was enjoying getting old. But then, he enjoyed everything."

But not his dying, Ben thought.

In a softened elegiac mood they walked more slowly.

Wilder. Upham. Lofts. And, like other old families, mixed up in so many combinations.

"But no room for Everett Wilder Upham, the last of a long attenuated line," Merran said unfeelingly, breaking the mood.

"Merran, look at that. I've never seen that before, have you?" Becca said, pointing to a small oval metal plaque, ornate with curlicues and dark green with age, that was fastened with screws to an Upham stone above the chiseled name Honora. The screws were shiny new, which was why she had noticed it.

"Anybody got a dime?" Merran said. Ben jingled the change in his pocket; handed him one. He applied it to the screws, removing one and letting the cover swing down from the other. "Oh boy!" he said, in the tone of one who makes an unwelcome discovery.

Ben stepped back. Whatever this one was, to whomever it pertained, he didn't want to know anything about it. The perfection of a fair New England day had been tainted enough already. And there was now a bite in the breeze, and the sunlight felt like winter sunlight, golden bright but coolly distant. He shivered, more shaken than he cared to admit by the events of the morning. There was only one thing to do—go home to Jane. Without a word, without even being noticed, he walked rapidly in that direction.

I'll call Merran tomorrow morning, he told himself. Take him out for lunch. Won't bother him with that letter, though. Guess my imagination's just been working overtime, like the rest of me. I'm sure everything's okay.

Perfectly understandable reflections and decisions. Only later did he wonder if he had been wrong.

Indeed he had been. It was equally true, though, that any other reflections and decisions would not have made the least bit of difference anyway.

▽

FOUR

IF I HAVE TO exercise, goddammit, Ben thought, early the next morning, standing sideways to the mirror and sucking in his gut, I'll walk. Cheaper and easier than swim—

Uh-oh. I owe John for that cap.

He let out his breath in a resentful *whooosh* directed at his wife and Fee, who smiled sweetly in their sleep, and reached for clean underwear. But as he dressed, he began, deep inside himself, to laugh and to give thanks for Jane, whose once-cropped hair now flowed over the pillows and who, in her late forties, was still as slender as an asparagus under the quilt, and for Fee, who lay determinedly on top of it looking like a great baked yam with mysterious appendages.

The glacially tormented terrain within a modest radius of his house was daunting, and he sighed at the prospect of tackling the harder half of Seven-Mile Hill, turning onto Adams Lane, which snaked up, down, and around like a roller coaster, then making the dizzying descent of Konomoc Road, and so home. He would pass Holdridge and Shaw, come close to Chester and near to Upham. How many miles would he cover—four? five? Anyway, enough.

The morning was clear and autumn-fragrant, the sun a pink glow in the trees when he shut the back door softly behind him. He yawned comprehensively, wishing he had slept better and longer. He was still concerned about Merran Shaw. He reviewed briefly other worrisome matters peculiar to public education. He mocked himself for even considering the superintendency, let alone actively seeking it. But he was grimly determined to be healthy so as to be up for the several catastrophes that stud the superintendent's professional and private life—in the event, he explained to himself, only in the event. So he took his pulse, then set forth, swinging his arms and breathing deeply.

Puffing and grunting, sweating profusely, resigned to another shower and more clean underwear, and convinced that the sole benefit in exercise was the discovery that there was none, he turned onto Adams Lane—and stopped. Coming toward him was a small figure in a designer jogging outfit and surmounted by a Medusa head of bobbing sausages tied up in curling ribbons.

Nora Chester. Twin to Val Elliot in gratuitous nastiness, which in Ben's view canceled any virtues they possessed and denied them any sympathy they might be entitled to.

Nora blocked his way, jogging easily in place and laughing at his unconcealed chagrin. Her skin was smooth and dewy, her breathing even, her eyes bright with malice. "You owe John three dollars and seventy-eight cents for a swim cap, Ben. You can't get out of it by walking instead of swimming." Her breasts bounced under the fantastic animals painted on the sweatshirt. He couldn't pull his eyes away.

She laughed softly. "Martha Burch. California artist. Like it?"

"Very fetching." He made to go around her, but she matched her steps to his as in a dance.

"John says it's free advertising for the shop. He likes me to take a different route every few days. You know what that bastard does? Makes me pay for these outfits out of my housekeeping money! Do you think that's fair?"

"I think that what I think isn't important, Nora. Now if you don't mind—"

"A Ben Louis statement if ever I heard one. You were always the careful one, Benjamin Franklin Louis. The judicious one. And the tallest, the darkest, the handsomest, the classiest. If I were Jane, I'd never let you out of my sight without a leash. What did she ever do to be so lucky? Do you want to know what *I* think—about that bastard I married and all the men I—"

All at once the malice and anger went out of her like water down a drain. The world froze into place. Then she sprang at him like a tiger, locking him in an unbreakable iron vise, arms around his neck, legs around his waist, strong hands grasping his hair and pulling his head down. Fiercely, hungrily, she kissed him, mashing his lips against his teeth, forcing his mouth open and exploring it with her demanding tongue while he stood helpless, arms at his sides, feeling nothing but revulsion.

A car chugged up the hill and stopped inches from them. The driver playfully tooted the horn, and Ben blushed as Nora released him and turned around.

The driver was Geraldine Carr, once a member of Ben's staff, now a vice principal in Westwood. "Hi, guys. Hey, love that shirt, Nora. A Burch, right? She's marvelous. Any more like it? I must get down to the shop one of these days."

Perfectly poised, Nora laughed. "You've been saying that for two years, Ger."

"This time I mean it, honest. I'll drop by some night on my way home. Provided I survive the traffic on 128. Okay, guys, south to the salt mines." She waved and disappeared around the curve.

Nora smiled up at Ben. "Guess I better be on my way too," she said breezily, and then her face crumpled and she ran off sobbing.

He stood shaken and nauseated, trying to spit out the inside of his mouth. He scrubbed it, and his lips, with his handkerchief, which he then dropped onto the road and walked away from. If exercise paid off in death, fury, passion, and littering, to hell with it.

Then he yawned until his jaw cracked and his eyes watered. Oh boy, it's a bad sign—I'm whacked before I start, he thought.

Ben might at least have slept a little better had he known that Merran Shaw, after eating meatball subs in the sanctuary with Becca Holdridge, had given her a leisurely, expensive dinner and had then gone home and bundled Val Elliot's possessions out of his house and into her apartment, waking her up to say they were through.

These sensible acts improved neither Merran's sleep nor his morale, and when Ben called him later in the morning, his furious "Yes, what!" came snarling over the wire.

"Oof!" Ben grunted, massaging his ear. "Look, I'll be free at one. How about I buy you a lunch? You've been sounding bent out of shape lately. Oh, and by the way, in case you still don't know, it was Carl Baker who died, and Everett's going to run for his seat on the Fin Com. He just stopped by to ask me to sign his petition. He's following your advice and running for the right to have the flag lowered when his time comes, as he put it. And Val Elliot is masterminding his campaign. He's very pleased and optimistic."

"Oh? Well now. Bully for Val and Everett."

"He also said George Taylor and John Chester were locking the barn door, as it were—bellowing at each other this morning about a wiring estimate for the dressing room. You didn't go today? Too bad. George called John a pennypinching crud who puts copper pennies in his fuse box, et cetera et cetera. I heard an earlier installment when I went for a cap. Those two old buddies seem to have quite an agenda to plow through when they get together, much of it cryptic, from what Everett told me."

"Well, he hasn't told me yet, so go ahead. Divert me. Cryptic is fun."

"That's a matter of opinion. George said—to John—'Now

that Blair's dead, you'll no doubt fish for an appointment to fill out his term. Nothing like being an incumbent when an election comes around. Saves money on campaigning.'

"John said he wasn't interested in selectman, that he was going after Carl Baker's seat because the best way to make policy was through—what else?—money!"

"Nothing cryptic about that."

"I'm not finished yet. Then, Everett said, John peered up at George and said, 'You look a mite peaked, fella. Little more strung out than usual? Why don't you get Doris to do you a favor—make you a nice meal, say. That ought to do for what ails you, what with everybody out lately.' They were arguing about house calls when I went in for a cap, I remember. Everett wants to know what's with those two. All I know is they went to school together and that George is the best electrician in town."

"A better electrician than husband or father, if you'll forgive an otherwise ethical person for saying so. What those two were arguing about, though, I don't know and don't care. But if, O Master, I may take a leaf out of your book this early in the day, you're diverting the dickens out of me."

"Not a bad pun, but you've got a way to go. Okay, the rest of the story is that George lifted John up by his shirt, punched him bloody, dropped him on the floor, and took off. Everett helped him up, and by way of thanks John said he was going to make mincemeat of him in the campaign. Everett said he and Val Elliot were going to show *him* a thing or two—and John just laughed while he wiped the blood off his face. And that's the end of that chapter."

"Sorry I missed it."

"Yes, it does make a nice change from education, where all is peace and sweet reason. Okay, come in at one. I want to talk to you about something. I'll order in something bracing. You need it."

"What's the point? None that I've seen for the last two months."

Two months ago Ricky Priest, a senior with whom Merran

had been working intensively for more than a year, had hanged himself in his room.

"The point," Ben said angrily, "the *point* is doing what we're supposed to be doing, as best we can. Which you did with Ricky. Who the hell do you think you are—Super-shrink? Even Freud couldn't win 'em all."

"All right, so I'm arrogant because I think I can. And should. And must. Like all shrinks, even Freud. You ought to know, you were one yourself, if briefly. We *all* believe in our omnipotence and our omniscience. It's implicit in our idiotic assumption that *we* know enough to tell other people how to live better. It's implicit in the hope we bring to every case. We know we shouldn't hope, we're trained not to hope, but we're human and we hope. And the next step's easy because we're also egotistical as hell or we wouldn't be in this racket in the first place, so we do expect to win 'em all. The suicide of a seventeen-year-old boy's a rotten way to learn how wrong we are, how wrongly placed we are. I'm getting out. I've had it."

"Not yet you don't. You have a contract, remember? Heal thyself, doctor. And you can start by getting your ass in here at one."

He put the phone down with a crash. To brandish Merran's contract in his face was only to give him a moral or ethical nudge; the town had no legal hold on him. Had Merran not been so depressed, he would have said so.

Damn it to hell, Ben thought, and turned irritably to his work, which had increased in complicated ways with the transfer of the sixth, seventh, and eighth grades to the high school, whose severely declining enrollment had created a lot of space.

But not all that much, he said, sighing over the cracks that had begun appearing in his dedication to his profession. Where the hell was the sense in upgrading himself from principal to superintendent in Manton or anywhere else? It would bring him more work, more worry, more tension, more money, higher taxes, and no time to smell the roses. He had not told even Jane, but he too had been thinking of quitting. Better call Mack Post, he thought, and take myself out of the running.

I mean, do I *need* this? he asked himself later, after three calls in a row from angry parents. If he had had the time, and a few less urgent things to do that should have been accomplished the day before yesterday, he would have quit on the spot.

In the middle of the morning, his busiest time, George Taylor barged past his three secretaries and into his office.

Taylor was a tense wiry man in his middle forties whose dyed curled hair, stovepipe jeans, brass belt buckle, and high-heeled boots presented an aggressive challenge or an invitation of one kind or another. So did his white van, around whose middle leaped flames of scarlet and orange outlined in black. ("Rorschach card of the month. A virgin being raped by the Devil," Merran said. "Taylor leads an active fantasy life, I'd say.")

"I been wanting to talk to you about what that shrink a yours is up to with my kids," Taylor said nervously, his eyes darting and sliding. He sat down, uninvited.

"Which is what?"

"I want him to go easy on my little girl—"

"Connie is in the middle school," Ben said coldly. "Make an appointment to see *her* principal. You know Mr. Tempesta, of course. And see Dr. Shaw. Now if you'll excuse me—"

"I don't like your attitude, Louis."

"Like you, Mr. Taylor, I see people by appointment. I don't have time for you now."

"Sorry. Guess I should've called. But I was going by and thought if I could just see you for a minute—"

"A minute, then. I really am busy, and I'm trying to prepare for a meeting. What's on your mind?"

"Well . . . why's Shaw riding my family so hard?"

"I'm not aware that he is. All I know is that he has your written permission to see what he can do for your youngest child, who doesn't talk, and also to interview the two older kids, who might be able to help him help her. Frankly, Mr. Taylor, under the circumstances your concern seems to be misplaced."

"I just don't trust shrinks. Don't know anybody who does. So what I want to know is, can you be there when he sees my little Connie? And the other kids? Keep an eye on him, like?"

Ben stared at him. "Mr. Taylor, there are several reasons for observing the professional performance of staff members, but none of them applies to Dr. Shaw at this time, and I have no reason to make such a request of him. It's highly insulting, if nothing else."

"Maybe. But it's either that, or I pull my Connie out of the whole thing." He looked at his watch and jumped up. "Boy, I gotta take off . . ." He went out as hastily as he had come, leaving Ben intensely curious as well as angry. George Taylor was clearly afraid of something.

Becca came in before lunch. "One item, Ben. Connie Taylor apparently doesn't give anything away except when the class sings or listens to records. She sways and hums a little but shuts down if anybody at all makes mention of it. So how about Merran and I doing some music therapy with her alone this afternoon? We've been talking about it, and Bill Tempesta's willing. That is, if you don't mind lending me out."

"I don't know, Bec. Taylor was in this morning. He's afraid play therapy's proving too hard on his little girl, and he doesn't want her to suffer any more than she already has. How, he didn't specify. Under a lot of bad manners he really sounded scared."

"God knows why he should be. Whatever deep dark family secret that child might be hiding, she'll never talk. She enjoys watching everybody trot out all their ploys and gambits to get her talking. It's a big game to her. She's as wily as a hunted animal. Also a master strategist and a malicious tease. Merran's come close to smacking her a time or two, and she knows it."

"How sweet it is to wield power—ask any school administrator. Silence evidently pays bigger and better grats than talking would. Well, I've no objection, but if you don't mind a favor for a favor, I'll have the piano put in Room 113. Nobody's doing any testing or observing in there at the moment, and maybe I can get Taylor off everybody's back if I look in just once, though I can't imagine what he wants me to do. I should have told him no. I'm sorry about this, Bec."

Merran came in, pale and subdued and too late for lunch. Ben, who never noticed that he had worked straight through his own, walked down the corridor with him to Rooms 112 and 113, the upper half of whose shared wall was a one-way mirror.

"That kid's as dumpy and colorless and boneless as a pudding," Merran grumbled as Becca and Bill Tempesta, principal of the relocated middle school, came into view with Connie Taylor in tow. "Never cottoned to her."

"Good. There's nothing in the canon says you have to. So you can expect nothing, hope for nothing. You can be detached and scientific and uninvolved because on one level you don't care. Maybe that'll sharpen your edge."

The child followed Becca Holdridge into the testing room. "Keep me posted," Tempesta told Merran, who nodded and shrugged and closed the door.

Bill Tempesta was a horsey-looking man with long straight silky hair, long thin arms and legs, prominent joints, and a heavy barrel of a body. "That kid sure has fun keeping shut, Ben, I'll tell you that. I've seen her in action. Her classmates're very protective of her, and of course they enjoy the drama of the thing. Wonder if she'll ever let go." His long head lifted and his nostrils quivered as if he were about to neigh.

"Well, fun and dependency aside, Merran has the Taylors' permission to get her talking, but that doesn't necessarily mean she has it too."

"Maybe this approach'll pry her jaws open. Time'll tell." Tempesta was curvetting with anticipation. "Well, if anyone can do it, Merran can. Catch you later, Ben."

Ben went into Room 112, turned on the speaker, and sat down before the special glass. He winced as Becca sang "Hel-lo-oh" and "Good af-ter-noo-oon" in her awful voice and the piano notes ascended brightly, filled all to hell with hope—to Ben the sound of sunlight.

He stayed ten minutes. Merran's voice alternated with, sometimes joined, Becca's. The child sat hunched and motionless in a corner.

"I wonder if it's the best approach," Ben said later. "All your communicating was open and cheerful and trusting—the way communication's *spoze* to be."

"Yeah," Merran said in disgust. "The whole goddam thing sounded like a reproach to the kid."

"Guess we'd better try another tack," Becca said. "We certainly didn't get to her with that one. Maybe she was just scared. It is a new departure, after all. What do you think?"

Merran got up and went to the door. "Oh, we got to her, all right. And of course she's scared. But she's also one very angry little kid. Now if you'll excuse me, I think I'll go get something to eat."

"But how can you tell we got to her, Merran? Once she sat down, she never moved a muscle."

"That's how you can tell." He left before Ben, who had opened his mouth, could say anything else.

Ben spent another troubled night. It began with Everett Upham waking him out of a delicious after-dinner doze in his favorite chair to tell him that John Chester was the buyer of the acre abutting the cemetery and would on no account sell Everett so much as a square inch of it to be buried in.

"Ben, *please* tell John that based on what he paid for that acre, I'll pay him twice the cost of a six-foot strip—so many square yards—I haven't worked it out yet, I'm too upset." He was almost hysterical with rage and grief. "Please, Ben? John will listen to you—everybody does! I have to have my place, Ben! I insist on having my place!"

"What else could I say but yes?" Ben exploded to Jane after putting the phone down.

Then, in the small hours, during an unseasonal thunderstorm accompanied by violent winds, he was awakened again by the faint but unmistakable smell of smoke and the shrilling of fire engines converging on John Chester's house nearby. But any hope of saving one of the town's finest antique houses was defeated by the wind before the firefighters were even in position.

Ben was too tired and troubled by now to care what was burning, provided it was not his bed. He rolled over and fell back into sleep.

▽

FIVE

"I EXPECT YOU KNOW what they're saying about John Chester?" Everett said with relish. "That he moved his family into the apartment over the shop with such dispatch that it looks as if he planned the whole thing for the insurance. That house was worth—at the very least—three hundred fifty thousand."

It was 6:30 in the morning, two weeks after the Chesters' house burned to the ground, and Ben was on his reluctant way—reluctant if only because he was giving up his one free hour in the next eighteen—to ask John to sell a fragment of his new property to Everett. In one of his pockets was the money he owed John for the swimming cap. I'll pay him, I'll ask him, and the hell with him *and* Everett Wilder Upham.

He said, deliberately irrelevant, "Gifford looks terrific, Everett. He'll make a big hit with the voters."

The boxer wore a silk paisley scarf in place of his usual leather collar, and sandwich boards over his sleek ribs, Everett's picture on one, his platform on the other.

"The rascal lost his collar somewhere, but I rather think I'll keep him in silk if you really feel his rig's an asset, Ben? That was a pretty nasty attack on me in the paper, you know. It could only have come from John. My attorney talked with the Bushes after Blair's death, and I don't know if I mentioned this to you, but they're considering taking John to court, not me. They're hardly the sort to pull a cheap, dreadful stunt like that letter. It's really set me back, and Val isn't sure I can recoup."

Everett's campaign for the seat on the Finance Committee had been developing well under Val Elliot's aggressive handling, and he seemed too happy winning back his place in the sun to worry about his hole in the ground. But a week before the Chester fire, a remark about Gifford's part in Blair Bush's death sprang out of nowhere and spread like a disease, followed by a smoothly worded letter to the editor by Name Withheld about dogs and dog owners and responsibility and the lengths to which political ambition could go. People had been listening to Everett, who spoke well, and for a while his victory over John Chester seemed certain, but now voters began backing off as if he had developed a bad smell. And Everett, as if struck by a mortal chill, again begged Ben to speak to John. "He'll certainly appreciate the extra money, given all the things he and Nora will have to replace because of the fire," he said, and Ben could not disagree.

In front of them were Merran and Becca. Merran pulled ahead impatiently as they passed the cemetery. "Right, Ev," he said over his shoulder. "But you can forget about John making money on that fire. You know what the fire marshal said—the thermostat on the heater in the back shed off the kitchen was faulty and didn't shut off, so the wire heated up inside the wall, but the fuse didn't blow because there was a copper penny in the fuse box. John swears he never put it there, but as long as he can't prove it, there won't be any insurance. But don't shoot your mouth off even to us about arson or letters to the paper from John, or you'll find yourself in court facing a charge of slander. And from that, believe me, John could stand to make a very great deal. Now let's for godsake get cracking!"

His mood had worsened, mostly because of his frustration over Connie Taylor, the sixth grader who would not talk. For days he and Becca had sung to each other and the four walls of Room 113, and on the small upright Becca had played anger and sadness and fear and trembling, but the child had made no progress, unless a hardening of her position could be called progress. Merran's attention was centered with an irrational intensity on this child; everything else was trivial. And in any case he had heard all he wanted to hear from Everett about his burial plot. Without another word he swung away from them and went around to the back.

Becca followed him, saying, "Good luck, Everett," but Everett ignored her, as usual, and Ben was tempted to leave him then and there.

Somewhere behind the building a dog barked and barked, the sound desperate, anguished, pleading. Everett's hands trembled as he tied Gifford to a tree. "God!" he said angrily and almost staggered as he stood up. He steadied himself against the tree and breathed deeply, a hand over his eyes.

"What's the matter, Everett?" Ben said. "You all right?"

"No. I'm not all right. It makes me *sick*, Ben, the way they treat that little dog. He could have—"

He stopped and shook his head. "Let's go in." He patted Gifford, then led the way into the shop just as Nora trailed down the stairs from the apartment, stony-faced, pale, and bitter.

John was perched on a ladder, settling the helmet onto a deep-sea diving outfit. Lovingly he twirled the bright brass handles. The puffed arms of the towering figure hung slack. The round face, its three windows black with emptiness, stared blankly at nothing. An impotent giant waiting to be activated.

"Nice, huh?" John said, getting down and shaking his arms after all the reaching and stretching.

"My husband's new friend," Nora said. "I think he's charming. Don't you think he's charming, Ben?"

"No," Ben said flatly. Solid and unflappable—in the full flower of maturity, in fact—he would even now clutch up when one of his movie heroes donned this sinister-looking outfit, as though the danger lay not in bold exploration or perilous rescue but in attracting some arcane oceanic force that would bend him to its evil purpose.

"Come on, Ben, try it on," John said. "It'd fit you just fine."

"You couldn't pay me enough to get in that thing, John. I wouldn't be caught dead in it."

"To each his own. I think he's quite nice, myself. Hello in there," John said, standing tiptoe to tap the front glass and wiggle his fingers at it. "Weighs three hundred pounds fully equipped."

"Impressive," Everett said affably.

John propped the ladder against the wall and put away the pulley and rope with which he had hoisted the suit into place by means of a heavy hook in one of the exposed low beams. With a sensual pleasure he began slipping ten-pound lead weights into the slots around the waist. "You wouldn't believe what this big guy cost me. Got it for a song. Somebody'll buy it before long. First principle of business—buy cheap, sell dear. Well, folks, what can I do for you?"

"*To* you is more like it," Nora said.

And indeed the look in John's eye said plainly that, given a chance, he would ream them properly. Ben wasted no time on amenities but gave him the money he owed for the cap.

"By rights he should charge you interest," Nora said.

Ben ignored this too. "John, I came on Everett's behalf to ask you to sell him a six-foot strip of the land across the way. Right down the boundary."

"Why should I?"

"I told you why," Everett said. "My family plots are full, and I'm the last of the line. You can understand that I want to be buried with them. Look at this, John. I drew it to scale." He took a sheet of graph paper out of his pocket and smoothed it flat on the counter.

The six-foot strip paralleling the boundary line was an insignificant part of the whole, and the coffin-shaped figure within it, halfway up the hill, was virtually invisible. "It'd be dead easy to arrange, John," Everett urged.

"It isn't really much, John," Ben said, "and I can't see that it would make much difference to whatever you plan to do."

"Can't you? Well, you thought wrong. I've got some ideas about that acre—like building a tavern to draw the golfers, provide a function room for funeral parties, that sort of thing. I'd need every single inch for parking and landscaping."

"I can appreciate that—" Everett began hastily.

Ben shook his head. "It's unlikely in the extreme that Planning and Zoning will give you a permit for any business venture there, John. And I think you know that."

"I do, if he doesn't," Nora said, "and I could use the money, John. If you think I'm going to live in that rattrap upstairs with that broken-down junk from Goodwill until you spring for some decent furniture, you can think again."

"We'll get furniture when I'm good and ready. Just forget it, Nora. Keep out of my business."

"Then what do you say to making a little bulge in that wall, John?" Everett said. "It isn't ruler-straight anyway, so a bit of a jog in it wouldn't show. What do you say to that? And I'll pay you the same as if you'd sold me the whole strip."

"I said no and I meant no. Ben, you're a sensible man. Will you explain to this little bastard that I've got too much on my mind to waste any more time on crap like this. I know a good few people in this town who're entitled to a spot in that cemetery that'll have to spend their eternal rest someplace else—and they're not pissing and moaning about it like Everett is. Now, I've got work to do, so if you'll let me get on with it . . ." He went into his office and shut the door.

"Another charmer," Nora said. Adding something else under her breath, she unclipped the velvet-covered chain across the foot of the stairs and, leaving it hanging, took them at a run.

It seemed to Ben that Everett's outlines were melting and slipping like the names on the old headstones in the cemetery. "Everett," he said before he could think about it, "come on, walk back with me and have some coffee. Jane would love to see you. And then I do have to get to the office. How about it?"

Everett nodded like someone in a trance but was quite collected by the time they reached Ben's house. He made pleasant small talk over the coffee and smiled when Ben and Jane's dog, Fee, inspected Gifford's sandwich boards and walked thoughtfully away. But he looked ill, and Ben insisted on driving him home.

"A great place you've got," Ben said, getting out of the car the better to admire it. "We were glad when we heard it was going to be lived in again. A house like this should be lived in. You've done wonders with it."

The house was one of the oldest in town, a two-over-two saltbox, its ancient clapboards stripped and stained a warm woodsy brown so that it melted into the enfolding trees. Most of the windows bore the original leaded panes, hell to clean but a source of pride to people like Everett. The grounds were manicured like a pleasure garden and backed up by woodland and wetland. Beyond lay the Atlantic.

An acrid odor, a dark-brown odor, came intermittently to Ben's nostrils, which twitched like a hound's.

"We're downwind of John's house at the moment," Everett said, noticing. "The ruins of it, rather. Even the trees smell. Just through the woods there," pointing. "But I expect you know that? Some more onshore breezes from the northeast will blow it away in time. I can't stand the stench, it suffocates me. You'll have to come in some day," he added listlessly, ushering Gifford out of the back seat. "I haven't had too many visitors. A house needs visitors."

"Yes, it does. And we'd like that. Okay, Everett, see you later. 'Bye, Gifford," Ben said and drove off, depressed and sad.

▽

SIX

IT HAD BLOWN A gale all the night before, and outside was a fairy world of glittering ice. Ben stood at the bedroom window, soaking up the unseasonal sight and blinking with the brilliance of it.

Several days of walking all by himself up and down long hills, plus that look out of the window now, convinced him that swimming in John Chester's pool was healthier than sitting at his desk for the better part of a ten-hour day with aching feet and knots in his legs.

So, a week after the failed meeting with John, he rolled his cap and trunks into a towel and hastened as best he could to catch up with Merran and Becca, Everett and Gifford, stilting along over the treacherous glaze and storm litter like a marsh bird. Exercise of any kind was no more inviting today than it had been yesterday, regardless of the weather, but he would at least be with his friends. That prospect, like the carrot in front of the donkey, had always lured him to school and to other invidious duties—and he had gotten to eat the carrot.

Furthermore, he had become curious to see what was going to happen in this suddenly intense (to him) little world. The intervening days had been oddly free of gossip from or about Everett, Merran, Becca, the Chesters, or anybody else. Or maybe it was just that he had been too busy to hear any.

As he puffed along, he saw Everett slumped on the cemetery wall, Gifford's head in his lap. He called out, and both sat up.

"Tell Giff good morning, Ben," Everett said, perking up and twinkling.

"Good morning, Gifford."

The dog jumped down off the wall, tail stump jerking passionately; bowed; sat down; offered Ben his left paw.

"Now, Giff," Everett said, mock-reproachful. "Not your left paw. Your right paw," and Ben could have sworn that the dog winked as he obeyed.

He stroked the shining head and said "good boy" (Fee, Jane would have said, would consider such stunts beneath him), and the dog jumped back up onto the wall.

"He really is a good boy," Everett said. "The best dog I ever had. I worry about him sometimes."

"He seems in great shape to me."

"Oh, he is. That isn't what I meant. No, it's something most people worry about—who will take care of the animals when we die, don't you see?"

"I never thought about it. Maybe I haven't wanted to. I expect people make some provision in their wills."

"Yes, but you never can be sure how it will work out. Family or friends may agree and then refuse the responsibility when the time comes. But even if they don't, an animal may not survive its own grief." He put an arm around the boxer, and the handsome head nestled like a confiding child's against his chest.

"Sufficient unto the day, Everett," Ben said briskly. "Now I think we'd better get with it. It's a gorgeous day, weather notwithstanding. Actually, it's getting warmer. Ice'll be gone by noon."

They found Merran and Becca at the pool door with some other regulars. Beyond the building a dog barked insistently, as usual. Everett seemed not to hear it this time.

"Locked out," grumbled one of the jocks. "We've been waiting fifteen minutes, and I'm getting blinded from all this glare. Somebody ought to tell John Chester a thing or two."

Chorus of sulky agreement.

It was a fine morning to wait in, bright and sparkling with birdsong, and Ben thought they ought to be grateful. "I'll give it a go," he said, and returned to the front of the shop and rapped a tattoo with the old brass knocker. Even as he leaned on the door, looking around and enjoying the scene, the door swung open and he almost fell inside.

Nora Chester, in nightgown and robe and a headful of springing curls, regarded him with increasing warmth.

"I saw you coming. It's no use asking me where John is, dear Ben—dearest Ben—because I don't know. But I would love you to come in and spend some time with me. I wish I felt better. I ache all over, and my head's killing me. I think I've got the flu. You could cure it, I know that."

The last woman Ben had flirted with was Jane, some twenty-five years ago, and no one had interested him since. "Yes, well, we only wondered if something's wrong—"

"Wrong? Wrong? After all we've been through?" Her laugh was sharp and mirthless, her eyes welled with tears. "How could anything be wrong? Yesterday the insurance company told us they won't pay off on the house because of that penny in the fuse box—can you believe it!—and then Everett asked John again about the land and he said no, so we won't even have a few dollars from that! So how could anything possibly be wrong!"

Another swimmer appeared.

"Go around. We'll be along," Ben said. He moved Nora gently back from the door and closed it behind them. "At least you're safe and you've got this place. In no time John'll have it all done again—house, furniture, the works. You know that."

"Oh yes," she said with an exhausted irony. "John'll do it, all right. It's just . . . I can't get that smell out of my nose.

I smell it all the time. Such an awful smell, so bitter. I keep washing and washing my hair. Ben, I don't think I can ever bear to live on that lot again. I want to sell it and go somewhere else, but John—" a tear rolled down her cheek. "I adored that house, and now I feel so sick, and we're so cramped upstairs."

"It won't be for long. Hold the thought. You say you don't know where John is?"

"Last time I saw him, he went downstairs last night to see someone—there was someone at the door, and they started arguing. I'd taken sleeping pills and the kids were in bed, so I paid no attention and went to bed. I've been so tired since the fire, but I can't sleep without pills. None of this seems to bother John—no matter how late he stays up, he's at his goddam cash register at the crack of dawn. He didn't come to bed, I know that, because his bed hasn't been slept in. Did you know he actually found a buyer for that diving suit? The guy was going to take it away last night, so maybe John went with him to help. But even so—oh Ben, *I* don't know," she wailed. "What should I do?"

"What would you like me to do? There's a crowd out back. Any one of us could check the water, start the pump. Or would you rather close until you see what's what?"

"Close? And give rebates? John doesn't give money away, Ben, he takes it," she said between clenched teeth. "Guess I better get going—I know the routine, I do it every day. It saves John time, and time is *money*," clenching again. "Just give me a few minutes. I'll go get dressed and see the kids are ready for school, and then I'll be right down. You can all get ready—here's the key—but tell everybody to stay out of the water till I take a sample. God, I feel sick. I think I have a temp." Hunched up hugging herself she went up the stairs.

Ben stood for a moment thinking that nothing would keep John away from hearth and home all night and part of the morning unless he had found it intensely profitable to be somewhere else. Or maybe he and the suit buyer had hoisted a few too many at a bar after loading the damned rig into a truck or whatever, and he was still sleeping it off somewhere.

No, John would never do that. It was cheaper to drink at home, where you didn't have to take turns buying, never mind give it away for nothing.

To hell with John, Ben told himself, more truly than he knew, and headed for the door at the back of the shop, threading his way through a maze of clothing racks, cartons, and cabinets. Oh boy, he thought. The fire marshal would have a fit if he ever saw this. I should have gone out and around.

He was fed up with John and John's approach to retail and to Nora and to Everett, and he was fed up with physical fitness and physical fitness freaks and his own bad temper and just about everything else. What do I need this for! he grumbled. It starts out a perfectly nice day and I'm perfectly fine the way I am, and then I have to come here, and all of a sudden I'm Nora's social worker.

At least that—that *thing* is gone, and good riddance! John ought to clear out some of those cartons too, put some of that junk in his storeroom! Which is no doubt loaded to the gills with more, on his Buy Cheap Principle. Where the hell does he find it all? Railroad salvage, probably. Bet everything falls out when he opens the door.

Coming into the shop from the pool several days before to buy a swim cap, Ben had passed the storeroom without thinking anything about it. Now he ignored the STOREROOM—KEEP OUT sign and opened the door to see if he was right.

He wasn't.

The only thing in the room was the helmeted diving suit, which lay supine in the middle of the floor, an alien being asleep or felled by Earth's atmosphere. Good, and let it stay that way, Ben thought, closing the door.

Almost instantly the import of his fancy struck him. Every hair on the back of his neck stood up and the skin all over his body prickled and contracted and his breath became a hard lump in his throat. He opened the door again and tiptoed in as if loath to awaken the sleeper.

No chance.

The stiff canvas chest and belly should have been concave with emptiness, the arms more or less flat. The glass faceplate should have revealed to him only a reflection of his own face.

He bent over to look more closely. From the thing emanated a whiff of something rotten. Of something rotting, spoiling.

His preswim juice and biscuit exploded into his mouth. Swallowing desperately, he put out a tentative finger and gently prodded one canvas arm.

It gave back a horrible resistance.

▽

SEVEN

WINTER CLAIMED THE TOWN prematurely and hung on for a few days, and Ben, battling his windy way to the pool, asked himself what he was trying to prove. Since he was not expecting an answer, he did not get one.

A subdued Nora let the swimmers into the pool building. She was not so pale and ill nor did she move so stiffly as on that bright Friday morning when he had told her where and how John had spent the night. She thanked him and the other swimmers and shoppers who kept coming. "This flu's been a bitch, but you're keeping me busy and I appreciate it. I have to do *some*thing, God knows," she said. "At least until this is all over."

As if murder, Ben thought, were merely an object that could be wrapped up in inquest and funeral and stowed away in some dark lost place, to be forgotten forever. He shuddered at the image, and the fingertip with which he had touched the diving suit tingled horribly. He rubbed away at it, knowing that till the end of his life he would remember that day . . .

The little room, once a pantry stocked with housewifely treasures, was dominated by the huge supine figure. Ben willed himself to turn his back on it, telling himself it wasn't going to jump up and grab him from behind. All the same, the skin on his back crawled as he went out to John's office to call Police Chief Colin MacWhirter.

He watched the squad test the brass fittings and faceplates for fingerprints; there were none, of course. And then he held his breath until he thought his lungs would burst while they removed the helmet and set it aside and undid the other fittings and extracted the small stinking body, which was soiled by a little blood and a lot of excrement.

Minutes later the medical examiner, Dr. Ivan Cantor, made only one of two things perfectly clear.

First, that John had been struck on the left side of the head with a lead weight from the slotted belt. A fair assumption, one of these objects having been discovered bearing unmistakable traces of hair and blood.

"But why put the weight back without cleaning it properly?" the police chief grumbled, as if the malefactor had done something unreasonable.

"Possibly," Ben said, "with the thought that order, being, like cleanliness, next to godliness, might expunge part if not all of the sin of murder."

"Mmff!"

Second, "The blow could have killed someone with a thinner skull," Cantor said slowly, consideringly. "Even the victim, for that matter. But I don't know, it just doesn't look all *that* bad . . .

"I'd say—now, this is just a hunch, mind you, because even an autopsy may not necessarily give us a one hundred percent ironclad, watertight [That's a good one, Jane would have said] cause of death—"

MacWhirter was almost jigging with irritation. "Ivan, for godsake, say it straight out for once in your life! There aren't any witnesses, nobody's gonna 'cuse you of author's license or reckless flights of imagination and haul you into court. Just say what you think, and let's get on with it!"

"All right, then," Cantor said mildly, "but when I've done the autopsy, which in a case like this won't—repeat, won't—prove my hunch, just don't push me for a definitive blood or tissue—

"All right! I'd say John Chester died peacefully of suffocation in this rig and never knew it. Probably never even saw the blow coming in the first place, judging from where he was hit. Boy. How many people do we know, including us, who'd like to check out this way. Nice. Oh, very nice. I thought I'd seen 'em all, but murder in a snazzy deep-sea diving suit? My my."

" 'Beware of all enterprises that require new clothes,' " Ben said. "Henry David Thoreau. Right, Colin?"

MacWhirter snorted again. Everybody with kids in the high school knew about Ben and his history because every month or so he gave closed-circuit television lectures, with illustrative sets and costumes—another example of the frills and fluffs the taxpayer had to kick in for [the PTA ladies, led by Jane, did everything and paid for it out of dues] and never mind the growing interest in social studies and the higher marks pertaining thereto. "The question is, did one person hit him and then put him in the suit? Or did he take off thinking he'd killed him with that one blow, thinking his job was done? Did he even want to kill him? Would Chester've died if he'd been left there undiscovered till morning?

"Or did someone else come along and see that he was still alive and take the God-given opportunity to dress him up for his murder?

"Or were there two murderers, allies, who did the job together? Must've been two, 'cause how the hell could one person manage such a stunt unless they were Arnold Schwarzenegger?"

"I make that seven questions, Colin," the ME said with unusual incisiveness as he packed up. "And better yours than mine. You'll have my report soonest. See you around, Ben."

* * *

By the time Ben left his office late that afternoon, the town hall flag was once again at half-mast, there being no question that John would have won the seat on the Finance Committee had he lived. Not that anyone *liked* John Chester, you understand, people said, but after all, the widow and children of such a prominent man deserve this mark of respect . . .

There was no reactive ground swell of support for Everett Upham in the matter of the election, and the sandwich boards that Gifford had worn so proudly went into the trash. But at the overlong graveside service, during a pouring rain, Everett and even Gifford seemed genuine mourners, the raindrops running down their solemn cheeks.

"Touchingly appropriate, those two," Merran told Ben later. "In pleasant contrast to a couple of other people present who were hard put, flu or no flu, to keep from dancing a fandango."

"I noticed. You're not suggesting they had the same reason?"

"I'll give it some thought. If I have nothing better to do."

▽

EIGHT

A SECOND UGLY LETTER about Merran Shaw came in the morning mail. Until John Chester's murder, Ben had suspected that little weasel of sending the first one simply because it was probably he who had ruined Everett Upham's campaign with the anonymous letter to the paper about dogs. But what did John—or Nora?—have against Merran? Nothing I ever heard about, Ben thought.

A much likelier candidate was George Taylor, who, during his rude unannounced visit to the office, had made known his dislike, even his fear, of Merran.

Ben discarded this idea also. George was more likely to strike his enemy with his swift right cross than to sit still long enough to cut libel out of many kinds of type and paste the bits on fine bond.

Ben had still not shown the first letter to Merran, telling himself that there never seemed to be enough time. He had not shared the matter with the central office either, since he knew perfectly well what the upshot would be. It took him half the morning to do his duty and make the two calls.

Merran said he would be in at lunchtime.

The Superintendent was away, his secretary said, but would be glad to see them the day after tomorrow, at five.

No he won't, Ben thought, putting the second letter away with the first. But maybe not. After all, it can't mean too much, because if it did, he'd be calling me.

The reasoning was correct as far as it went. Which, he was to acknowledge later, turned out to be not very far.

Merran came in at noon with two meatball subs. "A reward for doing your first mile," he said, giving one to Ben. He flopped into the visitor's chair and regarded his fragrant portion without enthusiasm.

"Thanks. I rather hoped my achievement hadn't gone unnoticed. What do I get when I swim two?"

"Pheasant under glass. In advance. I've been invited to George Taylor's for lunch tomorrow. Heard great things about his wife's cooking and got him to invite you too."

"What's the occasion?" Ben said around a huge bite.

"I think he wants to neutralize me. Kill me with kindness, you might say. Should be interesting."

"Connie Taylor talking yet?"

"Bec and I tried something new the other day. I brought in a few things—paper bricks, a gun, some dolls—father, mother, children—you know the sort of stuff. Bec played—anger, mostly. I just watched. The kid built a wall with the bricks and hid behind it. Which makes a lot of sense. Thought you'd like to take a look in. Something tells me there's about to be a breakthrough."

"For a searcher who expects a breakthrough, you look singularly flat."

"I guess."

"You feel you need some backup at the Taylors."

"Yeah."

"You feel my input will be helpful."

"Yeah, I guess—get off it, Ben!"

Ben laughed, then stopped laughing as he took the folder out of his drawer and handed it over. "Take a look at these. The second one came a while ago."

Merran glanced at them. "Oh? Well well. Maybe the next

ones'll be in code. I wouldn't worry about it."

"Yes, well, but the Super might, so if you have any late afternoon appointments day after tomorrow, cancel them. We're seeing him at five. He has to know."

"He's probably gotten plenty of this sort of garbage himself. Goes with the territory." Merran tossed the folder onto the desk and took a bite out of his sandwich.

At one o'clock Ben opened his office door and prepared to go and settle himself in Room 112. He was pleasantly full, and the more comfortable for having watched Merran develop a degree of interest in his own food. But the sight of Police Chief Colin MacWhirter and George Taylor marching grimly toward him transformed his favorite lunch into a lump of cement that rose into his throat and anchored him to the floor.

An immensely fat man, MacWhirter looked trim and formidable in his well-tailored uniform. "Sorry to bust in on you like this, Ben, but I've got a notion you can help. Nora says John told her—the day of the murder—that George was coming over with his bill but that he could whistle for his money because John wasn't satisfied with the work. She says someone did come to the shop that night and there was a big shouting match, that her kids were asleep already, and that she'd taken a sedative and passed out in the middle of it. George says he went over, all right, but didn't stay more'n a minute, never went in 'cause they were arguing in there, and Connie was with him—she stayed in the van—and can so testify. So you can appreciate," he said, his suety voice rich with irony, "that after what Nora just told me, I couldn't take time to make an appointment to see you."

"You were lucky to find me in," Ben said coolly.

MacWhirter laughed. "Put it down to living right. Now then. I know Merran Shaw's been seeing Connie. So how about it, Ben?"

"How about what? You think the child will talk to him or you or me or anyone just because you ask her to?"

"She may be dumb but she isn't stupid, if you'll excuse

the expression, and I don't believe for one minute she'd refuse to help her old man, given a situation like this. No, what I thought was, you let us watch Merran Shaw work with her and see what he can do. She won't even know we're there. I know, I know—client privilege and all that. But in a case of murder, Ben—"

Reluctantly Ben picked up his phone and rang Merran's office.

The three men sat down in a row before the one-way screen, Ben quietly furious, MacWhirter skeptical, George a volcano dangerously a-boil. When the little fat girl, with Merran and Becca at her heels, entered Room 113, George jumped up and began biting his nails. He had so far said not a word.

Merran had brought more than a few things into Room 113. A high bookcase stood against one wall, its shelves covered with toys; the paper building blocks filled a carton big enough to hold a washing machine. In three minutes the child built a wall—a fort—with the blocks and hid behind it. Merran removed a block from the third course and sat back. The child stuck her hand through the gap. There was a distinct sound of a giggle.

George Taylor muttered something.

Bec played quietly, neutrally, waiting for a clue.

The child got up and went to the bookshelf. Her hands were locked behind her as if she had been told to look but not touch. Then one hand slowly came around and timidly reached for something Ben couldn't see.

Clatter of objects raining down onto the floor.

"It's okay, don't worry about it. Everybody drops things," Merran said from his chair, but the child sat down before the bookshelf silent and motionless.

Minutes passed.

Ben's attention wandered away. He thought about John Chester, felled by a blunt instrument while his wife slept, sedated and flu-ridden, hearing nothing of the violence developing below . . .

He thought about how powerful the murderer must be to have lowered that unwieldy stiff canvas-and-rubber suit with all those solid brass fittings and wood-and-leather-soled boots to the floor and wrassled John's body into it . . .

He thought that neither of the two people who felt they had cause to hate John was powerful enough—or even angry enough—for such a task . . .

He thought about the two people at the funeral whose satisfaction at the turn of events had been too irrepressible to hide . . .

He thought about the cemetery staff having had to dig the third grave in a row—Carl Baker's, Blair Bush's, John Chester's—with the cemetery's little backhoe, in preparation for John's funeral the other day, once the ME had released the body . . .

He thought Connie would look better in her pink sweater and skirt if she weren't so fat . . .

"Mm? Mm?" the child said, pointing, and Ben sat up with a start.

"Yes?" Merran said.

She tugged at his sleeve. "Mm. *Mm!*"

"Tell me."

"Mm!"

What was she pointing at? Ben leaned forward and squinted. Oh yes. That was progress indeed.

"Go get it," Merran said.

Scowling and foot-stamping.

"Listen, you little brat, you've pulled that helpless act long enough," Merran said (and George growled under his breath about the way Shaw was talking to his kid). "You want that gun, you have two choices. Ask me for it or get it yourself."

She glared at him. Then she stood on a chair and got down the gun.

"Swell," Merran said. "Now do us both a favor and don't try that phony act again. You're as capable as everybody else."

Full marks, Ben thought. He's as authentic in his crankiness with this pest as he would be with any other.

The child took the gun and went back behind her wall. Merran peeked through the gap and said hello. And found himself staring down the barrel of the wavering gun.

"Well?" he said angrily. "Shoot!"

Brief furious dissonances issued encouragingly from Becca's upright piano. Then came the unmistakable sound of the plastic trigger clicking once, and again.

Merran squatted on his heels, as the gun was withdrawn.

"Who am I?" he whispered. "Who'd you shoot, Connie?"

She stood up slowly, as if she ached in every part.

"Daddy," she said hoarsely, looking down at him with shocked eyes. "I shot Daddy—"

To Ben's astonished ears the gun made as much noise falling to the floor as if it had fired off a real bullet.

The child stared at Merran, eyes bulging with fear, then backed away, hands over her mouth.

"It feels scary, doesn't it, being mad at your father," Merran said softly. "But it's okay to be mad at him. Lots of kids get mad at their fathers. Their mothers too. Look, Connie. Your father's worried. He's very upset about something, and you can help him even though you feel mad at him. I think you know what your father is worried about and how you can help him. Tell me about it, Connie. You'll feel better, not so scared. You're safe here, you can't be punished for whatever you say to me, you know that."

The child shook her head and retreated, collapsing behind her wall.

George rushed out of the room and wrenched open the door to Room 113. Before Merran could organize himself, George yanked the child to her feet and shook her so hard that her head flopped up and down like a doll's and the wall of paper bricks tumbled down and scattered over the carpet.

"Tell him!" George shouted. "Talk! Talk, you rotten kid, lousy rotten kid! Tell him I didn't stay at John's place—tell him, damn you!"

She stared up at him, terrified. Then the terror in her expression faded into hatred. For a fraction of an instant purest malice gleamed in her eyes. Then, still in his grasp, she wilted and began to cry.

"That's enough," Ben said, taking charge. "Colin, get that man out of my school. I'll be in touch with you." He switched on the microphone. "Miss Holdridge, take Connie to the lav, wash her face, see she gets to class."

When they had gone he joined Merran.

"Poor little bugger," Merran said, neatening up. "But now what, Ben?"

"I think you should see the two older kids now. Before she gets home—or they do, or George does, that stupid son of a bitch. I'll have them called down here one at a time. Be right back."

A few minutes later, back in Room 112, he saw a remarkably beautiful girl enter Room 113 and close the door. She was dewy, velvety, delicious, a peach right out of a hothouse. She sat on Becca's piano stool, her back straight, feet flat on the floor, knees virginally together, hands writhing in her lap like creatures caught in a snare.

Merran was momentarily stalled by the force of her impact. He took out his little notebook and pen and settled his foxy-grampa glasses halfway down his nose. Ben watched, amused and impressed.

"I expect your parents told you I'd be wanting to talk with you," Merran said, looking as dry as an old bone.

He got nowhere. All his questions and remarks the girl answered with every youngster's most powerful weapon, the one-shoulder shrug, whose verbal equivalents are the I-don't-know, the I-don't-care, and the you-can't-make-me.

"I understand Connie was a late starter in the talking department," Merran said. "How was that, do you think?"

The shrugs did amazing things to her full young breasts. Again she shrugged, and Ben crossed his fingers, but Merran's eyes never left the girl's face.

"She was talking quite a bit when she was about three.

You'd have been ten then." Merran smiled an ancient dusty smile. Ben uncrossed his fingers.

Shrug.

"Sometimes," Merran went on conversationally, "little kids find they don't have to bother with the hassle of learning to talk because everybody else does their talking for them. Know what I mean?"

Shrug.

"Well, suppose a little kid, let's say Connie, points to something she wants. Peanut butter, for instance. Someone says, 'She wants the peanut butter, don't you, Connie?' and passes it over. Next time she wants the peanut butter, she points to it and gets it because she's so cute and knows just what she wants. Soon she learns that she can get her way in lots of things without having to talk.

"Now, the less she talks, the more dependent she becomes on everybody's knowing her signals. Which means she gets babied and protected because she seems so helpless because she can't talk, but she likes that too. All in all, she's pretty powerful because she makes people do what she wants. Anything like that happen in your house?"

Shrug.

"There's another thing can happen to keep a child from talking," Merran went on, weighty and professorial. "She can see something or hear something that frightens her, shocks her into silence. Or she can be blackmailed into silence by threats of punishment for having seen or heard something."

The lovely eyes glazed with fear.

Merran put aside his notebook and said very simply, "Joy, what's the matter? Please let me help you."

Her lips parted and trembled as if she were about to free herself of a terrible burden. Then she shot out of the chair and out of the room.

Merran looked at the one-way screen. "Well, Ben? One of two things'll happen when she gets home. She'll say, 'Dr. Shaw asked me some questions about Connie. He's real nice but there wasn't anything special I could tell him, and I missed half my art class too.' Or, 'That guy asked me some pretty weird things, like, y'know? and I don't want to see *him* anymore.' Right?"

Ben switched on the microphone again. "Probably. And then George will stop by and tell me to tell you to leave his kids alone. Okay, the boy's on his way down." He switched off and sat back.

The junior George was friendly and cheerful. His mother was the greatest cook in the world and worked too hard. Joy was the pits, like all big sisters. Connie was the pits, like all little sisters. His father was a good guy but he was always out. "But when he's home, man, yuh gotta watch his right," the boy said proudly and with the greatest good humor. "Man, when he's mad, he'll deck yuh soon as look atcha. He's got a right cross'ud cream yuh."

"Well, Ben?" Merran said from Room 113, standing up and stretching when the boy had gone. "Got any theories?"

"I never theorize unless I know all the answers."

"What about luncheon *chez* Taylor tomorrow?"

"We'll assume it's still on," Ben said, and went back to his office.

The next morning at the pool Everett Upham told Ben that Nora Chester could make no commitment about selling him the land he wanted because the matter had to wait on probate.

"Naturally," Ben said. "Might be as much as a year."

"But that could be too late, Ben!"

"Nonsense. But opt for cremation, just in case. There's bound to be room enough in the right place for your ashes," Ben said firmly and dove into the water.

At one o'clock George Taylor corraled Ben and Merran into his home with a nervous heartiness that made all Ben's teeth hurt. "Sorry about yesterday, Dr. Louis, Dr. Shaw. I was a bit upset, as you can imagine. Well now. This is sure a nice change for the wife and I in the middle of the day. You just come right in and sit. Better'n any old office for a little chat. But we'll eat first. Don't want to spoil a good dinner with business, now, do we?"

We're to have a nice cozy social luncheon, and isn't that swell! Ben thought. These people have a daughter who doesn't speak and another daughter with another big problem, but not for them the waiting room, the secretary, the silence, the chairs without arms, the old magazines that countless strangers have handled, the closed door behind which who knows what unspeakable things are disclosed. That's for sick people, crazy people.

They were escorted into the dining room by dumpy, faded Doris Taylor on one side and George, spruce, tense, and youthful in his skinny jeans, on the other, as if they needed help or might think twice and decide it was better to be elsewhere. And maybe I do, Ben thought. He seemed to be walking through a swamp of words, through air clotted with the happy couple's nervous effusiveness.

The table was set to a *House Beautiful* formula, and the flowers and doilies and mint dishes and wine glasses were wildly inappropriate to the occasion. On the other hand, a meatball sub such as Ben often counted on to brighten his day would have been a vulgarity in that astonishing house. It was a large, custom-built colonial, formal and frighteningly clean, and choked with fussy flocked wallpaper and expensive brocaded upholstery. Clearly George enjoyed it, and enjoyed sharing it, and there was, Ben thought, a likable innocence in that.

They talked about this and that through the ham with raisin sauce, the chilled rosé, the perfect coffee, and the lemon chiffon pie that trembled exquisitely, more than three inches high, under its tender blanket of whipped cream. By this time Ben regarded the wallpaper with a more appreciative eye.

"You're one hell of a cook, Mrs. Taylor," he said reverently. Merran, who had eaten less well, echoed him weakly.

"Cooks this good all the time," George said, patting his flat belly, and Ben recalled Everett Upham's description of George decking John Chester for twitting him about his wife's cooking. Why? Had she missed the other ways to her husband's heart? George was as taut as a violin string. One more little twist, and he might snap with a *ping-g-g.*

Ben swiftly reviewed a possible scenario. George interrupts noisy argument with John Chester to remove blunt instrument carefully from slotted belt. Deals killing or at least stunning blow. Replaces blunt instrument. Rejoins mute daughter waiting in van. Drives home as normal as baked ham with raisin sauce. Possible? Anything was possible. Only, George hadn't gone inside.

Ben pushed his plate away. "Well now, time's getting on, and we have to earn this wonderful meal. Dr. Shaw, perhaps you'll begin?" He almost heard the Taylor skeletons clattering in the closets.

Merran began with his usual tribute to parental patience and good sense in trying situations. But he had hardly finished his opening remarks when the front door slammed.

Joy Taylor came into the room. Seeing the guests, she stopped and stood uncertain, this beautiful seventeen-year-old with a strong resemblance to her mother.

George jumped up to hug her and kiss her lightly, possessively, on the lips. She stiffened, shrank back. And Doris Taylor lost light as her husband glowed with it.

George's Joy, Ben thought. George Taylor's joy. Oh hell, he thought, as a theory began to take shape. Oh bloody hell.

Part II
Merran

▽

NINE

DURING THE NIGHT A storm roared through Manton, and Merran awoke freezing. One of his favorite pines had snapped, landing on the power line. His telephone was also unresponsive. He dressed, shivering, and ran up the street to Becca Holdridge's house for a hot breakfast and the use of her phone.

"Sure," she said, smiling, ushering him into a house he knew as well as his own. "But it's getting late and—"

"We'll have flapjacks. And don't tell me we don't have time. No way there'll be school, Becca my girl, so let's get started. And all my clients will cancel if they have any sense. Oh, it's going to be a lovely day."

"But—"

He took out the griddle, clattered it happily onto a burner, and went for the mixings.

"We do have school, Merran, so don't get too comfortable. I just heard the radio."

"Live a little." He measured shortening into a bowl.

Laughing, she handed him the eggs. "I do. With you. Since we were ten, you've had a way of making me do what I didn't think I ought to do—and liking it. It's a worrying thought."

"Well, help me now and compliment me later. I love it,

especially from you, but not on an empty stomach."

He glanced at her, laughing, as he broke an egg into the bowl, and saw the red splotches on her scrubbed white cheeks spreading all over her face in a fiery blush.

What did I say? Did I say something? he asked himself stupidly.

Into the garbage with the eggshells went his pleasure in this enterprise, and something happened that had never happened before. He was stiff and shy with her. He avoided her eyes and fumbled his fork. His sentences collided with hers and broke. He apologized too much and left half his food.

"Your house must be an icebox by now," she said calmly. "Why don't you—"

"I think I better—"

"—call about that tree."

"—call about that tree," he echoed, confused as he had never been in his life. He picked up the phone. It was something concrete to do, and he knew how to do it and did it very well.

He reported his plight to the telephone and electric companies, thanked Becca for the breakfast, and was away like a rocket, feeling that he had barely escaped from something he couldn't even put a name to. Sighing, he went home for his car, and drove, reluctant but obedient, to the high school.

With an equine toss of his long head and manelike hair, Bill Tempesta, principal of the relocated middle school, waved Merran into his office. "God*sake,* Merran, what went on at your lunch with the Taylors? Mister called to say Connie wouldn't be in for a while, and he didn't sound all that hospitable anymore. You better back off."

"Why?"

"Well, look, Merran, if you're doing what they want, that's fine. Otherwise—"

"Otherwise a little kid's supposed to be frightened into silence? Maybe for the rest of her life? Tell me something,

Bill. If the Taylors were violent illiterate city-ghetto types of whatever size, shape, race, color, or creed, what would you call their situation?"

"Well, I—well, cruelty, I guess. Even parental neglect."

"Which we are required *by law* to report to the authorities, right? Even though it's happening in a right little, tight little, posh Yankee town?"

"Well yes, but—"

"But I shouldn't rock this posh town's boat, right?"

Bill Tempesta looked the way all school administrators look when pressed—as if he found himself standing on a pile of eggs. "Well . . . *yes,* dammit! The Taylors've put the kibosh on your show, so under the circumstances maybe you better just . . ." He looked down at his old brown shoes and shook his head, like a horse shaking a fly off its ear. "Oh, I almost forgot. Ben wants to talk to you. He'll be in his office at 10:30."

At 10:30 Merran appeared at Ben's door.

"You're pure poison around here, Merran," Ben said glumly.

"Who says?"

"George Taylor—who else? He called. It doesn't sort with the treatment we got yesterday, but my phone's still smoking. And this time he was very definite and to the point. He wants us to stay out of his family affairs."

"I hope that that last word won't prove to be the *mot juste,* after what we saw there. Can we in conscience do nothing about Joy? We're talking possible rape and incest, Ben, and you know it."

"I *don't* know it. There's nothing in her records or anywhere else that suggests a family problem of consequence. I've done some careful checking around."

"But dammit, Ben, you saw George's behavior toward her, you saw Mrs. Taylor's reaction to that behavior, and you saw her in Room—"

"Yes, I saw. But you're reaching pretty far, Merran, without hard evidence, and that way lies danger for the best therapist. Look, do yourself a favor and don't theorize or diagnose until you have all the evidence. Safer that way. Look, we'll go into it this afternoon with the Superintendent. Don't forget—five o'clock."

"Yeah. I have to see a kid here at four, but I'll cut him short. Talking about appointments, I'm late for one right now."

Ben said slowly, "Well . . . Go now, if you like. The Super—"

"The Super *what?* Am I supposed to stay out of everybody else's affairs too?"

"I'm afraid so. For today, anyway. I'm sorry, Merran. He should have told you himself. I didn't think it would come to this. But I'm going to put the arm on him, don't worry. He owes me a few. You can have a whole day at the Medical Center, if that'll help."

It didn't. When Merran reached his private office at the Medical Center, Jo Miles, whose secretarial services he shared with two other practitioners, told him that all of his afternoon and evening clients had canceled.

"They didn't even give any reason," she said, quietly angry. "What's going on, Merran?" Her life and marriage were solidly intact because of his counseling, all of it free, and her eyes were devoted and unflinching.

He shrugged as he unlocked his door. "Maybe they're all sick. There's a lot of flu going around."

"How about some nice fresh coffee and a doughnut?"

"Maybe later. Thanks, Jo." He went into his office and closed the door softly.

It was a good room to work in, small but cheerful with its bright yellow curtains and moss-green carpet. On the long wall opposite the door were blond oak shelves holding toys and books. On the short wall behind the desk were built-in cabinets filled with client folders, stationery, and divers stuff that he had collected along the way. Under the high windows, in which ivy flourished, were deep squashy chairs covered in durable forest-green sailcloth. Travel posters of Japanese gardens and the moors of Yorkshire, his favorite places (though he had not yet been to either), hung opposite the shelves. Below them was a child's desk: his own, which his parents had given him when he was three and deemed ready for scholarly pursuits. A good room. It had absorbed a lot of stress but remained peaceful, welcoming, supportive.

I'll have to move out if this keeps up, he thought, forgetting that until recently the office had seemed a prison. Well, I can always open my office at home. I've got the space for it.

But he knew he could not do that. He was being slandered and libeled while working in a school whose swinging half-doors to the toilet stalls had been removed, for crissake! Could he risk seeing clients—could he even expect to see them—in a house that had doors that locked, and beds and couches on which Sin could be committed? No. He would have to ride it out here until his name was cleared. Sooner or later it would be, he was sure of that.

Briskly he brought his notes about Connie up to date, wondering what would have happened had George not ruined everything. Then, thinking how long it had been since he had last published, he began roughing out an article on her case, focusing on therapeutic technique in general and on changing styles thereof.

But the day dragged, and he found himself missing the people—not cases of divorce or abandonment but the *people* he might never see again. When the Unitarian Church carillon on the common struck the third quarter after four, breaking the increasingly ominous silence in which he had struggled all day, he jumped up in relief. What awaited him at the Superintendent's office in fifteen minutes could not be any worse and might, he told himself, be a good deal better than what had gone before.

As he locked his door, he saw Everett Upham and Gifford sitting in the waiting room by the internist's suite. The boxer wore a handsome new collar. Everett, who had not been looking well since the failure of his campaign, seemed to be wasting inside his sagging gray skin. He smiled but was obviously in pain.

"Just a touch of stomach upset. Dr. Clarkson isn't overly concerned. How are you doing? Some nasty things being bandied around about you, Merran."

"Pay no attention. Some crank, I expect. Some miserable paranoid crank whose life's awry. Don't let it worry you, Ev. I'll straighten it out one way or another. I'll get the bastard who's behind it."

Everett blanched as he always did at obscenities but shook his head. "It's a serious charge. I rather think that no matter what you say, people will not listen. Have you lost many clients?"

"A couple. There's plenty still want me." Forcing a smile, Merran waggled his appointment book before locking it in the secretary's desk, as usual. "Not to worry."

"Afraid I will. It's a terrible feeling, being rejected. Abandoned. Believe me, I know the feeling." The internist's door opened and a nurse appeared, smiling. "Ah. I'm being summoned. I'll talk to you later, Merran. Stay, Gifford."

Merran was four minutes early for his appointment with the Superintendent and was kept waiting half an hour, while snatches of heated argument reached him from the other side of the door. It opened, and the Superintendent beckoned him in even as he was getting up, apprehensive now, and angry, to leave. By the desk, sitting motionless in an almost visible cloud of fury, was Ben. He was too upset to say hello.

"Forgive me, Merran, for keeping you waiting," the Superintendent said with his old-world courtesy. "Please sit down and make yourself comfortable." His spotted hands shook and his bald spotted crown gleamed moistly as he began fussing with a cigarette and a denicotinizing holder. "How is your father? Still in Florida? Please give him my regards the next time you speak to him."

Merran stayed where he was, just inside the closed door. "I haven't heard from him in a couple of months. The last time he wrote, he was okay. What's all this about?" But he already knew.

The Superintendent slowly brought one foot up to the mark. "I don't mind telling you I haven't heard anything like this in all the twenty-six years I've been in this office." He looked around as if concerned for the purity of the innocent walls. The cigarette holder slipped out of his hand. He bent gratefully to retrieve it.

"Anything like what?" Merran demanded, refusing to help.

Red with embarrassment, the Superintendent painstakingly fitted the cigarette into the holder and as painstakingly lighted it. He was a decent man and, because of his long friendship with the father, his cordiality to the son transcended, if only just, his deep suspicion of his Freudian orientation, indeed of psychology in general.

"Anything like *what?*" Merran said again.

"Uh, well, in fact, moral turpitude. A harsh charge. Undoubtedly undeserved. Oh, undoubtedly. There is no question of that in my mind. But the charge has been made and must be considered."

Merran sat down heavily. "Made by whom? George Taylor, I suppose?"

"George—? No, not to me. Although from what I've just been told, he's not happy with your work. Bill Tempesta and Ben here say he's told them he wants no more help from you. From people like you, to put it plainly. No, several other people—" He crushed out his cigarette and examined the filter with a worried eye.

"Who, exactly?"

"I don't know. They don't identify themselves over the phone to my secretaries, or to the committee members, who have also been called. They just say you, uh—forgive me, Merran—they say you're unnecessarily, uh, helpful, shall I say, to little, uh, little girls. Just like those shocking letters. Now, *I* know you're—"

"Clean? Wholesome? Normal?"

"I trust you. So does Ben. And Bill. And most of the staff, I'm glad to say. But you understand how I'm placed. At the slightest whisper of scandal, I have to bring things to a halt while I look into the, uh, situation. For your own good, Merran, I would suggest you take a short leave of absence—"

"Sure." Merran got up, feeling that every part of his body had been whipped. "Ben?"

Ben said, "I've been sitting here arguing for more than an hour, Merran. I've also talked with as many committee members as I could reach. Unfortunately Martin Guinness is leading the pack, so I couldn't get them to understand that suspending you without a hearing and withholding your salary too—oh yes!—are not just illegal moves but goddam stupid ones, that putting you on ice gives credence to rumor—"

"Now now, Ben, don't be hasty. It's not as if we aren't all sorry about all this," the Superintendent said.

"Why be sorry?" Merran said. "You're saving the commonwealth the cost and bother of a trial, aren't you? Never mind that your Star Chamber tactics're illegal as all hell and that I'll sue the crap out of all of you. What have you got to be sorry about!"

"Merran—"

"Yeah, sure, you're only doing what you have to do. I'll tell my father that when I give him your regards!" He flung the door open and went out.

No, goddammit, he thought, getting into his car, the old man isn't doing what he *has* to do, and he wouldn't lose anything by doing otherwise—after all, he's retiring in June. All he has to do is stand up to this town and affirm his trust in my integrity.

You kidding? Fat chance even the fightingest head honcho would ever stick his neck out for anyone in my position. The best of them are controlled by their committees, when push comes to shove. And this nice old guy's no fighter and never has been. He runs a conservative system, does a nice maintenance job, never rocks the boat or lets anyone else rock it, and even enjoys his job despite the professional hazards—of which I am now one.

I should feel sorry for him. Because even the best-liked superintendent's head is on the block every hour of the day, three hundred sixty-five days a year. His privacy is nil, and the cordiality tendered him by staff and town is as unsubstantial as smoke when so much as one chip is down. It's a lousy job at best. And Ben thinks he wants a crack at it? He's crazy!

On the word he slammed the door shut, and the remains of his self-confidence and optimism cracked and dropped off like a shell. Vulnerable, reckless with anger, he drove to the supermarket for a paper and a few groceries, and when several people, a couple of them his clients, looked through him as though he were invisible, he began to think that the anonymous letter writers and callers had broadcast his alleged misconduct to the whole town.

Whoever the libelers and slanderers were, though, he was sure that George Taylor wasn't one of them. Because clearly George was hiding something; he was not about to say anything to anyone that could boomerang and threaten what had begun to look like a desperate need for concealment.

Who, then? Merran asked himself. Who wants me out of the schools and out of private practice?

And why?

▽

TEN

NORA CHESTER CALLED MERRAN at six the next morning as he was about to leave for the pool. "I was pretty sure you'd be up, even if you haven't got much to do, Merran. Habits are hard to break. But I just didn't want you to come over here for nothing."

"What's the matter? Something wrong with the works?"

"Not mine. Yours. I'm sorry, Merran, I don't know what to say. It's just that some people feel you'll pollute the water if you swim in it."

"What are you talking about?"

"What I'm talking about is, if you come, they won't. I've had any number of calls since yesterday—"

"Who from?"

"*I* don't know—a lot of people. And I can't afford more trouble now. The pool and the shop are all I have to support us with, and until probate—well, I thought I'd spare you the walk over—"

"It's not like you to beat around the bush, Nora. Why don't you just say you don't want me to make any trouble at the pool?"

"All right, then. I don't want you coming over and making

trouble at the pool. All right? Look, I have to go now, they're starting to arrive—"

"Nora, will you tell me one thing? Just one thing?"

"Well?"

"Did any of them say why?"

"I expect you know the reason as well as everybody else does. Look, Merran, I really have to go."

He sat there staring at the phone in his hand. As he replaced it, it rang.

"Merran? Everett. I thought I might just catch you before you left. Sorry I couldn't call you yesterday when I heard about Nora's decision to bar you from the pool. It's—terrible! Absolutely unbelievable! I told her that if you couldn't go, I wouldn't either. So why not go to the Y in Beverly? It's clean and well-managed and the dressing room is better. I checked it out. We can sign up as members or pay by the day. What do you say? The worst thing in the world is to sit around and do nothing, I can tell you that. Look, I'll leave Gifford here and pick you up in two twos, all right?"

The desk clerk at the Y refused Merran entry.

"What is this!" Everett said. "By what authority do you keep Dr. Shaw out!"

"Never mind, Ev," Merran said. "Go ahead and swim. I don't mind waiting."

"Nonsense. I wouldn't enjoy it, knowing you were waiting outside. Let's go. Look, how about breakfast and then a spot of golf? Clarkson told me to exercise, and it's a fine day for it. If we can't swim, we'll walk."

"This afternoon, maybe, Ev. There's some work I want to finish, and I've a client at noon. And if you don't mind, I'll skip breakfast, I'm just not all that hungry. Look, I'll call you about one."

Disappointed, Everett drove him home, where he mixed a cup of instant coffee and stared at his notes for the Connie Taylor article. But the quiet defeated him. He left the coffee untasted on the table and went to his office, hoping to work there. And hoping his noon client would come.

The client came, with something other than himself on his mind. He cleared his throat nervously. "Dr. Shaw, I had a call the other day from someone—didn't give his name—said he was one of your patients too. And—and—"

"And he said I liked little girls."

"Yeah," wiping his forehead on his sleeve.

"But you're here."

"Yeah."

"But you're not all that sure I'm normal."

"Yeah."

"Well, for what my word's worth, you can be."

A pause. "Yeah. Okay, Doc. I've been thinking about what you said last time about my anger on the job—Look, if I get any chances to straighten people out, you can count on me. Okay, so where was I?"

Becca Holdridge arrived, hugging two meatball subs. "I thought," she said uncertainly, "I thought we could have lunch together. I wanted to tell you what I think of Nora Chester and a few other people in this town."

He drew her in and, moved by an inexplicable impulse, kissed her.

The splotch of red on her paper-white cheek flamed and spread. She turned abruptly away. "I had a set-to with Bill Tempesta. I said that if he said one more word to me or anyone else about you in or out of school, you'd sue him and everybody else for slander. I said I was writing to the committee, the Super, and the union, which hit him hard. I said if this was the kind of leadership and backup a person could expect from this town, it was time to leave. If he's still on his feet, it's because I didn't hit him hard enough. Here. I brought lunch. All right? You're not going out, are you?"

"No." He had forgotten, almost as he made it, his promise to call Everett Upham. All at once he was very hungry. Happily he set the food out on the table between the two deep chairs.

Becca's dark blue eyes stared unfocused at the Yorkshire moors. "It's true, you know. It is time to leave. For both of us, I think. People like this—! Damn them, they don't deserve us, Merran."

How beautiful she is! he thought. No man could have a better friend, a better sister. And when she added, "Wish I'd taken that offer from Juilliard last year," an unaccountable chill struck him over the heart.

"I think I'll start sending out my résumé," she said. "Juilliard might still be interested. What are you going to do?"

"I don't know . . ." He bit off a piece of the sandwich and chewed it absently. "Well, one thing. I can't leave here until this business is cleared up, I can't run away from it. I have to find out who's responsible, who's doing this to me."

"How?"

He looked at the sandwich in his hands as if he could not imagine what it was or why he was holding it. He put it down. "Haven't the slightest idea," he said, with a twisted smile. "Do you?"

"I haven't gotten to that yet. I'm still trying to deal with the why. I did have a fleeting thought—whether what's happening to you has anything to do with John Chester's murder. Does that sound strange?"

"No more than anything else does these days."

There was a sharp rap on the door, the visitor Police Chief Colin MacWhirter. "Saw your cars 'n thought I'd look in. Nice to see you, Miz Holdridge. Didn't get a chance to say how much I admired your playing the other day. Sure was a strange business all around, though," he said, seating himself behind Merran's desk. "Hey, hope I didn't interrupt your lunch."

"No no. And I was about to leave," Becca said. "I have Chorus."

"But not you, hey, Doc? Sorry about all that. But if you two'll give me a minute, I'd appreciate you telling me if you found out anything from George Taylor's kid, Miz Holdridge, when you took her away."

"She cried and cried. I didn't press. I don't think she would have said anything, though. And she hasn't been to school since that day."

"And you, Doc, were kicked out because it was your fault."

"Who'd you hear all that from?"

"My own kid, can you believe it?" The huge body shook with laughter. "My youngest. He doesn't write a gossip column, he's in the middle school, for godsake. But seriously, I got a nasty letter in today's mail about you, Doc. I called the Super, and then I went and talked to Tempesta and Ben Louis, and Ben showed me the two letters he got. Very inneresting. And a bunch of baloney. George didn't write them. He'll punch you out, but subtlety's beyond him. What do you think the kid *might* have said if she'd talked."

"If I could turn that family inside out, Chief, I'd know. I'm sure of that. All I can say now is, when I do find out—or think I have—I'll tell you."

"I bet that aging Casanova daddy of hers knows—and something tells me it's got nothing to do with the night John was killed. I know he and John fought for years. I know he decked him in the dressing room. But I think he told the truth about not going in, the night John was killed. If Nora hadn't said he was expected over with a bill, I'd never've thought he'd been there. The kid'll back him up eventually. Doris did, but that's worth diddley.

"Okay. But I can't let him off the hook officially until the kid talks—or writes, for godsake! But hey, did you happen to catch that look on her face when he shook her up? She can talk, all right, if you ask me, but she won't give him the satisfaction, she's really making him sweat. And I want to know why. But anyhow, when your suspension follows her absence from school, Doc, well, anybody'd think there was a connection, right?"

He grinned. His interest in human behavior, like Merran's, was rendered socially acceptable by his position and never flagged. Everyone in town knew that he enjoyed his job enormously. He was entitled: he handled it honorably and well.

"Incidentally," he went on, "I want to apologize for butting in the other day, Doc, Miz Holdridge, and I'm damn sorry it turned out the way it did. But I don't like murder-by-person-or-persons-unknown verdicts, although they're a damn sight better'n accidental death, because then I have a chance to catch that unknown sonofabitch who's walking around loose thinking he's home free. And I don't hold with client privilege in a capital case. By which I don't mean to infer that I disregard it or that I think George Taylor's guilty, like I said." He heaved himself up and took a last look at the meatballs. "You ought to be arrested, leaving good food like that. See you around."

"Damn it, Merran, I'm going to be late again!" Becca said. "Come over for supper if you haven't anything else to do. Maybe we can sort something out then. We have to do something."

He sank back into the chair and covered his eyes. "I just might. We have to put our heads together, Bec my girl."

He did not see her blush furiously as she let herself out.

Jo Miles said, "Merran, none of your afternoon and evening clients are coming. I called them all to confirm their appointments. In view of everything, I thought I'd better. And oh Merran, I'm so sorry. Not one of them gave anything like a reason. They either said straight out that they were canceling, or they just hemmed and hawed. I don't know how I kept my temper! I hate them all! Merran, what are you going to do?"

"Laundry. It's been piling up. If you want me for anything, I'll be home. And Jo, don't get shook. I'm not licked yet. Hell—I haven't even begun to fight."

At home he found a burst washing machine hose and water rising up the cellar walls. Feeling raw inside, he turned off the faucet and mopped up as best he could. Then, instead of telephoning Swiggett Plumbing for help, he drove there, because driving took him out of the empty silence he called home.

Pete Swiggett called out to him from a cozy little sitting room at the back of his shop. He was eating with hurried gusto and a plastic fork from an aluminum tray, his dog Sam watching him closely. "To make sure I'm doing it right, right, Sammy?" Pete said, rewarding his vigilance with a forkful of lasagna.

"Nice place," Merran said, sinking onto a welcoming couch.

"Home away from home. The wife fixed it up for me. Got everything I want in here. Little fridge, microwave, radio, everything, practically, 'cept her and a TV, which I don't have all that much time for anyway. Just having a late lunch. Or early supper, I'm not sure which. Between jobs, anyhow.

"Say, Merran, I been hearing about the frost people're giving you around here. Take my advice 'n tell the bastards to go to hell. You look a mite peaked. How about I micro you a Lean Cuisine? Weight Watchers? The wife buys all kinds of different ones for emergencies, 'n they're not bad if you don't take too long over them."

"I'm good, thanks." All the same Merran leaned back with a sigh and closed his eyes.

"What can I do you for?"

"My washing machine peed all over the cellar."

"Yeah, it happens. Every now 'n then the cold water hose blows if you don't turn off the water when the cycle comes to the end. If you can wait till maybe tomorrow, I can put a new hose on for you, but I'm flat out now. Don't know when I'll get home tonight, even. Only reason you caught me in here is I said to hell with the bastards, a man's gotta eat."

"I'm in no rush."

"Well, I am. Better check the book, see what I'm up to tomorrow. Here, Sammy, you can have the last bite," which the dog took off the fork with a crunch. "Oh boy, no rest for the weary," Pete said, groaning as he stood up. He led the way into his office.

The "book" was a big calendar. "The blue ink is scheduled appointments," Pete explained. "The red ones're emergencies, specially after hours or on weekends and holidays. The wife's idea—she keeps the books." He bent over the calendar. "Yeah, how's tomorrow afternoon—'round two? I can let myself in if you're not gonna be home. I know my way around that place—been there enough times when your mother was alive. Lessee, do I have your house key?"

He opened a shallow wall cupboard above the desk, disclosing a pegboard covered with keys neatly labeled and in alphabetical order. "Nope. Your Medical Center key but not your house key, Merran. I got practically everybody else's in this town. My wife set this up. Saves me all kinds of time."

"No offense, Pete, but there's not all that much security here."

"Haven't lost one yet. Or had one borrowed for a bit of B and E. And what with Sammy here most of the time, any thieving sonofabitch would take one look at him and skedaddle. Right, Sam?" The dog wagged his tail amiably and collapsed in a boneless heap. "Okay, I'll put you down for two, Merran. See you then. Meanwhile, don't take any shit from the bastards."

It was only midafternoon, and the weather fair. Merran went home and fetched his father's golf bag out of the attic. The little suede bags on the club heads were dusty, the whole outfit gray with disuse. Three years ago, for a dollar and other considerations, his father had sold it to him along with the house and everything in it. Then, encumbered by nothing more than a few clothes and a picture of his only son and newly dead wife, Garth Shaw had gone away. He wrote or called from time to time but never mentioned the possibility of returning.

Merran gripped the well-balanced mashie, its fine leather dark and smooth from his father's devoted playing. He almost felt his father's hands in his own, warm and strong.

He assumed the stance and swung, and wondered if Garth's loneliness, within the scanty limits he had walled himself into so far away, was any more bearable than was Everett's in his fine house on that beautiful country road in the town of his origins.

What about my own loneliness and depression, Merran asked himself, and suffered a poignant thrust as he considered the human dilemma in its several aspects. Then he slipped the suede bag onto the mashie and went out to his car.

There was a slightly bitter scent in the air around Everett Upham's antique house, a reminder of the Chesters' blackened ruin close by. Nora's revulsion for the property was understandable, drenched as it was in one of the worst of odors. What must she be feeling now for the apartment she was tied to, when for as much as ten hours she had been sleeping right above John's stinking body? If after probate she sold everything and moved away, who would be surprised?

Everett was out. Merran left the mashie at his back door with a note: "My father's favorite club. Sorry about this afternoon. Got tied up with the police! 18 holes and lunch tomorrow after your swim? Call me."

Hope it helps, he thought and went back to his car.

Abruptly he turned toward the back lawn and the woods beyond, wondering if there were a path to the Chester home.

There was, between two great rhododendrons and through stands of pine and hemlock, the air cool and dim and, to his surprise, fragrant. Presently he reached the edge of a large clearing. The trees around it were scorched and mutilated, the air here still rank with the old odor of a terrible fire. The roof of the once fine house had fallen in. Blackened rafters stuck up like broken jackstraws, and the walls leaned in and brooded over the ancient granite foundation. Another house would one day stand securely on it, but not Nora's. Someday someone will want it, he thought.

At top dollar too, he could almost hear John say.

He went closer for another look, and a heavy-gauge wire sagging between two scorched trees branded his neck with its cold touch. Startled, he stepped back and fell into a hole.

When he had righted himself, he saw that there were several other holes variously filled with debris. A large fire-blackened dog collar curled out of one of them. He touched it with the tip of his toe. The Chester mutt's, he thought, the one that barks all the time. My god. This wire's a trolley, and the poor mutt ran back and forth on it all day long, barking for attention, digging holes because he had nothing else to do. Must've torn himself loose when the fire got close. Lucky for him, or he'd've cooked. It's clear the Chesters didn't give him a thought.

Shuddering and almost unbearably depressed, he went hastily back through the woods to his car.

▽

ELEVEN

THE EVENING THAT MERRAN spent with Becca following the police chief's visit was a bore and a waste. Incompatible strangers thrown together by happenstance could not have had a more miserable time. By morning he had forgotten the name of the movie they had seen. Later, on the golf course with Everett, he quit after four holes and, to Everett's almost angry disappointment, begged off lunch.

Each day was like that worst of nightmares when the very air bars one's flight from terror. An inner voice commanded him to pull his socks up and get cracking before something horrible caught and destroyed him, but he was locked into a pattern and could not obey.

The quiet empty house became intolerable, and he spent more and more time in his office simply because real people came and went on the other side of his door. Yet he stopped answering the phone or even checking for messages on the answering machine. The only people he saw were those who went out of their way to give him the cold shoulder.

More than a week passed like this. Then one morning he awoke to a subtle change in mood and came into the Medical Center to deal with the problem that was poisoning his life.

He flopped into one of the deep chairs and, calmly regarding the vigorous ivy in the window above his head, let his thoughts take their own way.

The first of these was that every standing appointment had been canceled, which meant that his practice was in effect ended—all in the space of two or three days following the disaster with Connie Taylor.

The thought presented itself in a new light. Talk about patterns! Talk about predictability! It's almost as if the bastard, whoever he is, got on the phone and went down a list.

List?

He sprang up and went out to the crowded waiting room. No one but Jo Miles looked at him.

"Jo," he whispered, "did you by any chance put my appointment book someplace else recently? Or maybe leave the drawer unlocked?"

"No, Merran, it's always in the middle drawer on the left side. I've never moved it. And I always lock up if I leave for any reason, even if it's only for a couple of minutes. Why?"

He bent to examine the drawer in question. The lock showed no signs of having been forced, and the scratches around it told him only that the desk, though handsome enough, was old.

"What's the matter?" she said anxiously. "Did I do something wrong?"

"No, no. Of course not. I was just . . . wondering."

They stared at each other.

"It's almost as if someone knew who to call," she murmured. "Someone who hates you. Hates you enough to keep everybody away. Is that what you're thinking?"

"Something like that," he said and went back to his chair under the ivy.

A picture flashed up out of the murk of his subconscious but sank too quickly to catch. Something about keys . . .

Keys?

Damn it—what was it!

Not to worry. It'll come back . . .

He dozed for a minute or two, then came awake with a start.

Who hated him enough to want to break his career? A pathologically disgruntled client? There were plenty of those in all the helping professions—hell, there were plenty of them everywhere. People with an unassuageable grievance didn't stop at suing their doctors, their lawyers, teachers, shrinks, employers, fellow workers. They blew up their houses, bombed their cars, walked right up to them and shot them dead—and one or two more for good measure.

Have I missed the boat on someone? he asked himself. Was my diagnosis wrong? my approach? Plenty of people said Ricky Priest's suicide proved I'd been way off base.

In the cabinet behind his desk was a record of every client he had ever seen, with a few careful phrases about each. Without it he would long ago have forgotten many of the people he had treated. His eye raked the list. No one on it seemed paranoid enough or angry enough to have mounted such a vicious campaign against him.

The Priests?

No. Nothing, no one in the world, could prevail upon them to exhume what passed for grief by attacking him. It was precisely their distaste for strong feeling, their avoidance of it, that had brought them and their only child to such a pass. Emotionally dead and thus having no guilt, they needed no scapegoat.

No, it had to be someone else.

He put the folder away and leaned back and closed his eyes. Keys, he thought, gently prodding his memory—which said helpfully that the car needed a tune-up and possibly a battery. Sighing, he called Whit's Garage and made an appointment, then irritably resumed his favorite place.

Nothing offered.

All right, relax, he told himself. When the old sub-conscious is ready, you'll know it.

Once again an image of a key shot up, and once again it dropped out through the bottom of his awareness.

No time to wait, he said, and seized the word itself.

Keys. Doors. Privacy.

Closed-door privacy? Mail privacy? Telephone privacy?

Who besides Jo knows who my clients are?

A bank teller. The tellers know why I get—got—checks with a certain regularity. Suppose one of them, surrounded by money, hungry for it, sold some other hungry bastard a list of my clients, or maybe someone bribed a teller—or even my mailman—for a list, so as to look up phone numbers and make poison calls.

Have you heard that Dr. Shaw likes little girls?

Possible? Anything's possible. That's the kind of world we live in. But probable? Is my small practice such a threat that someone—who? another shrink?—would pay to close it down?

The notion was so absurd on its face that he resolved never to mention it even to Becca. In discarding it, he was no farther ahead, but he did feel better. Hungry, in fact; even cheerful. This suggested another course of action altogether. It would mean more cold shoulders and snide comments, but he set about the first part of it, then put on his jacket and went out to do the second.

Everett Upham, looking pale and tired, was sitting by Dr. Clarkson's door again.

Merran sat down beside him. "What's the matter, Ev? You don't look too swift. Where's Gifford?"

"In the car, behind the wheel, with a chauffeur's cap on his head. It's his latest trick. People get such a kick out of it that he's taken to waiting for me outside. He's marvelous, you know. Tremendous sense of humor. I don't know what I'd do without him."

Merran laughed. "I don't know what he'd do without you."

"You're looking rather more purposeful than usual, I'm glad to see. Where are you heading?"

"I just decided to give a dinner party tonight. Ben and Jane Louis, Becca, Guy McKay—he's on the Cemetery Board, remember?—and you. I just called your house, in fact. How about it? It'll buck us both up. And bring Gifford. I expect he could use a night out."

"Maybe you're right. I must say life's been a pretty grim business lately. Look, Merran, please don't take this the wrong way, but—if you need anything—money—I'd be more than happy to help you out."

"Thanks, Ev, I appreciate it, but I'm not hurting yet. I can hold out a little longer. Oh hey, what did you think of my dad's mashie? I faded so fast the other day, I never got to ask."

The internist's nurse opened the door and beckoned, and Everett got up with a grunt. "It's the best I ever had. *Why* doesn't Garth come home! We both need him. I'll let you know about tonight. And Merran, don't take any guff, my boy. You haven't done anything."

No one at the bank seemed to agree with that. Merely standing at the teller's window was like being stripped of his rank before the regiment. It was the same at the post office, the cleaners, the liquor store. At the market where the Shaws had shopped for years, the checker studiously joked with the bagger as she punched the register, and she would not touch Merran's money until he had put it on the counter.

"Thanks, kiddo, and have a good day," he said as usual.

She looked right through him, and someone somewhere said, "The nerve!"

He did not go home so much as flee home, feeling flayed, scared. It was all very well to tell himself, to hear Everett say, that he was innocent of any sort of wrongdoing. He could as easily have kept an ice cube intact in the palm of his hand.

Passing the Chester shop on his way, he wondered how Nora was coping and whether he ought to ask her to his dinner party too. I'm not the only one having a hard time, he thought, and I don't think she's mad at me. He turned back.

Nora was out by the trash bin enclosure, scooping dog food from a metal container into a dirty dish. Despite the dreadful upheaval in her life, she looked better than he had seen her look since their high school graduation, before John came into her life. But her temper had not improved. Somewhere in a little grove of trees beyond the building a dog was barking and barking. "Damn dog," she said, slamming down the cover of the container. "I'd like to stuff him in here and bury him, rotten useless animal. I knew I'd be the one to get stuck with him. You think those damn kids of mine have time to feed their lousy mutt? No way."

"So give him to the SPCA."

"He'd only be destroyed. It'd upset the kids."

A little mutt was tied to a tree by a rope as twisted up as an old telephone cord. At sight of Merran and Nora, he danced and lunged, barking and coughing as he tried to reach them. "Shut up!" Nora shouted, and he sat down and whined heartbrokenly. Then he got up and danced again, twisting the rope into ever tighter coils, his bark dwindling to a hoarse gasp.

Nora put the dish down near him and jumped back to avoid another lunge. "I was sure he'd died in the fire—wish he had!—but somehow he got loose, more's the pity."

"Nora, if you don't do something about that rope, he won't be able to reach his food pretty soon. He'll starve to death. And what about some water? He needs water."

"The rain fills up all those holes he digs."

"It isn't raining now."

"All right, all *right!* I'll get it, for godsake!" she said and left him there.

He was surprised and shaken by her criminal neglect. "Down," he said softly, patting the dirty head and gaunt ribs, "lie down, poor ol' boy," and untied the rope and went to work on it.

The dog's size surprised him, its bark having suggested a much larger animal. He talked quietly as he worked on the rope, making himself feel a little better but knowing that he was making it worse for the dog than if he ignored him altogether.

"What do you think you're doing!" Nora said, coming

back with a bowl of water. She almost threw it on the ground. "You better tie him up before he takes off."

"It wouldn't be the worst idea he ever had. Make up your mind, Nora. Either take care of this animal or give him away. He's in bad shape." Finished, he stroked the small shapely head and stood up.

"You take him, then, if you're feeling so overcome."

"Look, Nora, that rope's dangerous. If you're going to keep him tied on it, put swivel clips on both ends. Unless you want him to choke to death."

"I might," she said ambiguously. "Tell me, Merran, are you going in for animal husbandry now? Or did you have another reason for this visit?"

"Not especially. See you around."

He neatened the house, made a salad and dressing, put potatoes into the oven, showered and shaved, and was drinking Scotch and setting the table when the Louises arrived and folded him into their expansive warmth. Guy McKay, a large, merry-faced, openhanded lawyer, was next, with a huge box of candy and an armful of flowers for the table. A few minutes later Everett came, followed by Becca. Her eyes were as dark as lapis lazuli, her black curls beautifully combed—on one side.

It can only get better, Merran thought, and it did, although a chance mention of Blair Bush gave pause to their growing enjoyment.

"Seems so long since he died," Ben said, "but at the same time I can't believe the days have gone so fast." He looked at his watch as if it were recording only the lengthening interval since Blair Bush's death. "That was my first dunk in John's pool. My god."

"Ben swims toward death," Guy McKay said in a voice throaty with doom. "Sounds like a title for a mystery. *Swim Toward Death.* Or . . . *Initiation to Death.* How's that one?"

"Good, but it was hardly an initiation," Jane said. "Ben's got two other deaths under his belt in the line of duty, remember. They were murders, though, remember?"*

"How could I forget? Ben really wiped the chief's eye on those cases. (That was Arthur Hudson, Everett.) And while we're on the subject, maybe this is the time to change your vocation, Benjamin. Hang out your shingle as a private eye. As I get the story, the School Committee's damn near hopelessly split on the matter of your appointment. If it makes up its collective mind—either way—by June, it'll be a miracle. But even if you're a shoo-in, you just might want to change direction, the way things've been going around here. I'm not kidding."

"*We,*" Jane said, her green eyes flashing with warning as she handed coffee around, "are thinking about it, and *we* are most definitely not kidding either. *We* do not intend to complicate life at this stage of the game with a Trojan horse like a superintendency."

Becca had not been listening. "He would have been fifty-one next week," she said softly. "Which reminds me. I still haven't put the date of his death on the family tree."

Ben poured himself some brandy and passed the bottle. "We've heard about that thing often enough, Bec, so how come in all the years we've known you, we've never seen it?"

"I have. Hell of a great thing." Guy stretched his arms wide. "I bet everybody in town's on it."

"What exactly is Blair's relationship to you, Bec?" Jane said.

"Oh, a cousin. I'm not sure how it worked out. I haven't looked at that tree since Mother and Dad died. I feel very . . . strange having to go and sort of cross him off too. Wipe him out, you know?"

"How about we go get it, Bec," Guy said. "Share the trauma with you. Come on."

"No need for you to bother, it's only a step away."

Depressed again by the talk about Blair and by Everett's

---

* Read *She Should Have Cried on Monday* and *Nice Enough to Murder* by E. S. Russell.

growing, gray-faced silence, Merran jumped up. "Sit tight, Guy, I'll take her. And no buts, my girl. It's too far to go in the dark."

Ben laughed. "Well, it's about time you two—"

"Come on, let's clear," Jane said quickly and got up and carried the bowl of flowers to the sideboard.

Merran and Becca were out and back in minutes with a large metal cylinder. Becca uncapped one end and shook out a scroll. It was thick and crackly, like parchment, and its corners curled up stubbornly from its long confinement. They anchored it with coffee cups and the brandy bottle.

The "tree" was an enormous circle. At first glance it looked like a giant spiderweb irregularly hung with dew, its compartmented concentric circles radiating outward from a dime-sized one in the center and variously inscribed. The writing was faded, cranky, indecipherable in places.

"How the hell can anybody understand such a format?" Ben said.

Becca put a blunt-tipped finger on the center. "Start here, with the progenitor."

Eustace Holdridge, 1594. Lndn.

"London, Bec?" Ben said, squinting, and she nodded.

"My," Jane breathed, "oh my. Who started this thing—old Eustace himself?"

"My father's grandfather. He left trunks full of wills, bills, deeds, letters—tons of them!—that Mother and Dad loved wading through and puzzling out. There are some gaps, as you can see, but it took years of work to bring this up to date. All I can say is, I find the Messiah score a lot easier to read."

"Oh, such wonderful names," Jane said. "Peaceful Ames. Verity Furneaux. Lovegod. Plenty. Ithiel. Tabitha Holdridge. Gardiner. I love it! Oh, here's something, Everett—"

"I really don't—" Everett began in a strangled voice, half rising out of his chair, when someone rapped sharply on the front door. Guy was nearest, and opened it.

It was Val Elliot. She was dressed for a formal evening; her camera, a permanent accessory except at John Chester's poolside, hung around her neck. She sailed past Guy, breezily tossed her coat aside, and helped herself to his chair and his brandy. "Forgive me for getting here so late, Merran. I should have phoned first," she said, as if he were alone and waiting for her.

Merran had not seen her in weeks. She was so assured, so elegant, so brimful of thinly veiled mockery at his dismay. "Yes, you should have," he said. "What do you want?" Out of the corner of his eye he could see the deepening flush on Becca's cheeks.

"I wanted to—oh, what in the world is this?" Val stood up, brandy balloon in hand, to look at the great chart. "Why, it's a family tree. I've never seen anything like this, only the usual kind. Mind if I take a picture?"

Her flash went off once, twice, three times, and they sat gaping at her insolent expertise.

"Marvelous," she said. "No problem enlarging it, and then I won't have any trouble reading it. Maybe I'll do a story on your family, Becca. It'd be a great feature. Who're you tracking down?"

"Blair Bush. He was a cousin of mine. We haven't yet worked out how."

"You'll manage, Becca dear, I'm sure. You're the type."

"What's that supposed to mean?" Merran said. "And just exactly what is on your mind?"

"What's on yours? I heard about your preparations for this night's festivities, and I had to see how you really are. Do give me a statement. You too, Ben. If and when you become superintendent, do you plan to reinstate Merran?"

Merran went for her coat and thrust it at her. "Here. Write what you like."

The pointed little face hardened within its frame of sea foam; the hazel eyes gleamed maliciously. "Well, since you won't help me set things straight, I guess I'll have to figure it all out for myself, won't I. And you know I will."

In the silence she shouldered into her coat and went to the door. The bell rang imperiously and the knob turned in her hand. She opened the door and said, "Well *well!*" and stepped aside.

It's like an evil game, Merran thought, as Police Sergeant Dave Bates strode in. The talk turns to death. Guy lets Val in. Val lets the police in. Who'll *he* let in—the Grim Reaper?

Merran sensed immediately that Chief MacWhirter had assigned his underling too heavy a burden. Dave had gone to school with Merran and Becca and knew the others, yet he tried to cover his embarrassment by acting as if he had never seen any of them before.

"What's up?" Merran said.

"Call came about, uh, about you when the chief was about to leave for supper, so he sent me." He cleared his throat a couple of times. "Okay, Dr. Shaw," he said hoarsely, reaching for formality, "where is she?"

"Where is who?"

"Joy Taylor."

"Joy—! Dave, what the hell are you talking about?"

"I'm talking about a missing high school kid, Dr. Shaw."

God, he's pathetic, Merran thought. "I interviewed her briefly and for the first time—ditto the boy—a few weeks ago at school. Ben was there. I saw her a second time in her house, even more briefly, when I went to see her folks at their invitation. Ben was there that time too. I haven't seen her since, nor do I expect to."

"What did you see her about?"

"Come off it, Dave. The chief must have told you, so you know why. Nothing fishy about it. The Taylors gave me permission to interview the two older kids about Connie, the sister who doesn't talk. That's all there is to it. So what's this—invasion—all about?"

Bates's mouth was so dry that his upper lip was turned under and stuck on his teeth. He licked it and worked it loose. "Look, Merran, be reasonable. There's enough evidence to show probable cause for issuing a search warrant, way things've been happening lately—I mean, all the talk about you and, uh, I mean, that's the way it is. So why waste time going for a warrant? Be easier all around if I could go take a look, get it over with?"

Merran ignored the note of pleading in his voice. "Hey, wait a damn minute, Dave! That's the way *what* is?"

Bates licked his lips again. "Well, uh, we have information the girl came to this house. She told her folks at breakfast she was spending the night with her best friend. Before I came over here I called George to see if she went home after all, what with the weather and everything, you know, but he says when she wasn't home before supper, like always, he called around, but no such arrangement was made. The girl's best friend said Joy split after school. She headed for you, obviously."

"I don't see *obviously!*"

"Yeah, well, but I gotta—I mean, I better . . ." The sergeant shrugged apologetically at no one in particular and went out of the room, and moments passed before Ben could ask himself why Guy McKay, a widely respected and often feared legal adversary known for his knowledge, preparation, agility under fire, and success, had not demanded that Bates produce a search warrant or make himself scarce. Or was Guy waiting, quite properly, for Merran to retain him first?

But Guy, like the rest, had been immobilized by the swift and complicated derangement of a pleasant party, and Bates, interpreting the frozen silence he had created as permission to stomp all over the house looking for George Taylor's joy, did so.

Back again, he spread his hands sheepishly to show that he didn't have her either.

"Who told you she came here—George?" Merran said.

"We're, uh, we are not at liberty to say."

Finally Guy McKay spoke. "Chief MacWhirter may not have thought it essential to furnish you with a warrant, Sergeant, nor does the name of the informant have to appear on one so long as the judge considers that probable cause has been amply set forth, but you know, of course, that sooner or later the caller's identity must be made known.

But I am not waiting for that," he said, intimidating in his size and authoritative air. "I want to know *now* who called."

Bates swallowed hard and shook his head. "I don't know who it was. Caller didn't give his name and hung up before I could—well, before I could think of a damn thing to say." He had the grace to look sheepish, an endearing grace that Merran had watched him trade on since the first grade.

"And on the strength of *that* you come barging into my house!"

"Well, hell, Merran, it fitted right in with everything else they're saying about you."

"Which made it equally correct?"

"Well, I—"

"Get out. Get the hell out of my house. And when you and MacWhirter've learned something about character assassination and slander and items like that, you can both come back and apologize. Or better yet, put it in writing and send it to the paper. And good night to you too, Val."

He opened the door and had the thin satisfaction of watching the shamefaced police officer leave. Val followed, a cat smile on that lovely face of hers, and he knew that she was sharpening her claws, preparing, under the mantle of the First Amendment, to tear him to bloody bits. She had been waiting for the chance. He could not have presented her with a better one.

"Bitch," Jane said, and got up to fetch Guy a clean glass.

"This may sound inadequate, Merran," Ben said, "but I wouldn't worry if I were you. We can safely infer that MacWhirter wouldn't have sent Dave without a warrant if he thought there was anything to that call. He had to give the thing token attention, inasmuch as Dave answered the phone. Dave's just too stupid to catch on. It's all garbage, it'll straighten out. People will be falling all over you soon."

"And then he'll feel worse, and so will you, Benjamin Franklin Louis," Jane said acerbically, and with truth. "But in the meantime, the anti-Shaw campaign is assuming awful dimensions and aspects. Thanks for a beautiful dinner, Merran. It was lovely."

A few minutes later they were gone. A slashing rain poured down, renewing and increasing Merran's depression. He cleared the table, stood the cylinder containing Becca's family tree in a corner by the front door, and got started on the dishes, hating to be alone.

He was not alone for long.

Someone knocked on the door. He snatched up a towel and wiped his hands as he went to open it, assuming that Becca was back to fetch her tree—but if so, why didn't she let herself in?—or that Val the Cat wanted a picture of her prey in all his misery and alienation for the next edition.

But it was only another mouse.

It crept in frightened, soaked, bedraggled, but gorgeous nonetheless.

▽

TWELVE

"YOU SAID—YOU SAID you'd help." The girl shuddered and hugged herself with her bare wet arms. She was soaked, and strands of hair were plastered to her pale cheeks. "I waited till they left. The police and all. Then I waited till I thought—till I could"—her chattering teeth chopped up the words. Her nipples were erect with cold and poked through the thin blouse.

"Drum up the courage? Right. I can understand that. But first things first." Merran went to the phone. "Bec? Get back here fast. I'm sorry but I need you."

Would the police and everyone else be sure now that this girl was one of his regular visitors—one of the girls he *liked to help?* Angrily he took a heavy sweater out of the hall closet and almost threw it at her. "Why're you out in this weather without a coat? Put this on. I'll make you some hot cocoa. Had any supper? Didn't think so. Here," giving her the towel, "dry your hair."

When Becca came dripping in, he said grimly, "We have a guest," and went into the kitchen.

"Oh my dear," Becca said, slipping off her coat. Her raspy voice was filled with compassion. She put her arm around the girl and led her to the couch. "Tell me what's wrong."

Joy leaned against her and burst into a storm of tears. "I'm scared," she hiccuped. "I'm so scared."

Becca crooned over her until she had cried herself out. Then Merran gave her cocoa and slabs of buttered bread. She ate gratefully.

"Miss Holdridge is my friend," Merran said. "We sometimes work together. All right?" Her I-don't-care shrug suited him this time. "Good. It's handy having friends to go to."

"I couldn't go home. I couldn't go—there."

"Scary."

She nodded, her eyes on his. Then they went blank, focusing inward, seeing the frightening thing. The full lower lip began trembling again.

Sometimes a whole hour passed, sometimes days passed, while he waited for the next disclosure. But his welfare too was at stake. This was no time to be nondirective.

"Joy," he said carefully, "I think you're worried about your father."

"Yes . . . he . . . he's bothering me. He's at me all the time. I don't understand. He comes into my room when I'm dressing. He just opens the door and walks right in."

"You don't have a lock?"

She shook her head hopelessly. "I did. He took it off. He said he wouldn't have locked doors under his roof. Does he have a right to do that?"

"No, he does not. What happens when he walks in?"

She swallowed hard, and her limpid eyes clouded with panic. "He says he has to check that I'll be ready for school on time. But I'm never late. I've always been on time! He's always picking on me!"

"Really gets on your case, huh."

In her answering sigh was a hint of impatience for the old and foolish. "Like, I wear tights, right? They're hard to put on. Well, what I do, I lie on my bed with my feet up in the air so I can pull them on evenly. He said one day he thought that was stupid. *I* don't think it's stupid."

All at once the color drained out of her face. She bent over, trying to hide, rocking herself for comfort.

"And your father came in one day when you were doing that."

"Yes," whispering. "He was . . . in his underwear . . . and he—he—oh god!"

"And he got turned on."

The rocking stopped. The hands fell away. "I . . . saw. He stood there staring at me. There was such a—a look on his face. My own father. He—he lay down on top of me! He held me—I fought him off. I yelled but my mother didn't come. She didn't come! Connie came. My little sister came and hit him and hit him till he got off me. Oh god, oh god!" Fear and revulsion shook the shapely untried body. "Since then I stay out of his way. I don't let him kiss me anymore. I never will again! Last night I put a chair under my doorknob but he broke it down this morning. That's why I couldn't go home. I can't! Please, Dr. Shaw, don't make me! I hate my mother, I hate her! She didn't come and help me, she didn't come!"

Becca put her arm around the terrified girl. "You can stay with me, dear." She arched an eyebrow at Merran, who nodded.

"I can get a court order if necessary," he said. "It probably won't be, though. But your parents will have to know where you are. Take her home with you, Bec. I'll see to the rest."

"You promise?" the girl whispered.

"I promise. Feeling better?"

"Yes. Thank you." She got up unsteadily, his sweater big enough to cover two of her. "But why, Dr. Shaw? He punched John Chester out once for making a pass at me—well, John only said something, is all—and he wouldn't let me go swimming there anymore—but everybody else does, all my friends! So why is he doing this to me? Why?"

What could he tell her? The very core of a simple truth. "When a man and woman are really happy together," he said, "they treat their kids *as* kids, and with respect."

She smiled wanly, and in the shake of her head was an adult sadness. "My parents don't even respect each other. My mother's always cooking. Cooking and cleaning. She never does anything else—doesn't even talk to him."

"And your father?"

"He eats and eats and watches TV. And after work he washes and puts on clean clothes down cellar. My mother makes him. And last week when Connie wouldn't talk when he tried to make her in your office, she said that after what he'd done when Connie stopped talking, there wasn't *any* way he could wash himself clean. She wouldn't tell me what she meant. But an electrician doesn't get all that dirty, not most of the time."

"Last question. How do your parents get along with your brother and sister?"

"Well, this sounds weird, and maybe I shouldn't say it, but I don't think my mother loves any of us, even my brother. You'd think he'd be her favorite, y'know? I was always—*his* favorite." Her shrug this time was eloquent of the burden that preference had become.

And suddenly Merran knew—or thought he knew—why. It seemed so obvious. It always was, when you knew the *why*. But you couldn't help wondering which of the principals you felt sorriest for. Because you did feel sorry.

He couldn't tell MacWhirter, though. Apart from the matter of client privilege, what good was a strong hunch? He had to present the chief with a certainty.

When Becca had taken the girl away, he called the Taylors and told them where their daughter was, and why, and what he was prepared to do about it. He did not bother notifying the police. He called Ben instead.

"I'd apologize for bothering you this late, Ben, but you might as well get used to it—it's what a superintendent's life is all about. Anyway, you have to know," and quickly he told Ben what had transpired.

"My god—do you realize how lucky you are, Merran? If

Bates had seen that kid hanging around in the shrubbery—!"

"I'd've been lynched. But never mind about that now. We know something shut Connie up when she was three. It has to have been about sex, of course. I think she witnessed George raping Doris or she herself was raped. And what's more, I bet you anything you like, Ben, that those three kids were the result of rape. They couldn't've been conceived any other way.

"I'm as sure of it now as if I'd been a fly on her fancy wallpaper. I think she made the poor bastard pull out all those years—and not too often at that—and probably scrubbed herself afterward with a wire brush! God, Ben, the rawest kind of sex act accompanied by mutual bitterness and disgust and anger, while a ripening girl like the one he married or thought he'd gotten is growing up right under his nose!

"Yeah . . . I think his hair-trigger temper and surprising leanness—considering how he eats—and the goddam flames on his van can be explained by extraordinary sexual tension! Remember what happened when Joy came home while we were there? How he kissed her? How Doris looked? Yes, I'm sure you do.

"As for the hair dye, the boots, the skintight jeans, the belt buckle—George was staying young, unconsciously wooing his daughter Joy, a girl he could never have. Then one day she innocently has her legs up in the air and he can't stand it and makes a move on her and Connie's a witness to that too and is scared all over again, right out of her tree. It's pathetic, Ben."

"Yes, it is. And you think John knew all this."

"Knew it or guessed, knowing his man. Those two had a peculiar relationship, the kind where they tell each other everything but hate each other's guts yet can't let go, like some kind of addiction. And it's likely John said one more thing, and George went for him, after all, with one of those lead weights out of the diving suit. But whether he left and someone else put John in that suit, or he came back later and did it—

"Damn it. I wasn't going to tell MacWhirter, but I can see I may have to. And if I do, I'll have to tell Joy I'm going to have to tell him. And Connie has to talk.

"But Ben, what scared that little kid into mutism when she was three? I wonder. . . . Could they have been involved in some public scandal? What sticks in my head like a burr is the way MacWhirter called George an aging Casanova. Now. You recall anything big in the scandal department happening around here eight years ago?"

Ben reached back into his vast memory for trivia.

"Hm . . . maybe I do. George was caught turning on a prominent Manton matron. Working on her electrical impulses, you might say. Augmenting her circuits—"

"Ben. Enough already. Who blew the whistle on him, do you know?"

"No . . . don't think I do. The library—or the paper—has all the back issues on microfiche. One of us should look it up. I think we're onto something."

"I'll do it first thing tomorrow. Maybe Connie was involved in the disclosure, so it's fair to suppose she saw something, and George threatened to have her head if she ever opened her mouth again, and she took him literally. And learned to love it. I don't knock her loyalty to her big sister, that's valid enough, but she can use it to feed her anger and mask her guilt. Nice, the way people hang on to neuroses. Kids are very good at it."

"Makes sense. And you know, maybe that scandal connects with John's murder. I'll bet George never stopped playing around these past eight years, and John needled him every chance he got. I'm thinking of my first day there, when I had to get a new cap. I tell you about that? John was badgering George—said George had made thisthatandtheother stops so far that week and owed him—John—money. And George said sure, but they weren't home, they don't stay home anymore, they go out and work. I think we may take it that 'they' are the ladies of the house. George was furious. But John kept pushing him."

"You're saying he got fed up after eight years of this and—pardon the expression—put John's lights out?"

"Doused his glim, you mean? He might have. Psychology isn't always right. People aren't all that predictable."

"True. I didn't think George was an ironclad candidate and neither did MacWhirter, but I may have to change my mind, and I think he will too when I tell him what Joy Taylor told Bec and me.

"God, I'm bushed, Ben. Really whacked. I'm not even sure anymore exactly where we are after all this palaver."

"I know where I am—I'm in bed and about to sleep the sleep of the just. I have this day put the finishing touches to my next TV lecture on Star Chamber tactics, slander, libel, and assorted cases like yours. It was a heroic effort, believe me. I'm giving it in the morning, and it'll either cure the committee or kill it—"

"Ben, they'll wreck you! You'll never be a superintendent here or anywhere else if you—"

"—whereas you," Ben continued serenely, "are off and running. No kidding, Merran, you've accomplished a lot tonight. You know the likely reason for Connie Taylor's mutism. You've snatched a fine girl from the very jaws of incest and worse. And whether or not George is a murderer, you've got the parental George by the shorts and you'll certainly be reinstated. Enjoy it, it doesn't happen all that often. 'Night."

Merran regarded the dirty dishes. "Heroes don't do dishes. They sleep the sleep of the just," he said, and went to bed.

And dreamed, again, about keys.

▽

THIRTEEN

HE HELD A SMALL key in his hand. Just as he thought he recognized the lock to which it belonged, it grew bigger and bigger until it was too heavy to carry and was dragging on the ground. He hoisted it onto his shoulder like a length of board, but it kept growing, so Pete Swiggett took one end and helped him carry it along. Pete's dog, Sam, gallumphed over and batted at it playfully with a gigantic paw, so they held it up like a vaulting bar and he rose into the air and cleared it—but very slowly, as if he were suspended in an invisible cradle and being lifted over through a highly viscous atmosphere. He barked and barked, and Merran opened his eyes.

A dog was indeed barking. Merran stumbled to the window and leaned out into the sunlight.

Gifford, full of ecstasy over the bright day, was excitedly summoning him to come out and play.

"How about some golf?" Everett said. "It's a fine morning, not too breezy."

"Okay, great, Ev. But are you sure you're up for it? Last night—"

"I'm perfectly fine. Clarkson thinks we caught it in time—some odd virus—and he told me to keep active. What does upset me is your situation."

"I've some good news about that. Be right down."

His news was the quid pro quo he had exacted from the Taylors the night before. They would inform the Superintendent and the press of their appreciation for his work thus far with Connie. For his part, he would withdraw his threat to take them to court provided they embarked on family therapy and Joy stayed indefinitely with Becca Holdridge. But he made it absolutely clear that he would discuss the entire matter with the chief of police.

This cheering news was not proof against the arrival of a beery foursome, and Everett sliced viciously. A divot flew into the air, the ball into the rough. This put Merran off his stroke, and another divot flew.

With or without permission, Gifford always accompanied Everett over the course, sitting neat and attentive to one side while he teed off, fetching the rare divot, and walking at Everett's heel with a small bag of balls around his neck. He fetched both divots now, to the loud chaffing of the waiting four.

"Hard luck, guys," one said. "But no fair if the mutt helps you out there too. Not on a lousy l'il par three."

"Come, Giff," Everett said tightly, pulling his wheeled bag behind him.

Boozy laughter followed them down the fairway.

As they waded into the rough to look for their balls, someone called to them from the cemetery.

It was Pete Swiggett. He waved as he threaded his way around the gravestones, and vaulted the wall easily. Sam loped down the hill after him but stopped to decorate a bunch of chrysanthemums, after which exertion he collapsed in the shade.

"Morning, Merran, Mr. Upham," Pete shouted through the trees. "I was just putting some flowers on my father's grave when I happened to see you. Saves the wife a call. Part you ordered finally came yesterday night, Mr. Upham, so I can put it in anytime you want. Seeing it's you, I'll just let somebody else wait."

"Thank you, Pete. Come at your convenience, you have the key. Now I'd best get out of this." He dismissed the plumber with a nod and a smile, then, with Gifford waiting honorably on the fairway, poked around for his ball.

Merran, a little beyond him, gazed in dismay at a vigorous spread of poison ivy. Tentatively he parted some greasy leaves with the head of his club.

"Got it?" Everett said.

"No. Find yours?"

"Just this minute. Take the penalty, Merran, and let's go. We're better out of this."

"Oh, I think I see it—" Merran said, and then he heard five sounds in close succession.

First, the unmistakable *crack*, clean and dry, of a well-hit ball.

Then, Everett moving with care in the thick growth.

Then, from the loud group on the tee above and behind them, a "Fore!" followed by another cry, of triumph or derision.

And then a muffled *plonk* as a ball fell almost at Merran's feet.

As he turned angrily, something hit him behind the ear. He might have heard that too except that in the very same instant he seemed to be plunging away from the sound at great speed, face down into the poison ivy and past it, until he was at the bottom somewhere and could not fall any farther or hear any more.

"Take a lot to break *that* bone," Clarkson said, plucking Merran's hand off the bandaged pain behind his right ear. "Concussion and a nice hematoma but no fracture. Leave it alone."

"Guess that ball ran out of gas by the time it got to me," Merran whispered weakly.

"Lucky for you," the doctor told him repressively, as if the whole thing were his fault.

Merran looked around dizzily at the white bed covering, the white wall, the doctor's white jacket. Everything began to spin. He closed his eyes. "Everett get me here?"

"Carry you? He couldn't carry a baby. No, it was Pete Swiggett. Who may have damaged you more, carrying you off that course instead of waiting for the EMTs," Clarkson said hopefully. "Nauseous? It'll pass. Rest. Sleep."

His whispered name brought him back from the door.

"Yes?"

"About Everett—he all right—all this golf—?"

"Best thing he can do for his type of heart. Worry about yourself."

"Doctor—"

"What *now,* Merran?"

"I fell in some poison ivy."

"I'll give you a shot. Sleep."

Get the job done and on to the next constituted Dr. Clarkson's bedside manner and working style. He was gone before Merran could delay him further with a thank-you.

He slept through the shot for the poison ivy and dreamed that a huge ball was hurtling toward him. He ducked, and it turned into a key that got smaller and smaller until it fitted into his ear. It turned, as in a lock, and the ear opened and through it he saw—something.

He squinted. More keys hung in the air. All sorts of keys. They vanished, and he woke up.

That's twice now, he thought. So what about keys? Whose keys? What keys?

Thinking hurt and made him dizzy. He fell asleep again, gratefully, and the pain and nausea and dizziness continued without his knowing anything about it.

Warm lips on his cheek kissed him awake.

Becca, looking somehow different. Thinner? Neater? Anyhow, wearing a pretty dress he had not seen before and carrying flowers and a bowl of bright oranges.

He reached for her strong blunt-tipped hand. "Hey, Bec, you look terrific. Wear that outfit when I take you to the Ritz. We have to celebrate."

She blushed and withdrew her hand.

"What's up?" he said uneasily.

"Nothing. Why?"

"I feel something's going on. And that I'm not going to like it. Come on, give. You didn't get all dressed up just to come in and see me."

"No. But you first."

"Who's my successor?"

She blushed again. "It's just an interview. I told you I was getting fed up. I decided to look around."

"Where?"

She tossed an orange from one hand to another. "Oh . . . New York."

He turned cold under the thin blanket. "Juilliard?"

She began peeling the orange and did not look at him. "Well, you know, they offered—again. It's hard to turn down a flattering offer." She handed him a piece of the orange.

He pushed it away. "I suppose you think there's no politics down there? And what kind of time is this for an interview? Seven o'clock at night, for godsake!"

"Don't get upset, Merran, it isn't good—"

"What do you mean, don't get upset! Of course I'm upset! Who wouldn't be upset!"

"I should think you'd be glad I have a chance like this. I always wanted to get back there." She ate the piece of fruit he had rejected and put the rest down. "It isn't very sweet. I'm sorry. Maybe another one—"

"The hell with the goddam oranges. You can't make a plan like that and waltz in here and tell me you're off and running just because some jerk calls you up and makes you an offer."

"The head of the piano department, Merran."

"Big deal."

"You're angry."

"You bet I'm angry!"

"You feel I ought to stay here—"

"Damn right I do!"

"—and be your old buddy for the next thirty-two years."

"Damn right you should!" he shouted, and his head began throbbing violently. Everything went fuzzy, and he blinked and blinked and rubbed his eyes.

"You feel you aren't seeing too clearly," she said. Her raspy voice had an edge he had never heard before.

He stared at her, saw the paper-white skin, the not-so-plump-anymore cheeks with the red splotches on them, like rouge applied by a child. He saw the eyes, still as blue as lapis lazuli but sparkling now with anger. Saw an unusual tautness in the good, long-familiar face. Saw the shiny curls for once not so tangled as a floor mop. Saw so much and missed so much more.

"You'd better sleep, and I'd better go or I'll be late," she said, all the flash and sparkle gone like flame doused by cold water.

"Right," he said sullenly.

"See you tomorrow."

"Sure."

The door closed noiselessly.

Clarkson discharged him in the morning. "No golf, no swimming for a few days at least, Merran. Not too much walking around in the house, either." He permitted himself a small smile, possibly because he knew that inaction would greatly annoy his patient. "Call if there's any change—head, skin. Upham'll drive you home." He was gone like a whippet.

Merran washed and gathered his few things together and sat down to wait for Everett. He thought about Becca—disloyal! egocentric!—who needs her!—and such anger raged in him that he had to stretch out dizzy and nauseated on the bed.

* * *

Noise filled his ears. He groaned, and the noise stopped.

"Sorry, dear. I'll be as quick as I can," someone said.

He lifted his head and looked around. A cleaning woman, splayfooted and shapeless in blue and white mattress ticking, kicked a vacuum cleaner out the door and flapped a rag over the windowsill, raising puffs of dust.

"Oh," he said, holding onto his whirling head. "Good morning."

"It's 12:30, dear."

"But—I was supposed to leave at eleven."

"You been discharged? My. Way you been sleepin', dear, I thought they just brung you in."

"I've been waiting for my ride."

"You ain't heard the news, then?"

"News?"

She all but licked her lips. "A murder, dear. Awful thing it was. They brought her in early this morning, but she won't be leavin' like you. Pretty head all bashed in. Terrible shame it was. And in such a nice town too."

His hand went involuntarily to the bruise behind his ear. "Bad things happen in all kinds of places," he said indifferently.

"Bad things," she said huffily, "comes a women tryna be men. They shouldn't oughta be pokin' around the old station all hours a the night, takin' pitchers, buttin' in. That's men's work, is what I say. Serves 'em right, all that foolishness 'bout equality." She stuffed her dustrag into a pocket and went muttering to the door.

"Wait," he said, his voice sounding peculiar. "Who was it? Who was the victim?"

Mollified, she turned instantly. "A reporter, dear. Name of Elliot. Everybody knew her, just about."

Val the Cat. He had loved her once, or thought he had. He had hated her, or thought he had. He lay back and closed his eyes again, and the cleaning woman said happily, "Thass right, dear, you get a nice nap now," and shuffled away.

* * *

When next he opened his eyes he saw Everett reading patiently in the chair at the foot of the bed. He sat up and apologized.

"No need," Everett said tonelessly, slipping his book into his pocket and collecting the oranges. He looked more worn and pale than ever. "How are you feeling?"

Merran stood up. "Bit shaky, but okay, I guess." All he wanted was to be home. To call Becca, for one thing. To thank her for the oranges and the flowers, he told himself. I owe her that, he said.

Dave Bates appeared in the doorway. "Sorry, Merran. Afternoon, Mr. Upham." Bates was more assured than he had been two nights before. "Look, I know you're under the weather so I'll make it fast. It's about Val Elliot. She was murdered sometime yesterday."

"Yes, I heard. The cleaning lady told me. You suggesting I did away with her after I finished stashing the Taylor girl in my house, Dave?"

"Sorry about that, Merran. The chief said to say I was out of line and to apologize. I thought I knew what he wanted, but I guess I was wrong. But about Val Elliot, you and she were pretty tight, I understand."

"A long time ago."

"Yeah. All I wanted to know, could you tell me anything that might give us a lead of some kind?"

"No. I wish I could."

"You don't know what she would have been doing down the old railroad station?"

"How the hell would I know that! If she was on assignment—"

"Editor said she wasn't. Said she was off duty two nights ago, and there was nothing that'd put her down there that time of night with or without her camera anyway."

"Two nights ago? When you were at my house?"

"She was killed very late that night or early in the morning. Some kids found her this morning when they should've been in school. A coupla good blows to the head, and another one after death—a good dent but no fresh bleeding, see—so she may've been killed elsewhere 'n dumped there. Clothes not messed up—no rape.

"And here's something real weird. Her keys're in her car, which is near the body, and there's a hundred bucks in her wallet, ditto, but her apartment's cleaned out. No camera or TV, no typewriter, stuff she'd be bound to have. Looks like the killer does her in—at the old station or wherever, cleans her place out, stashes the loot who knows where, and leaves the car *by the body!* Would you believe? Clean, neat job. Dead easy zapping somebody who don't happen to be looking. Now, you don't know about anybody she might've been mad at or had trouble with?"

"No. Sorry, Dave. I'm really sorry."

"Yeah, well, just thought it was worth a shot. Take care. You need help getting out of here?"

"I'll take care of him," Everett said, and did, without offering to exchange banalities about the woman who had served him so well during his campaign. He only said as he opened the car door, "Oh. They gave me this at the desk. I almost forgot." He fished an envelope out of his pocket, gave it to Merran, and told Gifford to quiet down and sit in the back.

The envelope contained a telephone message from Becca: "Back for dinner. You rest, I'll cook. Ben says the committee forgives you because of Taylor statement."

Merran angrily crumpled up the note and put it into his pocket.

Everett drove him home as carefully as if he were a giant egg with a crack. "Now, rest," he said, helping him into the house and settling him on the couch. "I'll let myself out. If you need anything, call right away."

When he had gone, Merran felt in his pocket for Becca's note but did not reread it. Reinstatement as a worthy member of his community did not reassure him, because he knew that he would never get back as much as his short-lived downfall had taken away. He felt vulnerable, used up, and badly shaken by the news of Val Elliot's death. He wished that Everett had stayed with him. He thought about his father and his flight from painful memories, and of how much he missed and needed him, and this awareness, renewed and sharpened by exhaustion and weakness, was another physical blow that he felt in his whole body.

And Becca was in New York and might go there to stay.

He lay shuddering from head to toe with the cold that comes from shock and fear, and warm sunlight filled the big room and the birds sang. He recognized the sweet song of a robin; the chirping of finches, quarrelsome and greedy; the flutelike tootling of a jay. Calmer and warmer, he went into the kitchen for bread and peanut butter and hot cocoa. Nothing in the world was saner than peanut butter. Slowly he began feeling better.

He looked out at the backyard while he ate, remembering how his parents had always worked on it together. His father should be working on it now and letting himself grieve instead of lopping off the living past, his son along with it, and running away in agony.

I'll call him, Merran thought. I'll tell him to come home. Everett would like that too.

But Garth Shaw did not answer his phone.

And Becca was in New York.

And Val the Cat was dead.

Damn them. Damn them all for complicating my life, he raged, making himself dizzy again. He lay down and slept because there was nothing else to do.

Kitchen clatter and good smells woke him. He threw off the blanket—he did not remember covering himself—and said, "Who's there?" and a raspy "Just me" filled him with joy. He went into the kitchen; leaned against the doorframe; said, "How was New York?"

Val Elliot couldn't have said it any nastier.

"Exciting," Becca said evenly, spearing chicken onto a platter.

"And?"

She went by him to put the platter on the dining room table, which, he saw now, was invitingly set. "I don't think you're supposed to have any wine yet."

"Have some for me."

"No, I'm sleepy enough already. How about water—or milk or orange juice? Decaf coffee? I don't think that would charge you up. The thing is, alcohol and caffeine are both bad for a concussion—mask the symptoms."

"What's all this teamilkjuice business? I asked you a question, Bec."

Her hair flew around like a crazed floor mop but that lapis gaze regarded him steadily. "They offered me the job again. Being on the piano staff. They liked my Brahms particularly. And my Debussy. I can start in May, if I want to, although they'd like me right away. I said I'd think about it, that I may be getting a better offer."

The beautiful meal she had made might as well have been canned spaghetti. He pushed the food around on his plate and said, "Val's dead."

"Yes." She put down her fork and stared at it. "Yes, Ben told me. She wasn't my favorite sort of person, but she didn't deserve that."

Everett had said the same thing about John Chester. It was the kind of thing one said.

They went on eating, and silence grew between them.

At length Becca pushed her plate away and got up. "I never could stand your moods, Merran—they're the second worst thing about you—and I've had a full day. Do you mind if I leave now? I'll clean up tomorrow. Oh—where's my chart? I forgot to take it the other night."

He examined his distorted reflection in the back of a spoon. "By the sideboard, I think. Or the front door. Around here somewhere."

"I can't find it. Never mind—I'll look around tomorrow. 'Night."

The phone rang, and he threw down the spoon.

"Merran? Everett. Feeling better? Good. I take it for

granted you're going to bring an action against the fool who hit you? I have his name and address. I've seen all too much of these beer-guzzling golfers. They're a menace on every course, and injuries like yours happen everywhere and often. We should stop them if we can."

"Well, I hadn't thought about it. Don't know if I should, Ev. After all, it was an accident."

"Yes, but they teed off too soon, and that makes all the difference. We were both easy targets at that range. I have the ball that hit you."

"Well, now—"

"My attorney will handle the whole thing, Merran. I can recommend him with utmost confidence."

He's being fatherly and helpful, so why not? Merran thought. Isn't that just what I need? "All right," he said slowly, dizzy again. "Uh-oh—think I better go lie down, Ev. Will you call me tomorrow?"

Late next morning the front doorbell woke him, and he went carefully downstairs. He had not shaved in two days—what difference did it make? It wasn't Becca, or she'd have let herself in—his right cheek hurt, and the bright day seared his eyes when he opened the door.

The man on his threshold was one of the golfers who had laughed him and Everett off the tee: a loose-lipped, flabby man with the eyes of a steady drinker and a habit of glancing constantly at his watch as if checking the time for his next highball.

"I'm Andy Ross," he said anxiously. "Your buddy called and told me what happened, and listen, Dr. Shaw, it was a goddam irresponsible thing I did, teeing off too soon, and it won't happen again. I admit we all had one beer too many but I swear it wasn't my ball that hit—say, what the hell's the matter with your cheek?"

Merran felt it. It was hot and swollen. "Come on in," he said, his tongue oddly stiff, and went to the nearest mirror.

Beard and grubbiness aside, he looked terrible—like a

squirrel with a full pouch—and the eye above it was swelling shut even as he examined it. Whatever Clarkson had shot him up with hadn't helped. He was going to be out of action for a week.

"Just a minute," he said and called Clarkson, who told him to come right to the office. "I'm not up for driving—"

"Cab," the doctor said and hung up.

"Look, I'll drive you," Ross said, fascinated by the increase in Merran's cheek. "But first just take a look at what I showed your friend. The ball he said hit you just had a blue dot, right? Well, here's mine."

The ball was handsomely, even gaudily monogrammed.

"Kids gave me a gross of 'em for my birthday," Ross said proudly. "I don't use any other ones. 'Sides, you'd expect the one that hit you to be where you fell, right? Where he said he picked it up, in the pee eye? Sure. But mine was maybe eight feet away, and no pee eye at that spot, and that's the honest truth. Now, wanna dress first or go as you are? Don't matter to me. You're the doctor, harharhar!

"And talking about doctors," he added in an offhand way as he helped Merran into his car, "Ben Louis just got canned on account of some lecture he gave. Whaddyuh think of them golfballs!"

Part III
Ben

▽

FOURTEEN

TWO DAYS HAD PASSED since Ben's summary suspension by the School Committee and the simultaneous reversal of a move to reinstate Merran.

Guy McKay, driving to his office after a late lunch, saw them ambling, aimless and dispirited, through a fine autumn afternoon and ordered them into his car.

"We'll have a brandy. Before anything else happens around here. Not to worry, lads," he said happily.

He led the way into the stone house inside the cemetery gates and made for a moth-eaten wreck of a chair whose springs dangled like roots that had been rudely torn out of the stone floor. But it was one of the few chairs that embraced his big body with no more than a friendly murmur of recognition, and he would not hear of its removal. He lowered himself into it with anticipatory pleasure. "Those pitiful bastards don't know which end to think with, and I—ah, thank you"—accepting a balloon of brandy from Merran—"I am going to teach them."

"How?" Ben stared into his glass as if it contained a dose of hemlock.

"Easily! Did this or any previous committee ever tell you what you could or couldn't say in those TV lectures of yours?"

"No. I described them loosely, and that was that."

"Good. We may therefore infer that their absence of comment over the years is an expression of absolute confidence in your judgment rather than an unprofessional display of disinterest. The judge will have no trouble seeing this.

"However. The present committee never communicated with you in any way about any lecture that pleased or displeased them? Never, that is, until you got to your office yesterday and found the door padlocked, at which time your secretary merely passed on a verbal message that you'd been suspended?"

"Right. I was surprised to hear that this group had seen all the lectures—eight or nine, I think, since they've been serving together. Either they're the most unmannerly, unprofessional bunch Manton ever had—which doesn't take all that much doing [What Ben doesn't know about school committees, Jane would have said, isn't worth knowing—and neither are the committees]—or someone deliberately stirred them up by representing this particular lecture as an ad hominem attack masking some hidden evil purpose of my own. I meant to hurt them, I admit it, but I used a boomerang instead of a cudgel."

"No you didn't, Ben, and they'll learn that when we bring two civil rights actions—one for you, one for Merran—under Section nineteen eighty-three in Federal Court, seeking damages for deprivation of your constitutional rights to freedom of speech under the First Amendment and to due process under the Fourteenth Amendment. Has a fine ring to it, don't you agree?" He cackled with joy. "Just as well you didn't get yourself organized right away, Merran, because now I can give the bastards both barrels! We'll seek preliminary injunctions ordering your reinstatements pending final disposition; that is, either going to trial or settling and withdrawing." Another joyous cackle. "O yesyes*yes!* They'll settle quietly."

"Great," Ben said without enthusiasm.

"What's the matter, Ben? Did I use a bad word?"

"Reinstatement," Merran said shrewdly through his stiff puffy lips, and laughed.

Guy looked surprised. "I don't get it, Ben. Isn't it what you want?"

"Damned if I know. Carry on. What's Section nineteen eighty-three?"

"The Civil Rights Act, Ben. It gives cause of action to anybody deprived of his constitutional rights by the government or by a governmental actor, that is, by an official acting under color of law, such as a chairman of a school committee. Color of law. Love that phrase! After all the years I've been in practice, I still love the language of the law. Color of law. Beautiful." He held his glass admiringly to the light, as if its glowing amber contents were a distillation of the Constitution of the United States of America. "You'll both seek money damages, naturally."

"Oh?" Ben said, no less miserable. "Hadn't thought of that. What are we looking at?"

"A mil, maybe a mil and a half, for you at least. Possibly more for Merran."

"A mil? A million? That's—that's crazy!"

"Don't knock it, Ben. The Supreme Court has held that even the smallest deprivation of First Amendment rights is an irreparable harm. As to rights to due process, each of you was entitled to notice of the charges against you and to a hearing at which you'd have the opportunity to cross-examine and rebut, and those stupid bastards went ahead and acted as if the Constitution had never been heard of. Well, lads, they can't be allowed to get away with it. What they did to you two constitutes a ve-r-ry serious breach of the law. You know it, and when I'm through with them, they'll know it.

"Look, Ben. This'll take a few weeks to get in train. It may be four to six weeks before our application for two preliminary injunctions comes up. So treat this interim as a vacation. Take Jane on a trip. Smell the roses. Enjoy yourself in another way for a change. There's more to life than education, for godsake.

"Your situation's a little different, Merran. How are you feeling, by the way? You look like a squirrel packing for the lean times."

"Oh, it's better," Merran said, fingering his swollen cheeks. "Little stiff. A few more days, and I'll be good as new, Clarkson says. I've had pee eye before, but this is ridiculous. And what strikes me as even more ridiculous is that Everett wants me to retain Percival Jessiman to sue the pants off the guy he says laid me low with a dirty old Wilson."

"Oh? So? And?"

"So how am I supposed to sue somebody who uses nothing but brand-new gorgeously monogrammed Spaldings?"

"The discrepancy does present a problem, but hey, if litigation looks good to Everett Wilder Upham, why should a detail like that constitute an impediment? People have sued for reasons you wouldn't believe."

"I can believe anything, Guy. You were saying? About my situation?"

"That it's a little more complicated, what with the libel and slander and its effect on halting your practice. I can't promise anything—that is, if you want me to do this. Even if you do, we may not get to first base, but I look forward to a good go. Libel and slander. Guh-reat!" and he clapped his big hands merrily as if the best part of Merran's life were the nastiness that had flooded it.

"What comes first?" Ben said, smiling despite his depression.

Guy grinned like a wolf about to sit down to a tasty fat haunch. "We schedule depositions for immediately following the return date—the date when your cases are added to the court's docket. We depose the Super and every member of the school committee. We seek admissions from all of them, including their statements to the press and in committee meetings calling for your summary removals. We get clippings from the papers for the last three weeks about you two and the committee. We get the editor to certify that these clips were printed in specified editions of the paper. Long before which time, they'll back down and talk settlement. I'm telling you, it'll be a long day before any of those stupid bastards thinks of running for office again.

"A toast, lads. Cheers, and no looking back. From here on in, it's downhill all the way. And to make that happen, I've got to pop off now!"

"You're not thinking of dropping this, are you, Ben?" Merran said as they walked away. "Because it looks like you don't have a thing to worry about. There's all that money we're going to rake in, and I'd lay odds the committee'll elect you without even bothering to discuss it."

"The way they do everything, you mean?" Ben laughed harshly. "You're probably right, but I wasn't thinking about my professional future. As for all that money, whose pockets do you think it'd come out of? The poor old taxpayers', that's whose, including yours and mine. I wouldn't touch a nickel of it. No, it may be downhill in one way, but I think it's all the way up in another. Things have gotten very complicated around here."

"I don't follow."

Ben heaved a sigh. "I mean that I just heard myself say something I said a few minutes ago. What reason would anyone have to convince the committee I had a nefarious reason for giving that lecture? Talk about nefarious! Talk about hidden! devious! Doesn't the manner of my suspension and yours smack of some other devious happenings around here? That letter to the paper that ruined Everett's bid for office. The letters and smears about you that just about put you out of business. Two murders. And not just two murders but the modus operandi! Reminds me of *Macbeth*. The sun's shining down on us right now, but everything seems dark, cloaked. It doesn't feel like a sunny day to me. I swear, if John Chester were still alive, I wouldn't put it past him to have engineered all this."

"No way, Ben. He may have acted like something that crawled out from under a rock, but he never had a hidden motive in his life. Look, I've been around and around this and gotten nowhere. You're the expert on mystery and murder, you figure out who's doing what, and why. Take a vacation first, though, as Guy said, before you start sleuthing, or Jane'll have something to say."

(There's plenty of time for both, Jane would say, so start *now.*)

Ben thought for a moment, then actually smiled. "Elementary, my dear Watson. We start with a list of everything that's happened so far, and all the questions we have. Come for supper. Jane's lasagna has a way of clearing the head for thinking. Might even do something for that face of yours. And Bec may drop in."

Neither of them came.

Sensing, the moment she got home from school, that her house had been entered in her absence, Becca Holdridge spent hours going over every inch of it from cellar to attic to see what was missing. Nothing was, but her uneasy feeling remained.

And Merran was lying near the smoldering remains of the little garden shed in his backyard, with another murderous dent in his skull and blood and dirt in his thick brown hair, which effectively drove from his memory his intention to tell Chief MacWhirter about George Taylor's motivation for murder, or to look in the library microfiches for scandals involving his sex life as it pertained to his work and his mute daughter.

"I was going to have supper with Ben and Jane," he told Dr. Clarkson and Ben, somewhere around midnight. His swollen face was as white as the hospital pillowcase, his eyes closed from shock and exhaustion. " 'Fore I left, called Dad. Trying for days to get him, he's never in, but this time line was busy—'less something's wrong with it. Going to try again in ten minutes, so I just sat in the kitchen, staring out the window. Something moving out by the shed—a shadow.

Behind a big hemlock. Then a little light—not flashlight, more like striking a match. Went out to see and—*pow!*" His lips tightened in pain.

"A good thing I went back to look for you," Ben said. "I had a feeling something was wrong. You say you didn't see who was in your yard. Did you see anyone, talk to anyone, on your way home? Was there anyone in the neighborhood, or a car, anything that didn't seem quite right?"

Merran's eyes opened, closed wearily. "No, nobody. Oh. Nora. Jogging. Bitch. Murder sure doesn't agree with some people."

The doctor glared down at him as if being laid low a second time deprived him of the right to criticize anyone else. "You were hit in the same place, Merran. I hope neither of us has to answer for the consequences. Now sleep. Benjamin, it's late. Go home."

Ben went.

▽

FIFTEEN

JANE PUT THE BREAKFAST dishes in the sink. "Don't get up, Ben. Let's do what you told Merran you were going to do—list everything that's happened so far and every question, every thought, we have about it plus anything else we can think of. Merran, Becca, Everett, Nora, Guy, the chief—everyone can add to it, once we've got going. It's bound to produce something helpful. Too bad Val Elliot isn't around anymore. She must have known an awful lot about the people in this town."

She sat down opposite him at the kitchen table with paper and pencil and was about to write a heading when she noticed the look on his face.

"What?" she said, pencil poised.

"Nothing. Why?"

"You had a strange expression on your face."

Except that she was now a little grayer and stringier (as Ben had known she would be), she had not changed since their first meeting. Which suited him just fine. But now was not the time to say so. He said, smiling inwardly, "I was only thinking how much I love you, is all."

"Thank you, and vice versa, but no getting sidetracked. Now. John Chester, our first murderee of the fall season."

"And Manton's premier moneymaker."

"Premier in intent, maybe. He'd never have made it to the top. He thought small. A mean, small-spirited man."

"Right. I think he got more nasty satisfaction from needling George about his sexual activities than he ever got money from blackmailing him about them. Also, Nora said he made her pay out of her housekeeping money for the running suits she wore to advertise the shop. He really made her sweat, wouldn't you say? Which reminds me. I ever tell you she threw herself at me a few weeks ago?"

"I'm surprised it took her so long. Since those brats of hers were babies, she's made a move on almost every man who crosses her path. John has to have substituted money for sex after they had the kids. Why'd he have kids anyway? Kids cost."

"He'd screw you as soon as look at you, if I may be allowed such a modest venture."

"Ben, please. That was the second one, and it was dreadful, far below your usual low standard. No more, okay? All right, what else?"

"Well, John couldn't have been nastier to Everett about the burial plot—and Ev made a perfectly proper businesslike offer that Nora wanted to accept then and there—called Ev a bastard—"

"Ben, we have to do this chronologically. John's house burned down because of his penny-pinching, but Everett asked him the first time before that fire."

"The fire marshal never established the absolute cause of that fire. Maybe it was the penny in the fuse box, maybe it was the faulty heater in the shed. George claims it was both. John denied both. Naturally the insurance company chose to think the fault was John's on both counts."

"Suppose somebody else was responsible? Nobody liked John. God, this list is a mess. If we're going to be chronological, Ben, we've left out Blair Bush's death by electrocution in the dressing room due to John's penny-pinching."

"And Blair's vanity. Professional hairdryers are much

more powerful than the kind you get in any department store."

"True, but never mind that. So we sum John up with one word, 'money.' And there are three suspects. George. Nora. And Everett, poor old sweetie."

"MacWhirter's virtually certain George really has an alibi. Everett has a heart condition, Merran said, although Everett told him he had some weird virus. In any case, I don't see that tired old man bashing John's head in and then dressing him up for a spot of deep-sea diving. Six feet under."

"Ben, *please.* All right, but remember, Everett could have bashed John and someone else could have done the rest, whether they actually did it together or did each act separately and alone. MacWhirter said so."

"Yes, but it's out of the question that Everett was involved. There's never been a murmur about that. And I wouldn't say he was overjoyed when John was buried. He's clearly not that kind of person."

"Nora, then. If anyone despised John, she did. And if anyone was overjoyed to see him buried, she was. You saw the expression on her face at the funeral. And lately she's been looking better than she has in years."

"I'm not a Nora-watcher, I wouldn't know. But she was sick when John was killed. She was so pale and stiff with flu, she could hardly stand up. And she's small-boned and short. What—five two? five three? If someone in her condition could've wrested him into that suit, then I, as they say, am a Dutchman."

"I guess," Jane said, unconvinced, finishing this last note on John Chester. "All right. Next victim. Val Elliot. Over to you."

"A bitch to all but Everett. She handled his campaign well. He had great regard for her. And to be fair, so did I, professionally speaking. She was damn good at her job."

"Merran told her they were through."

"You could understand why if you ever heard her play that recorder of hers."

"We need your incisive Harvard-honed thinking now, so let's don't you be frivolous, Ben. What else?"

"Well . . . the only thing I can think of is the way she crashed Merran's dinner party, took pictures of Bec's family tree, made nasty cracks to her—"

"She was nasty to everybody that night. I wonder if she was that way to people on the paper. Nastiness detracts significantly from professionalism, seems to me."

"Maybe MacWhirter knows. Make a note to ask him. Also, who could have gotten her down to the old railroad station? Was the murderer in a car too, or on foot? Had he hitched a ride with her? Was he someone she knew? Could anything be made of any tire tracks or footprints at the murder scene? And exactly what was stolen from her, and how was the stuff carted away—her car, the murderer's, what?"

Jane's pencil flew over the paper. "Whew!" she said, shaking her wrist, and read over what she had written. "Speaking chronologically, we left out those letters you got about Merran. The first one came before anything else."

"Ah yes. I had the idea once that John had written them—the first one, anyway, though I didn't see any motive. Then I thought George did. Then I thought Val might have. But John was killed, George can't sit still for three seconds except to eat, and Val was killed."

"Everett, then? Or Nora? And could either of them have set fire to Merran's garden shed?"

"Everett treats him like a son, Jane. Why would he want to hurt him? And what was in it for Nora? Money? Hardly. She told Merran not to come to the pool again, which means less money for her, not more. Not all that great an amount, but still. As for sex, Merran has no use for her, never did, and she knows it."

"A woman scorned could have written those letters and made those phone calls and burned down that shed. Better ask him."

"If he's up to it, I will. Think I'll get over to the hospital now. Clarkson may allow him to go home today."

She nodded absently, still looking at her messy list, and he kissed her and was almost out the door when she said, "Ben, John got hit on the head once, and Val too. And Merran got hit twice if you count the golf ball—which reminds me that we forgot to put that business down. Could Everett have done it? Because two different balls don't add up, you know."

"It bothers me too, but again, why Everett? No way. Anyway, I think it's obvious he simply picked up the wrong ball so as to get the hell out of all that pee eye. Not deliberately, I don't mean that, but one that was close enough to where Merran fell so that he thought it was the one that hit him. My god, Jane, there must be a million balls in that poison ivy. Any golfer would rather take the penalty than spend time looking around in it for a lousy ball, it isn't worth it. But you were saying?"

"About what?"

"About head-bashing."

"Head-? Oh. I was just wondering. All that hitting on the head. Could the same person have done it? And/or was the basher righthanded or lefthanded?"

"Make another note to ask MacWhirter. He might know something useful by now. Because, if you'll pardon my saying so, in this past half hour we sure as hell haven't made any noticeable *head*way."

He darted out laughing as she threw her pencil at him.

She folded the list and put it into her pocket, not dissatisfied with the start they had made. It lacked a few important items, and others on it they had misinterpreted. Even so, she would have kissed Ben, pun or no pun, had she realized, on looking at it again, that his parting estimate was wrong.

She would have given his handsome head a good clout, too, if she had known that, in discovering the unconscious Merran by the ruined garden shed, he had unknowingly ("Thoughtlessly" would be a better word, she would have said) obliterated two easily identifiable footprints.

▽

SIXTEEN

BEN MET BECCA COMING out of the hospital.

"How's it going, Bec?" he said, worrying, surprised to see her away from school at any time in the morning. She seemed distracted and the red patches on her cheeks had faded. That she was ill was a possibility he rejected with all his strength.

Her smile failed utterly. "School just isn't the same without you around, Ben. And this town isn't the same either, not anymore. Something's happening—something's already happened. When you were locked out, the whole staff should have left—all of us, even Maintenance and the bus drivers. You're the best part of this system, and everybody knows it. But nobody made a move, nobody! Including me! I feel just—I feel sick and ashamed."

"Got a minute to talk?" he said. "Come on in, and I'll buy you a drink."

She did not hear him. Gripping the bannister between them, she started down the polished granite steps. "You know about the offer from Juilliard? I've decided to accept it. I'll start right after New Year's. Meanwhile, I have quit. And please don't say anything about contracts, Ben. They're meant to protect the employee, not the employer, and an employee can't be forced to work against his will. The committee will have my formal resignation in today's mail, those miserable—and that Martin Guinness is the worst of them! Ever since that nice boy of his dropped out, he's had it in for you and Merran." Tears glittered in her dark blue eyes.

He tugged her gently by the arm, led her into the hospital, planted her in a quiet corner of the cafeteria, and fetched coffee. "Okay, let's talk."

She smiled a little. "Thanks, Ben, but I don't think even you can talk me out of—"

"Leaving? I wasn't going to. And not necessarily because I've been thinking of doing the same thing. You're quite right, Bec. When working here—or anywhere—becomes intolerable, it is proper and entirely legal to leave."

"Oh, Ben!"

"Why not? Would this place be any more tolerable for me with you gone? And Merran? Anyway, I've been here a long time, maybe too long. I'm getting stale."

"Not you. Never you, of all people."

"Ben Louis, the iron man?" He smiled but shook his head. "I guess we've all been feeling pretty bruised lately. Speaking of which, Jane and I missed you last night. One of us should have called."

"No, I should have called you." She told him why she had not. "So this morning I got to school late, and the first thing I heard was that Martin Guinness had expressed his pleasure that Merran was back here again—and can you tell me how news gets around so fast? Well, I thought I'd better look over his house too, but I couldn't find his spare key—I keep it by my kitchen phone, and he has one of mine—so I came here to see if I could get his key ring. The charge nurse got it for me. She adores him, and she said she wasn't letting anyone bother him with trifles. You should hear *her* talk about the committee! As far as she's concerned, they're the ones responsible for his condition. She despises them as much as I do." She paused. "Ben, know what I thought when I walked out of that school—walked right away from a *class*?

I thought, the hell with them. The hell with all of them!" She blushed guiltily.

He laughed at the color flooding back into her cheeks. "Bec, as I said once—about a hundred years ago, it feels like—you have the nicest superego in the world. Never mind about school or Guinness. Look, I'll dash up and see for myself what's what with the wounded one, and then we can check over his house together and then you come home and have lunch with Jane and me. We can use your help. Tell you about it later."

The charge nurse, a gray-haired mite as tough as an ox, told Ben that Merran was being detained due to a possible skull fracture. "I'll let *you* say hello, Ben, but that's all. He isn't allowed visitors, actually, and to tell you the truth I don't think he cares a damn. He's enjoying being out of it awhile, and so he should, what with the bad time those swine have been giving him, poor lamb—and you, for that matter. This town ain't what it used to be, Ben Louis, and you can quote me. And if anyone else wants to see him, they can't, and you can quote me on that too."

"Dreamin' 'bout keys again," Merran murmured, drowsy and content in his railed cocoon. "Keys 'n Swiggett's dog. Of all people." He waved a limp hand. "Tell you 'bou' tha', Ben?"

"Rest now. You can tell me later. I'll be back."

They met Everett Upham in the parking lot. As always, Everett greeted Ben cordially but gave Becca the barest nod. "I heard about Merran," he said. He looked deeply tired. "Thought I'd see if there's something I can do for the lad."

"I don't think so, Ev. I just found out they aren't letting him have visitors. Say, why not come over for lunch. Around one. Jane would love it, and besides, we can use your help. We're about to canvas everybody who's involved for their thoughts on what's been going on around here. How about it? And not to waste any time, did Merran ever say anything to either of you about keys? In any connection?"

Bec shook her head. Everett, paler than before, said, "Keys? I don't think so. Why?"

"I don't know why. Okay, Bec, let's get weaving. I'll follow you to Merran's. And Ev, don't forget. Come by at one. We have to put our heads together."

Apart from the garden shed, whose charred remains would have to be carted away, there was nothing untoward in or around Merran's house except a mountain of dust and another of dirty laundry.

"I'll do it later," Bec said. "He probably has nothing left to wear."

"Place needs a woman's touch," Ben said pointedly, transparent in his hope that Merran propose to Becca before it was too late.

"What it needs," she said matter-of-factly, "is Garth. I wish he'd come home."

"Garth'll come home when and if he can. Look, Becca, turn on some lights, and the radio too, in case the bastard who burned down the shed is thinking of coming back to complicate Merran's life a little more. A few lights might not be all that much of a deterrent, but still, why give him a *break?* If you follow my drift."

"Ben. Shame on you."

"My only vice," he said tranquilly. "Okay, do the lights and radio. I'll call Jane and tell her we're coming."

Jane's lasagna was even better for being a day older, but Everett ate almost nothing. He seemed to be dwindling away, and his hands shook.

Jane gave out typed copies of the happenings and questions she and Ben had begun listing after breakfast. "I added a few items, but I didn't have time to put them in order. I expect we can neaten up as we go. Okay, look 'em over. Four heads have got to be better than two." She put a can of pens and pencils in the middle of the table and sat down.

The kitchen began to vibrate with concentration.

Everett said, "Ben, what is this about John blackmailing George? Am I reading it correctly? Blackmailing? Good grief! Whatever for? What grounds would he have for doing such a horrible thing?"

Ben as well as Merran had entirely forgotten to search the library's microfiches of either the local newspaper or the Boston *Globe* for information about George Taylor and old scandal. He remembered his intention now but was unwilling to bring the matter up. "I don't know, Everett. But John would do anything for money."

"Anything but sell me a bit of land."

"He had a nasty streak, Everett," Jane said, patting his arm reassuringly, feeling its fleshlessness through his tweed sleeve. "But don't worry about it anymore. The Cemetery Board will work things out, right, Bec?"

"Yes," Becca began.

Everett interrupted bitterly. "Provided I can fit into a take-home doggie bag when the time comes? Well, I don't *want* to fit into a doggie bag. I want to stretch out my full length—properly! I want what I'm entitled to!" He pushed his chair back and stood up. "I'm terribly upset—terribly! I'll—I'll attend to this later, if you don't mind, Ben? Jane? No no, my dear, don't bother seeing me to the door. I'll call you." Clutching the paper in a palsied fist, he rushed out.

"My fault," Ben said. "Sorry. One day at the pool when he was going on about not getting that goddam burial plot, I told him there'd at least be room among his people for an urn, and then I dove in before he could say anything. God. When I think how important it is to him to be listened to, and how angry and hurt he feels because he's retired and nobody listens anymore, I'm ashamed. It was an insensitive thing for me to say."

Jane said, "He's gone on and on about it to me too, but can we be expected to deal with his monomania like clinicians? Even Merran goes off duty now and then. *And* is sometimes rather less than sensitive to people's needs—not excluding his own." She very carefully did not look at Becca, who blushed.

"Monomania's the word," Ben said. "So what's the reason for it? There has to be a reason for it. There's a reason for every behavior, whether it's good or evil or anything in between. Let's see. What facts do we have about Everett anyway? That he was born here but spent the years from ten or twelve to seventy away. That he has a passionate love for the town. That his mother's buried here—"

"And that he appears to be related to you, Bec," Jane said.

Simultaneously Becca and Ben said *"What?"*

"Remember at Merran's that night, when you went home and got your family tree? Well, two things happened almost at once. I'd just seen Everett's name in very tiny writing stuck in among some Wilder-Holdridge combos—he got very excited when I started to point it out—when Val Elliot barged in. Then that jerk Dave Bates came looking for Joy Taylor, and then we all left and I clean forgot to tell you about it. Bec, you look absolutely stunned. You never saw that entry?"

"If I did, I don't remember it. Oh dear. The last time I really looked at that tree was long before Everett moved in, and now it's vanished. There's no way I could reproduce it."

"Yes there is," Ben said. "Val took pic—nope, wrong. According to the paper, nothing seemed to be missing from her purse, but there was no mention of her camera on or near her body. So either she left it somewhere—which I doubt; that camera was as much attached to her as her hair—or it was stolen along with a lot of other things from her apartment. Looks like you're out of luck, Bec. No one's ever going to see those pictures."

"The murderer might develop them," Becca said hopefully, and laughed at herself.

"Don't laugh. Stranger things have happened. Which reminds me. I just this minute realized none of us went to Val's funeral, not even Everett, and he had a high opinion of her, higher than anybody else did."

"Never mind about her now," Jane said impatiently. "What else about Everett?"

"I think I know something you don't know, Ben," Becca said slowly. "Remember after Blair died, when we walked around in the cemetery? And I noticed that plaque on Honora Upham's tombstone? And you left just as Merran saw what was underneath? He hasn't mentioned it to you, has he?"

"No. I didn't want to know any more about anything just then, and I'm not sure I want to now. If he didn't sound best pleased, why should I expect to be?"

"Tell me, Bec," Jane said.

"Well"—looking uncertainly at Ben—"there was a photograph of Honora—Everett's mother, could we infer?—and a man under that little metal plaque. An old one, all brown and faded, but it was clear enough to see that she was very beautiful. Her hair was piled up and there was what looked like a cameo brooch on the high collar of her ruffled blouse—all circa 1900, you know? You'll have to see it, Jane. But the man's head was all scribbled over with ink, as though whoever did it was really furious—and on top of that, the face was gouged out to make certainty more certain, Merran said—right down to the cardboard backing. Gouged with a knife, I thought, but Merran said it was more likely done with his fingernails."

"His?" Ben said.

"Well, Merran thought so. He said it was as Oedipal as anything I'd ever see. The ink looked old, faded, but we both thought the gouging was recent because of the color of the backing. And you saw the screws, Ben. They were new, no question about that. But I can't believe Everett did any of that."

"But who else would?" Jane said. "And who was the man—her father? her husband? her lover?"

"Or one of her cousins, whom we reckon up by dozens, or an aunt in drag—"

"Ben!" Jane said, throwing down her pencil.

"Right. Sorry again. Okay. If Merran thinks Ol' Oedipus is at work, this suggests that the man was Honora's husband—"

"Or lover?" Jane said, "and that Everett knew which?"

"It isn't likely anybody who buried Honora would put a picture of her lover on the stone. It's not even likely Everett did the gouging, and if that isn't likely, then he probably didn't do the scribbling when he was little. Kids scribble over what they reject, I know, but I don't see Everett as that little kid. Look, I'll ask Garth. No, I do *not* think," as Jane began to say something, "that even Garth, whom Merran says Everett has expressed a strong wish to see, could ask him directly so as to tell us. But what's this got to do with two murders and/or the two attacks on Merran?"

Jane picked up her pencil. "Okay, Ben, call Garth and see what he knows, but first let's add three items we know. Everett never uses bad language and is shocked when anyone else does. He has beautiful manners. And he never talks to you, Bec, or even looks at you."

"That last might have bearing, but I'm telling you in advance," Ben said, putting up his hands and laughing, "that it'll sound like a syllogism, so don't shoot. If—*if*—Ev is related to the Holdridges, Bec, he's related to you, by blood if not in law. But if so, why would that fact give him anything but gratitude? And why, given his exquisite manners, has he made no attempt to hide his feelings?"

"So are you saying," Jane said, cranky with confusion, "that because Everett doesn't like Bec, who looks like being related to him, the *bearing* those two observations have on two murders and two attacks on Merran is that Everett committed all four?"

"I don't know what I meant. It just popped out, so maybe it's significant and maybe it isn't. I'll have to think about it. But I've said it before—I don't think Everett murdered anybody or hurt anybody, no matter whom he's related to or how he felt about his mother. Okay, can we think of anything else about him?"

There was silence for a few moments.

Jane said dreamily, "The lady doth protest too much," and wrote something on her list.

Ben and Bec looked at her and waited.

"Everett's monomania," she said, "consists of a seemingly inordinate desire to be buried among relatives—although he appears not to cherish his one living one—in a town he urgently wants to be honored by, a town he almost reveres as sacred ground. Of which latter commodity he will accept no less than his full measure. Yet he did not come back here even to visit until he'd retired. Why?" Her green eyes were sharp with challenge. "No takers? Well, to me the operative word is 'claim.' I mean, to Everett a place in the cemetery is his by right. He makes much of that. But—"

"You mean legal right?" Ben said.

"Yes, that's what I mean. Haven't you noticed that every time a certain word is used, he always gets upset? The word 'bastard'?"

The clock above the stove ticked away the moments while they looked at each other.

"You mean he *is* a bastard—he's illegitimate?" Ben said.

"The thought occurred. But only just now. So how about this? Everett is illegitimate. He's afraid I stumbled onto it because of Bec's family tree. *He* knows about his connection with her but isn't sure she does and doesn't want her to find out. He resents her superior status in the family by virtue of her legitimacy and snubs her at every turn, regardless of its causing talk and even suspicion. Therefore he steals the tree. Now, can we prove any of this?"

"Everett told Merran he was born in '22, so we could start by checking the birth records at Town Hall," Bec said.

"We could, and I will," Ben said, getting up, "but remember, a father can acknowledge and give his name to his offspring without marrying the mother. Whether she can give his offspring his name without his consent, I don't know. Assuming she can, we still won't know very much. And we won't unless we can contact Garth. He always knew more about this town than anyone else around. I have his number somewhere. Might as well try it before I go."

He found the number and dialed. There was no answer.

Municipal regulations elsewhere required town clerks to stop Ben at the counter and then, draping the requested information as in a surgical field ready for the scalpel, give him one look at the line and no more. But Sarah Smith, a gray-haired, sweet-faced little lady in Manton Town Hall, told him he was free to help himself, as usual.

Laughing gently, she watched him go through the gate quivering like a hound on a hot scent and launch himself happily at the Records Room.

This room was like somebody's old attic: a small, airless, dimly lit warren stuffed with unwieldy archives and golden oak, and redolent of history. Ben could have spent weeks there.

A card file contained the names of all those who had been born in Manton, together with the number of the volume in which each birth had been recorded.

There was no card bearing Everett Wilder Upham's name.

Well, so what? Ben asked himself, not at all dismayed. The file, a recent addition to Vital Statistics, was designed to facilitate search, but the odd name could easily have been omitted when thousands of names were copied out of the original archives.

He turned to the big heavy canvas-covered volumes that leaned crazily on a shelf in a dark awkward corner. With some difficulty, two ladders having been abandoned there after recent renovations, he pulled out 1912–1930 and made space for it on top of a high cabinet by pushing away a pile of books and papers. These were determinedly pushed back, and another searcher stood up and regarded him from the other side. "Oh. Sorry," he said and withdrew 1912–1930 fractionally. The sheer discomfort of the place increased his pleasure in the task.

Not knowing the month of Everett's birth, he began necessarily with January of 1922 and ran a fingertip down the fourth column from the left (*Name of Child—If Any*).

Nothing.

February.

Nothing.

March, April, May, June, July, and on through December.

Nothing.

He went back through 1917 and forward through 1927, lingering over parents' places of birth and fathers' occupations, marveling at the good solid stock from away which had peopled this town, awed by the beautiful old penmanship in which the information had been recorded, amused by a son's prideful upgrading of a father's occupation from machinist to master mechanic half a century before. So this additional task was anything but tedious, and only partly because the population until well after World War II numbered less than fifteen hundred souls.

But it would not have mattered had the town been as big as it now was. For nowhere in those ten years did Everett's name appear.

Why? Ben asked himself, thoroughly mystified and pleased as Punch.

He returned the book to its place and leaned against the ladders, shifting his weight from one long leg to the other, staring at nothing, letting his thoughts roam at will. Presently he took out Jane's typed notes with his penciled additions and read them through carefully.

"What we're looking for," he told himself half aloud, again disturbing the other man—who was having plenty of his own troubles, not least because a volume of Land Records fully opened is more than four times wider than one of Vital Statistics—"what we're looking for is a significant inconsistency in behavior or motivation. Something that'll underline or point to something else. Damn it, I sense one. I know it's here!"

"I hope not," the other man said dryly.

Ben laughed and apologized again, and read his notes through a second time.

And found the inconsistency he was looking for.

And fitted it into the pattern being forced upon him.

And irritably rejected the result for being as absurd as it was logical.

And rather inconsiderately said "God damn it to hell!" as he rushed out.

▽

SEVENTEEN

MACK POST CALLED BEN just before dinner. "Ben, I have an offer you can't refuse."

"If it's from my committee, I can," Ben said, leaning back in his deep chair and contemplating the joys of independence.

"Those jerks haven't come to a decision yet. No, Elderkin just called from Ann Arbor. If he keeps this up, Ben, you'll have to retain him as an agent. He bumped into Aitch-Jay, who was in a rush as usual and asked him to convey an urgent message to you. I swear, Ben, I'd leave my wife and kids for the kind of job Aitch-Jay's offering you."

Ben began to glow with pleasure. Robertson Hartley-Jones, renowned psychiatrist, university-hopping professor of psychology, quintessential British gentleman from the crown of his bowler to the tip of his umbrella, had long ago invited Ben, his best Master's Degree candidate, into a seminar open only to doctoral candidates. It had proved an incalculably rich experience as well as the foundation for a friendship between mentor and student that time and distance had not weakened.

"What's it all about?" he said.

"Planning and administering a psychiatric clinic-cum-hospital, pal, from the ground up. Including organizing and allocating the space in the little shack it's going to be in. Including hiring much of the staff. Including the planning of programs reaching into surrounding communities to work toward a variety of goals. Research, social work, treatment, teaching—all kinds of stuff."

"Where?"

"Would you believe my old stamping grounds?"

"You can't mean Stockbridge?"

"Got it in one. Stockbridge. In our glorious Berkshires."

Walls fell away, horizons loomed, the air freshened, the blood sang in Ben's veins. "What else?" he said casually.

"*Else!* We are a greedy bugger, aren't we. There shouldn't be any *else,* but there happens to be a very big one. At least it would be for me. Never did like my house."

"Residential, I suppose?"

"Residential as all get-out, Ben. A sort of castle, crenels and all. Baronial. A huge country estate with umpteen acres of the Berkshires' best, and gardens like you wouldn't believe. My best friend since first grade became caretaker there and took me around many times. Most gorgeous place I ever saw, like something out of a book. To live there would be heaven. To work there, ditto. But both together? The word hasn't been invented to describe it, and you're the lucky son of a bitch who can have the whole thing on a silver platter."

To calm the riot in his insides, Ben addressed himself to crass matters. "What's it pay?" he said coolly.

"At least half again what you're getting now—and no fixed expenses like heat, electricity, house insurance, mundane stuff like that. You can live in the carriage house or a suite of two or three rooms in the big house plus an office. Either way, you two wouldn't be cramped for space or privacy, and there'd always be a bed for the kids when they visit. Even with a max of twenty live-in patients and maybe three or four in-house staff and the cook and housekeeper, I mean it's like *big.*"

"Who's bankrolling?"

Mack laughed. "Ever read a Sydney Sheldon-type opus, Ben? Husband rich as Croesus. Wife with fifteen years of shrinkage and no improvement. Despair all around. Wife referred to famous shrink. In less than three months is stabilized psychologically as well as medically—one of those subtle chemical imbalances that cause schizophrenia, bipolar syndrome, split personality, et cetera. Prognosis excellent. Grateful husband creates foundation, settles it on famous shrink. Truth is stranger than fiction, right? Enough already. Call Aitch-Jay at this number right away, Ben. The man's off to London any minute now but wants a word with you before he goes. Keep in touch."

Ben sat looking at the phone. There has to be a catch, he thought. It's too good to be true. I always thought I was lucky—until now, at least—but this is ridiculous. Too rich for my blood. And anyway, I'm a public school man, it'd be like deserting a sinking ship . . .

Immediately Conscience leaped to the other side. You were going to quit anyhow, it reminded him. You were in fact even considering becoming a private eye, as Guy McKay suggested.

On that he picked up the phone again and dialed the number Mack had given him.

Minutes later he was happily arranging a flight to Detroit. He was about to go and tell Jane when the phone rang again.

"Ben? Becca. I hope I'm not interrupting your dinner, but I had to know what you found out about Everett."

"He isn't on the books here, Bec. I looked through ten years' worth, just to make sure."

"Oh? Oh. Well, Garth would know. Why don't you—"

"Right," Ben said, and without another word broke the connection and dialed Florida.

"Supper, Ben. Everything's getting cold," Jane said at the study door. But that bloodhound look was on his face, and he was drumming a rapid tattoo on the arm of his chair. She came in and sat on the edge of his desk.

The tattoo slowed; stopped. Ben sat upright clutching the

phone. "Garth! Ben. Glad I got you. Look, I have to leave soon—have to catch a plane—so I only have a minute. I'll fill you in when I get back, if you haven't heard about the situation here from Merran. You haven't? Then this may sound strange, but where was Everett Wilder Upham born? Yes, he's back, bought the old Andrew Hopkinson house on—

"Yes, that's the one. . . . Who did? . . . Well, I'll be damned. But never mind about that, just tell me about Everett—

"True, but everybody's crazy, so we'll let that pass. Come on, give. Where was Everett born?

"In—! You're kidding. Because that's where I'm going, that's why. Small world, right? Okay, what else do you know about him?"

He listened for several minutes, his face grave.

"Poor bastard," he said. "He should've studied *Hamlet.* You should've too, if you don't mind my overstepping the bounds, old friend. But since I have, I might as well be shot for a sheep as a lamb so I'll go ahead and ask you when you think you'll have had enough of that living morgue. Being a beach bum or a recluse doesn't fit your image, pal.

"You're a what? A bank messenger? Not at all. Why the hell should I mind? Meet a lot of people that way. And anyway, it's a damn sight better than lying around getting skin cancer. Okay, gotta eat and pack. Oh, she's fine. I agree—the best. Another good reason to come home and see for yourself. Look, will you be home tonight? Good. Wait for Jane's call. There's a lot to tell you about what's going on around here. A lot you should know."

He put down the phone and stood up stretching luxuriously.

"You're flying where?" Jane said carefully.

"God, I'm starved. Come on, let's eat, I don't have much time," he said, putting an arm around her shoulders. She was stubbornly anchored to the desk. He laughed and kissed her. "Detroit. Very unromantic. You wouldn't like—all right, all right! Want it here or with supper?"

"Here. I can't stand it another minute. I've been waiting all afternoon to know what you found out. And what was all that about Hamlet?"

"Hamlet said—quoting now—there is nothing either good or bad, but thinking makes it so. Which is true, when you come to think about it. Take—oh, take cannibalism, for instance. To our culture one of the worst and most repellent of crimes, but to certain tribes in West Africa and—"

"Benjamin!"

"It seemed an appropriate topic, eating, although it's actually not about eating at all, but okay." He sat down again and drew her onto his lap.

"I waded through ten full years of Vital Statistics, but Garth said Everett was born in Jerome, Michigan, not here. The Uphams of Manton had two girls, Honora and Dorothy. Garth's mother and Honora were best friends, which is why he knows all this. When Honora was seventeen she went out to Detroit with her mother, ostensibly to visit relatives. About six months or so later, her mother returned with the news that Honora had married an Upham cousin who had a farm in Jerome, a little place about sixty miles from Ann Arbor, which isn't far from Detroit, and expected to stay there. But a few months later Honora came back with a bouncing baby boy—Everett—and the news that Warren Upham had been thrown by a horse and killed. She had no pictures of Warren and was vague on details, so people began to talk.

"Now, everyone knew she and Gardiner Holdridge—a handsome rakehelly, Garth's mother called him—had been seeing a lot of each other before she suddenly went west. Anyway, she stuck it out in Manton for ten years or so with Everett, but finally the talk drove her out of town. She was buried somewhere in the Midwest, but her family put up a stone here on one of their family plots because they felt it was the right thing to do. And the picture on the gravestone was of the two lovers. Originally, Garth said, it was just a picture of Honora, but the spinster older sister, Dorothy, told Garth's mother she made the switch. Another romantic. Just like you." He kissed her again.

"Oh come on, Ben! And Gardiner Holdridge? Just who was he?"

"One of Bec's great-uncles. Garth said that unquestionably Ev knew this."

"Oh boy. Poor Everett. Obviously there was no wedding out in Michigan, Ben, or Everett wouldn't behave as he does. Certainly not to Bec. Oh boy." She was silent for a moment. "But dammit, other people have been illegitimate—famous people like Alec Guinness the actor, for one. I read his book. He doesn't seem to have been all twisted up by it."

"You want to talk about a famous bastard, how about William the Conqueror? His truth was just as unpalatable as Everett's, he just handled it differently. And there was Dunois, the Bastard of Orleans, who fought with Joan of Arc—and when people called him Bastard, it was a title of respect—"

Her lips on his interrupted the lecture, and that exercise ended in a combined and irrepressible giggle.

"Okay okay, we'll eat!" he said. "Mmmmm, I think I fancy your left biceps," fingering the strong shapely part.

She looked at him critically. "You *are* crazy, you know, but I could always see past the unimportant stuff to the gold. Come on, I'll feed you and pack your bag, provided you tell me why I should."

He told her what Mack Post had said, and voiced the guilt that had assailed him at the thought of leaving public education.

"Where is it written that a person can't change careers whenever he wants to!" she demanded. "Look at Somerset Maugham. Look at A. J. Cronin and Conan Doyle and Richard Gordon. Doctors, all of them. Trained to heal the sick. And chucked it all when they found they liked writing better, or it paid better. And look at Gauguin—he'd been a banker or a stockbroker. Look, Ben, in twenty-three years in education you've given of yourself in spades, doubled. You don't owe Them anything. Only, if you *want* to stay where you are, it's okay with me provided you have a better reason than guilt."

So, with an eye on the clock, they talked, and the food grew colder, and neither of them noticed, or cared.

▽

EIGHTEEN

ROBERTSON HARTLEY-JONES FOLDED A pair of elegant striped trousers and with the greatest care placed them in a scarred leather suitcase that was plastered all over with names of faraway places. With a measuring eye on the pile of clothing on the bed, he closed the lid experimentally and shook his head. As he did so, he saw Ben looking at the labels. He laughed. "If you value the civilized life, Ben, travel simply isn't in it. From right here in Ann Arbor to Abu-bloody-Dhabi, hotels look the same, cost too much, serve dreadful food, break one's back on lethal mattresses, and stink of tobacco smoke. And since I have had rather less time than money to see more than is visible on the ride to and from air terminals—when a meeting wasn't in the terminal, that is—I generally leave with a confusion of impressions, possibly a bad cold, and the trots.

"Which are cogent reasons for my embarking on this new venture, which I've tentatively called Thornwood. No? Perhaps the symbolism is a trifle obscure. We might put our heads together and think of a better name? But whatever we call it, I intend to put down deep roots, Ben. I may go forth from your mahv'lous Barkshires"—giving it the British pronunciation—"to give the odd lecture, but I do intend to grow roots. For the first time in my life since I came down from Oxford.

"Furthermore, and most important, I will run my own show. I will have no board or committee to answer to. I will see my patients to the end of their treatment instead of being forced by bureaucratic lunacy to relinquish them in the middle to incompetents who make them crazy by pushing them in antithetical directions. I will see them housed in surroundings conducive to their progress. *And* I will assemble the kind of staff—beginning, I trust, with yourself—capable of implementing and improving the ideas I envision. I ask your pardon for repeating my—credo, would you call it?—but my god, what happiness!"

As if he could hardly wait to begin it, he stuffed the rest of his things anyhow into the case and, applying the full weight of his lean bent frame to the lid, bounced down on it to close it. Ben was too tired to help him.

"So, Ben, what do you think?" he said, smoothing his beautifully barbered silver hair as if the exertion had disarranged it.

"It sounds great, Rob. Really great," Ben said, listless from exhaustion. His two-hour-and-ten-minute nonstop flight from Boston to Detroit had been mysteriously delayed in Logan Airport for over an hour; had been interrupted by an unscheduled landing in Toledo due to engine problems; had been further lengthened not so much by the airline's need to change aircraft as by the fact that a plane with inadequate seating had been chosen to complete the journey. Since none of the passengers had volunteered to be bumped, more time had been spent wheeling the plane away and readying a larger one for flight. At last, at two in the morning they had touched down at Detroit Metro.

Too whacked on reaching Ann Arbor to shower or even to put on pajamas, Ben had had a broken sleep in his underwear and then an hour of feverishly exciting talk with the psychiatrist over a cup of indifferent coffee. And soon he would have to make the return trip.

Ordinarily he relished minor aggravations like these. They

were, in themselves, often interesting; they enormously enhanced, by way of contrast, the return to comforts; and they were almost always graced by unexpected bonuses—in the humor department, mostly, that he could chuckle over for days. But right now he felt worn to a frazzle by nothing more nor less than profound inner conflict.

"Before I went to the airport," he said slowly, "Jane and I built a whole new life, a whole new entirely unexpected life away from Manton—"

"And I fancy she's readier for it than you are! You know, Ben, she'd be a tremendous addition to Thornwood, have you considered that? Oh, not because she was a splendid English teacher—the woods are full of such—or even because of her considerable creative energies, but because a Thornwood—indeed any closed society—cannot help but generate a miasmic atmosphere that needs her brisk, unsentimental sanity. If she did nothing but be visible at all times, her very presence would affect it like a tonic."

"Yes. Yes. But . . . I'm just not sure yet. How long can you give me to make up my alleged mind?"

"Will the end of the month do you? I shall have returned from London by then. I've no other candidate in mind, and I'll not begin the search for one unless you have definitely opted out, so you'll have no pressure of that sort. Indeed, from what you've said—and have not said, if you'll forgive the liberty, old chap—your superego will prove to be the biggest impediment to change."

"You and Jane! But you're both right, of course. Guess I just need some time to get to feel what I know. It's always damned uncomfortable when the head and the gut are out of sync. Pass each other like ships in the night, so to speak." He moved restlessly, irritably, in his chair and massaged his foot, as if the trouble lay mainly in that quarter. "It'd help if I could figure out the situation back home. It wouldn't be possible for me to walk away from that. How about I run it past you while we have breakfast? I need some serious refueling for the flight back or I may ditch in Boston Harbor."

"By all means! But we'll eat at the terminal, if you don't mind. You do look a bit peckish, but I always have a dreadfully compulsive need to be two hours beforehand. And I leave here in the very nick, my boy. Those damned APA establishment jackals began nipping chunks out of my British backside the moment I stepped foot on this campus, and I do *not* fancy ending my career in Ann-bloody-Arbor. It's grown too big, for one thing. And the bah-stards are too full of themselves to see past themselves. Great bloated bullfrogs." He flourished his hazel walking stick at Them—the Enemy—like a sword, then blew on the carved ram's horn handle and gave it a vigorous polishing.

Ben laughed. "It's the way you dress, Rob. You're as conservative as they come, but to the Midwest Establishment you're outrageously original. Or maybe they don't like your intractably radical views on family therapy—particularly where alcoholics are involved. No one wants to hear you say that alcoholism isn't a disease but a lousy coping mechanism, a rotten means of manipulating others, and a slow form of suicide. It simply isn't the fashionable view. Alcoholics Anonymous has seen to that."

" 'Where there is a disposition to dislike, a motive will never be wanting.' Remarkable psychologist, my countrywoman, I always thought?" There was sly challenge in his gray-green glance. The questioning lilt in his voice reminded Ben of Everett Upham.

"Yes, I always thought so. Too bad she never finished that book. Pity it was her last," Ben said sweetly, foiling this literary ambush, a favorite game of Hartley-Jones's.

The psychiatrist grinned at him, well pleased, whereas Everett, had he set the trap, would have been offended by the ready response that deprived him of the chance to say, "Who? Jane Austen, of course. And the quote? Why, from *Lady Susan*. I'd have thought you knew that, Ben."

Not until they had settled their bills and were in the limousine did Ben begin recounting Manton's recent history. By the time they were on their second cup of weak tepid coffee in one of the airport cafeterias, Hartley-Jones had a succinct yet admirably complete picture of the principals involved in murder and old scandal, greed and obsession and malice, loneliness, lies and evasions, love unrecognized and love spurned.

"Oh, well done!" he said. "You haven't lost your reportorial touch, Ben. You're better than ever, if that's possible. And by the bye, I like the sound of your Merran Shaw. He'd make a fine assistant to you at Thornwood, wouldn't you say? Pity he's having such a bad time of it. Yes, it's a nasty tangle, but it won't occupy you for long, I shouldn't wonder. Apply Sherlock Holmes's dictum, and you're home and dry."

"Oh? Hm. Ah. Eliminate what's impossible, and whatever is left must be the solution, no matter how improbable it may seem."

"Bang on, old chap. The path to Truth is generally trod with short hesitant steps, but you will get there." Reflectively Aitch-Jay scraped burned toast. "You say that Everett's name does not appear in Manton's birth records, but has it occurred to you that it may very well appear in those of Jerome, Michigan?"

"I've only come as far as Detroit. Too tired to think farther," Ben said and laughed at his little joke. And then he clutched the psychiatrist's arm and pointed at the crowd surging past the window at which they sat. "I don't believe it! It can't be!"

The psychiatrist detached the clutching hand from his excellent worsted, which he examined anxiously for signs of jam or butter. "Cannot be what? Or whom?"

"Everett Upham—sorry!—I'd swear I saw him go by. Now why . . . ? Could he possibly know I checked Vital Statistics back home? Something tells me he's getting upset enough to sense things. He just might guess . . ." He looked at his watch and jumped up. "Rob, there's plenty of time. Hang on. I better call Jane. Something tells me . . ."

He dashed out and was back in less than ten minutes wearing his bloodhound look and clutching a road map. "Jane said Everett called last night to apologize for his behavior at our kitchen meeting. He wanted to talk to me, and she told him where I was headed. I wish she hadn't said anything."

"I can't think why. You look enormously pleased—and rather less tired than before. What are you thinking about?"

"Something very farfetched. That Everett's birth was indeed recorded in Jerome and that he's going there to delete it. Does that sound crazy?"

"Not at all. Whether you saw him just now or not, clearly he is disintegrating, and such a direct and logical answer to his needs, such a simple answer—the sort that would satisfy a child, or a man in his condition (which often comes to the same thing)—would make perfect sense to him. Further, if he were thinking of doing that, he would also think of enrolling himself, so to say, in Manton, would he not? Call your Mrs. Smith. He may have added his name to the roster by now. And call Jerome. Vital Statistics are public records, after all. They might be willing to give you the information over the phone."

"Worth a shot. Be right back."

He returned shortly and, shaking his head, sat down and opened the map. "Couldn't get Sarah—line was busy—so I called Jane and told her to alert Chief MacWhirter. But the only likely number to call in Jerome is the police station, damned if I know why, and that phone was busy, dammit, and then nobody answered. I let it ring fifteen times by actual count. Guess I'll have to go." Plainly he was not displeased. "Have to go through Jackson," he muttered. "Looks like the best . . . mm, yeah, 94 to 127 to 12, then south a bit. Have to rent a car . . ."

He jumped up again, nerves a-twang.

Laughing, Hartley-Jones caught Ben's arm in the ram's horn handle of his stick. "I'll call you without fail on the first of the month, Ben. Good luck, old chap. To us both. I rather think, though, that your friend Everett did not murder—"

But his estimate of Everett's criminal potential in whole or in part was not enough to detain someone as single-minded now as any four-footed tracker on a hot scent. Ben snatched up his case and was gone in a flash, almost taking the doctor's stick along with him.

▽

NINETEEN

JEROME, MICHIGAN, IMPRESSED BEN as a drab dead place unimproved by its few unimpressive hills (which was only one man's opinion) and populated largely by retirement couples (which was true). He acknowledged that he was pretty whacked and may have missed its virtues (he had), but after driving the better part of ninety miles in a Chevy he would never come to love, he was too tired and too preoccupied with map and mission to refine his first impression or to wish he were somewhere else.

And—when he found that the information he sought was some fifteen miles farther away, in the courthouse in Hillsdale—too angry: by the time he got there, Everett, who would, of course, have known exactly where to go, would have been and gone. He didn't think to ask himself if he really had seen Everett at the air terminal, or if he was prepared to confront him in Hillsdale.

"And Everett wouldn't have bothered taking time to pee before he got there, either, damn it to hell!" he swore loudly, looking for a likely place to stop. He had not yet admitted to himself that he was actually enjoying all this excitement tremendously. At length he parked at an unpromising little diner and went in.

He discovered while he was washing his hands that he was hungry again, so he ordered a medium-rare hamburger ("And hold the onions and french fries, please") and coffee.

"We don't have no onions left, and anyway the fryer's broke," said the girl behind the counter, her pale eyes anxious. "But you can have it without peppers if you want, okay?" Reassured by his cheerful nod, she yelled to the cook, who was not five feet away from her on the other side of the pass-through, "One medium-rare burger, hold the peppers," and went for the coffee.

The roll was spotted with blue mold, the meat could have soled a shoe, the coffee had the color and consistency of beef broth, the cream was a mite sour, the spoon greasy: a meal that definitely came under the Bonus heading. Ben laughed to himself as he scraped off the mold.

A nagging thought shot up out of the mental murk, possibly fueled by an excess of gassy indigestion: he had almost forgotten to make still another call, the result of which would probably deprive him of happy hours wandering about in Hillsdale's Vital Statistics. He had never even remotely expected to do this anyway, but he growled inwardly as he jumped up and went to a pay phone near the door to call Chief MacWhirter.

"Your wife," MacWhirter said irritably, "called with some kind of a screwy message 'bout Everett Upham's birthdate. Would you mind letting me in on whatever it is you're up to, Ben?"

"No time, Colin, I'm in transit. You get the date? From Motor Vehicles? Great. November 16, 1922? Well well. It wasn't in the Stats yesterday but it may be there tomorrow. No, I can't explain. Ask Jane. Look, I'm on my way to the Hillsdale courthouse. Will you vouch for me in case they don't want to give an outlander the time of day? I should be there in half an hour or so. Thanks. 'Bye."

"I couldn't help hearing where you're going," the little waitress said shyly, as she took his money, "and it's a real nice place, if you don't mind me saying so. It's got a clock tower and a widow's walk halfway down and beautiful woodwork inside too. Like quaint, everybody says, y' know? And stop by the college on your way. We're real proud of it around here. I mean, Ann Arbor ain't the only place on the map with a good school."

"I'll try," Ben said politely and hurried out and drove away, feeling faintly ridiculous. Presently he turned onto Route 34 and headed south.

The Hillsdale courthouse, a stately structure in the Greek Revival mode, was, for all its white trim and cream-colored brick, hardly what he would have called quaint. But architecture concerned him less than the possibility that Everett was crouched in a car in the parking lot, watching him right now, or peering at him around a window frame inside the building.

Well, what if he is? he asked himself, the flesh crawling up his spine, as he went through the big doors and gave not a thought to the handsome woodwork. The important thing is, if I really did see him and he really has come here, has he had time to do what I think he came to do—or do I have to wait around until he does? And if I do see him, what do I say—that I just happened to be in the neighborhood?

The matter was settled, if not definitively, when he entered the office of the county clerk and came face-to-face with Everett Wilder Upham, who was just turning away from the counter as a clerk behind it walked off stern-faced with an enormous volume in her arms.

Everett turned as white as paper and his breath came in rough gasps. He clutched at his chest and sank to his knees, his shocked eyes still on Ben's face. And then his eyeballs rolled up into his skull and he crumpled to the floor.

The resulting drama was more than Ben had anticipated. But a high school principal knows what has to be done, and he did it.

By the time he had seen Everett installed in the hospital and resting comfortably, it was too late to return to the courthouse. He found a shabby motel, booked in, and called home, full of complaints.

"Don't kid me, Benjamin Franklin Louis," Jane said. "I can tell you're having one hell of a good time. When do you think you'll be back? This house is an empty shell without you."

"Thank you. A couple of days, maybe. The attack wasn't serious but I'll have to stay till he's well enough to travel. I certainly can't abandon him here. He said, by the way, that he came to visit cousins. He got very chatty after a while, but he was careful not to ask me what I was up to. Oh, he left Gifford boarding at the vet's and asked if someone would call and say he was delayed."

"I'll do it, tell him. I take it you didn't get to the records. Do you think he did anything to them?"

"From the look on the clerk's face, I'd say he tried to. I'll certainly find out in the morning. Then, well, then I'll see."

"*What* will you see? If he was born there and he is illegitimate, I mean, so what? Or have I lost track of something? You were sure to the point of adamant that he didn't, couldn't, wouldn't hurt anyone, and I happen to think you're right. So what's the point of all this?"

"I don't know. Rob started to say something about how he didn't think Everett had murdered—and that's when I took off. Whether he meant Ev had murdered John but not Val, or vice versa, or neither one, it didn't hit me till I was on the road and he was halfway to London. I swear, I'd call him if I knew where he was. Did you give Colin a rundown? Thanks. 'Bye, darling. I'll call you after I've been to the courthouse."

He ate a midwestern supper whose ingredients had been killed rather than cooked and that prepared him inadequately for a brief but charged visit with Everett and then an endless night on a bed like an old dirt road. In the morning a tepid halfhearted shower restored him enough to down a breakfast that seemed to consist mainly of grease and acid. Thus fortified, he drove to the courthouse possessed of a savage joy in the certainty that he would discover nothing at all in the volume in which Everett's name should have been entered all those unhappy years ago, and that the county clerk would insist on vetting him first anyway, and that he would have to wait around, maybe for hours, for clearance, because Police Chief Colin MacWhirter, some eight hundred miles to the east, would be home eating lunch while his office phone was ringing.

The small boy in him was honest enough to giggle at his disappointment when delay proved unnecessary. One of the busy clerks asked him pleasantly what he wanted, and only nodded when he asked if it would be possible to bypass the index and go right to the volume of birth records that included November 1922.

"You see," he said earnestly, fingers crossed behind his back, "I'm running down some family history—a cousin on my mother's side, but I'm not sure of the name. Not sure of the town, if it comes to that. I believe it's Hudson, but I could be wrong." He did not want to give Everett's name in case she was the clerk to whom Everett had spoken yesterday. "But I know I'll recognize it when I see it. I think it's Upcross or Upshaw. Or am I complicating your life, Miss, uh?"

"Hartwig. Emma Hartwig. And it's *Ms.* Not at all," she said politely and went away, returning presently with a canvas-backed monster similar to the ones at home. "Take your time," she said and moved away to help someone else.

His heart banging, he turned the big pages carefully, noting that the column headings were the same as those in the Manton books. Where the November births began, he went slowly from one page to another until he reached the sixteenth day.

And there it was—Upham, Honora Wilder. *Place of birth,* Manton, Massachusetts. *Occupation,* none.

Not even a dash had been entered under *Name of Father.*

Under *Child If Any,* Everett Upham. The middle name, though, was not Wilder but Holdridge. And halfway through it ran a thin wavering line of ink.

Ben caught the clerk's eye and beckoned, and she came back to him. He said innocently, pointing to the ink, "Now who would do something like this, Ms. Hartwig?"

"Someone who either doesn't know the rules or—oh, I recognize you!" she said, smiling. "You helped that old man that had the heart attack yesterday! And this was the book he asked for. Well, what a coincidence. Millie over there just happened to catch him with a pen in his hand when my back was turned for a second, and she called him on it. He looked so upset, poor old guy. Wanted to show me his driver's license, but I said that wouldn't do, that he'd have to go through a whole procedure in order to make any change at all. You can't just walk in and change the books, just like that, even if your name was misspelled, say. Or suppose you found that a relative should be in the book but for some reason isn't. You have to have two substantiating documents to prove your point—marriage license, baptismal record, record of military service, things like that. And you have to make special application through the State before the book can be changed in any way."

"What did he say his middle name was, then?" Ben said carelessly. "Do you remember?"

"No. Oh . . . Wild, Wilding, something like that. He said—he practically insisted his father died before he was born, as though that would explain anything, know what I mean? Or as though it was any business of mine. It wouldn't've made any difference anyway. Procedure is procedure. Still, I felt sorry for the poor guy. Well. Did you find what you were looking for?"

"Uh, no. No, I didn't." Ben closed the book and pushed it toward her. "No big deal, really. Just some old family history I was trying to track down. But thank you, you've been very kind."

▽

TWENTY

A WEEK LATER, AT about the same time that Sarah Smith was explaining to Everett, as to a child or a simpleton, why he could not amend Vital Statistics *just like that,* Police Chief Colin MacWhirter was wedging his vast behind into an armchair at Ben's house and eyeing the spread of cakes and pastries on the great round dining table.

"Sarah and I decided it'd be best," he said, zeroing in on the chocolate cake and swallowing hard, "if she handles Everett Upham the simplest way possible when he shows up, and just tells him no, he can't write in the book. Why question him or threaten him? The guy's nuts, at least on this family business. It hasn't got anything to do with anything.

"Mind if I start? I gotta be home in time for supper. Ben, if you'd be good enough to cut me a piece of that cake. I really shouldn't, though. I'm still on duty."

Jane put a cup of steaming coffee by his plate. "Then work late tomorrow, or start earlier, to pay the time back. Unless you'd like to ease your conscience and go over a few things with us now. Which is why you're here, I thought?"

The chief grunted at sight of the folded paper she took from her pocket and spread out under his eye. It was the list of happenings, comments on character, and questions that she and Ben had begun a few days before. She had retyped it, done some more thinking, and messed it up all over again. MacWhirter looked at it without pleasure, folded it up, and pushed it over to her.

"First of all," she said, "who hit John Chester, Val Elliot, and Merran—a lefty or a righty? And was he tall or short or what? Did the ME say?"

Carefully, reflectively, MacWhirter licked a smear of butter icing off his fork. "He thinks—he isn't sure, naturally. You saw his style, Ben, right? That guy really gives me the pip. Never saw anybody so scared of pinning himself down! Someday he'll look at a stiff and say he doesn't want to commit himself is it dead or alive, it could be one, it could be the other, maybe a little bit of both, for crissake—

"Anyway, he thinks John and the Elliot woman were hit by a lefty of certainly no more than their own height, and they were almost of a height, those two. For a woman she was tall, for a man John wasn't. Everett's about their height, but I don't know if he's a lefty or a righty."

He regarded his fork. "Little squirt, John was. Slimy little squirt." He made a face, then took another forkful of cake, possibly to correct the taste in his mouth. "Merran is what—six two, six three? And he was hit bang on the crown of the head both times, so he might've been hit by the same short person if he was bending down or the hitter was standing on a chair. Maybe they were both kneeling—who the hell knows! If the ME does, he isn't saying. As for that business about two different kinds of golf balls, well, all I'm really sure of is that I'm sitting here eating the best goddam chocolate cake I ever had in my life."

"Thank you. But we have to try to be more sure. I've noticed Everett uses either hand. I do myself, some things. So does Ben. But who do we know who's out-and-out left-handed?"

"Connie Taylor is," Ben said. "That gun she shot Merran with—remember, Colin?—she was holding it in her left hand."

"And not too steady, either. If I didn't know she does well in school, I'd say she doesn't know her ear from her kneecap, let alone which hand is which. I take it you aren't suggesting she bashed anybody's head in? Good." MacWhirter examined the tines of his fork from all angles. "George is a southpaw, now I come to think about it, but I still don't think he murdered John. As for the Elliot woman, he said their paths never crossed and he never did any work for her. Said he wouldn't've wanted to. Don't blame him, either—I bet she laughed at those silly boots and belt buckles of his. She was one nasty broad, except to Everett. . . .

"*I* don't know. We couldn't get anything more out of the kid than Merran did, and Doris Taylor's statement about George taking her and the bill over to John's but coming home in practically no time flat and staying home don't mean diddley. She don't seem to care all that much about her three kids, but she's the most houseproud hausfrau I ever saw, and she cares plenty about that overstuffed clean house, plus what has to be a reasonably lot of money to spend, so why shouldn't she give George an alibi and protect her territory? It adds up to I don't have anything to arrest him on, even if he had two left hands and even if I think he did it, which I don't think I do. . . . I *think* . . . oh boy. I sound as bad as the ME.

"But anyway, I don't hold with any of that left-right-up-down crap. Someone could be layin' on the floor and you could be sittin' on a chair either facin' 'm or the other way, and lean over and whack him on the back of the head *or* the left side or the right side with a lead weight or a golf ball or anything else that's good and hard, and how tall would that make you—or him—and how hard is it, anyway, to hit the target with either hand when it's big enough and close enough so you can't miss it?

"Or say he's standing up and you're swinging from the chandelier—and ditto, so you could hit him with your foot and lay him low if you hit him hard enough. Furthermore, if he—or she, for that matter—was am-bye-dexterous, which in case you didn't notice, George Taylor more or less is—ever watch him work? In a tight spot he's a real switch hitter with a screwdriver or a wrench. He could put in a screw with his eyelids, for godsake—

"Where was I? Oh. I don't think it proves anything, I never did. Fingerprints prove things. Blood types, semen, stuff like that. But not always, either. Otherwise, about all you can say is, Subject was hit on the head from behind or the front or above, or wherever, and from the left or the right or smack in the middle, by someone who *appeared* to be about so many feet tall and may have been right-handed or left-handed—which don't tell you anything you can take to the bank.

"You make those custard tarts too, Jane? In that case I think I'll have a taste. Just a corner'll do."

Jane said, "That's all you deserve, you're not being very helpful," but gave him a whole one. "Next. Anything from the Bush family about John's dressing room wiring? Claims against his estate? Isn't Guy McKay the Bushes' attorney, Ben?"

"I think so. That reminds me. Everett said something about Diana Bush considering suing John but not him and Gifford. But then John was killed."

"Well, here's something inneresting," MacWhirter said, "and may God forgive me if I'm running off at the mouth to you two. I spoke to Guy right after Bush's funeral, which is when Mrs. Bush began going for all she could get from John, and his death makes no difference to her. She don't give a good goddam about Nora and her kids. She says Nora knew as much about John's doings as John did himself because she did all his office work—"

"She didn't," Ben said. "He was as close with her as he was with everybody else. He made that very plain."

"Oh? Well anyway, she says Nora not doing anything about that wiring makes her as liable as him even if he's dead as a mackerel. Bush had all kinds of insurance, which John didn't have, so Diana Bush and her kids aren't going to starve. But Blair was earning at least two hundred and fifty big ones a year, so if you figure he was good for at least fifteen years more, say he planned to retire at sixty-five, his widow and kids're out damn close to four mil', gross, to say nothing of a damn good husband and father—because there's no possible way Nora didn't see that arrangement in the dressing room. She had to've known *that*, all right, and didn't do zilch about it. Guy could make a good case on that."

Ben was aghast. "Nora knew all this—about Mrs. Bush?"

"Before John croaked, you mean? Betcher ass she knew it, and something else too—that *John* was going to sue *Everett*—because of the dog. Which meant even less money going to her for furniture or building a new house or anything else, what with lawyers liking a good chunk of money up front, which I don't think John had, unless he mortgaged the shop and pool, which he'd stand a good chance of losing all of too, he being the one that opened the door and let the mutt in. Proximate cause, it's called.

"Which suggests Nora had more than enough motive for wanting him dead. You're not surprised, are you? We are talking suspects, right? Well, all that stuff makes her one hell of a suspect where John's concerned. Oh yeah.

"She also knows that even if she finds buyers for all the three properties, she can't close any deals for a long long time. She'd have to get permission from Probate Court to sell anything *before* the estate is closed, plus she'd have to show that its total value was more than enough to cover any claims against it *after* it was closed. Which it won't be if Mrs. Bush goes for the works. The fact that Nora and the kids 'ud be left with nothing might or might not cut any ice with a jury. There might be a settlement out of court, Guy said, but either way, Nora's stuck. If I liked her better, I might feel sorry for her. But I don't think there was any connection between her and Val Elliot's death."

MacWhirter looked at his watch and pushed his plate away. "You sure can bake, Jane, but if I'm not home in fifteen minutes, my butt'll be in a sling for sure. Mary likes to serve at six sharp so's she can finish the dishes and be at the tube by seven, which means alls I get's a cold supper and clean up if I'm late. Anything else on your mind? Because there's a few things on mine, I can tell you."

"Like what?" Ben said glumly.

"Well, George Taylor's so-called alibi, for one thing. And Nora's, for another. I even caught myself wondering if there was anything between those two. After all, he's been in just about everybody's pants in this county, and I hear Nora's made a few moves on more than one person, you and Merran included, if I may say so. You know anything?"

Jane giggled and Ben turned red. He said, "I know Everett looked a damn sight sadder at John's funeral than George and Nora did. It could have been an act, of course. Everett has good manners. But even if it was an act, I don't think it means anything sinister. Everett with his heart condition and his depression and his monomania never killed anything larger than a fly."

"Anger makes people very strong, don't forget, Ben, and a person who acts on their anger can be as strong as a gorilla. Anyway, what also gets me," MacWhirter said, "is the—the kind of copycat thing in all this. Well, not all of it's copycat, but . . . John's house burns down. Merran's shed burns down. Everett's smeared with poison pen letters and loses the campaign. Merran ditto, and loses his job. And you got you suspended because of that history lecture you gave on his behalf, Ben. And did the same person write all those letters, or was it two different people, what about that?

"Then, John gets hit on the head. Val Elliot gets hit on the head. Merran gets hit on the head—twice.

"Then, there's two dogs here. Everett's dog gets treated like the king of Romania. John's dog gets treated like a piece of garbage—which Everett despised John for—and so do I.

"Then, Nora's asleep—from the strain of the fire—while her husband's being murdered downstairs, and George is in too delicate a condition from the strain of a normal workday to suffer waiting through an argument John's having with somebody and then go in and take up the cudgels on his own behalf by presenting his bill. Not that by cudgels I necessarily meant anything."

"Yes. And there are other coincidences," Jane fretted. "Val crashes Merran's dinner party, takes pictures of Bec's family tree, gets killed. One two three.

"Then, the tree goes missing and so does Val's camera. One two. It hasn't turned up anywhere, has it, Colin—her camera? In one of the local junk shops or pawn shops or Goodwill?"

"No. And I had Merran go through her apartment—he says a few things were taken, a portable TV and some other stuff—but not even a spare camera there either. So whether she had it on her when she was murdered or she went out and for once left it home, it's gone."

"Okay, Colin, so here's another one-two. That photo on Honora Upham's tombstone, Ben—Colin and I went to look at it while you were in Michigan—something crucial in it is missing—a man's face—and the pictures Val took of Bec's family tree are missing too. If we assume Everett gouged out the first—in an Oedipal rage, according to Merran—might he have destroyed the camera and the film in it because it bore on his parentage?"

"It wouldn't have to be an Oedipal thing," Ben said. "A woman scorned could have done the gouging. Anyone other than Honora's sister, that is, since Garth Shaw said she put up the tombstone and the picture on it. But it's unlikely. If there had been a woman scorned, seems to me Honora's face would've been gouged out. I only include the possibility to exclude it.

"But here's another thing. Was Val's apartment robbed because her killer took her keys along for whatever else he could grab, or was the burglary just window dressing to cover up taking the film? If it was that, doesn't the murder point to Everett whether we like it or not? After all, that family tree upset the hell out of him, as Val's picture-taking did. I saw him, he turned gray."

"I thought," MacWhirter said, passing his plate almost absentmindedly to Ben for more cake and pushing his coffee cup vaguely in Jane's general direction, "I thought you said Everett didn't have the strength to hurt a fly.

"But here's something else bothers *me.* Elliot's wallet was still in her purse, with about a hundred bucks at least in it. Can you imagine anybody leaving a hundred bucks on her but driving her car to her place to rob it and then—"

"How do you know that?" Jane interrupted. "I mean, do you really *know* that, Colin?"

"Yeah. The tire tracks we found backing and forthing near her body were made by her tires, nobody else's."

"You didn't say anything about that before," she said reproachfully.

"Uh-huh. Okay, can I go on? Where was I? Hm. Oh. The murderer drives her car to her place, robs it, and then parks her car *back* at the scene of the crime and goes on foot for his car, wherever it was, and assuming he had one? No, the burglary was window dressing. Had to be."

"If the same person killed Val as killed John," Ben said, "leaving her wallet intact could either have been a red herring or a stupid oversight, and I don't think we're going to come to an agreement now. But I don't see how the same person could have done both murders. One seems carefully thought out—hit John on the head, put him in the suit—and the other—

"No, that's wrong. Someone carefully lured Val to the old station and—

"There's too much we don't know. I don't even know what I *think!* I mean, if we eliminate the impossible, and what's left, no matter how improbable, has to be the solution, then what've we got? A sick little man with enough motive to put John Chester into that diving suit *and* bash Merran twice *and* burn his shed down and *lure* Val Elliot to the lonesomest place in Manton, for godsake, et cetera et cetera et cetera. I'm sorry, I just don't buy it. Not about Merran, certainly. Merran's like a son to Everett, for one thing."

"Then try this," Jane said. "Nora and George Taylor have been having a fling, and they kill John. Nora, because she's had it with that little skinflint, and George, because he's tired of being blackmailed. But if both murders were done by the same person or persons, is there a single thing that links him/them to Val?"

"I don't know," MacWhirter said. "But here's something else sticks in my craw. Another pair. You said Everett talked so much about his rightful place that you got the idea he was illegitimate, bogus, which he seems to be. Well, the same thing applies to George Taylor. There's something bogus about the way he acted with that kid of his. It wasn't normal, if that's the word I want. Like, he never took her with him when he went out on calls, so why did he take her the night John died? By accident, or because he had something in mind—something like murder? Boy. The way he went for her in school that day, Ben—not like he was all that anxious about a little kid with a big problem but like he wanted her to prove something for him—and not because it *was* true but because it *wasn't* true. Or am I making myself unclear?"

"No. It's a good point. You might have cause to arrest him after all, if you work at it."

"Yeah. And then there's Nora's alibi. If the argument George says he and Connie heard was so loud outside that he had to go home—and I seriously question whether Connie could've heard it in the van—how come Nora didn't stay awake 'n' hear it inside. She'd only just taken sleeping pills and was in bed just about right over it. Or her kids? It wasn't all that late, what with the next day being school and a kid waiting in the van, so prob'ly the Chester kids were still up too. And even if they weren't, if it was such a loud argument, they'd've been waked up by it. After all, *they* weren't taking sleeping pills—

"Jesus. Maybe Nora put some in their supper milk—and *they* were asleep, not her. Maybe it was Nora having the argument with John—"

"Unless it was Everett," Ben said. "He could've gone back

alone for another go at getting some land out of John. He wasn't satisfied after my attempt, he just wouldn't let go of it. Maybe he and John were arguing, and Nora heard them. She may have come down and joined them. She wanted Everett's money, she said so. Or maybe she came down after Everett hit him and left him for dead and went home, and then George returned and between them they got John into that suit—"

"You saying Nora called George to come finish him?" MacWhirter said.

"Why not? She hated John and she hated that suit, and putting him into it would've appealed to her twisted sense of humor. She couldn't have done it alone, but even if she only helped George, that would account for her stiffness the next day. She said it was flu, but—"

"Ben, you just said Everett didn't have the strength to bash John's head in, no matter how mad he was," Jane said, cranky again. "Why are you contradicting yourself?"

"It's wrong, I know, and I apologize. In any case, John died in the suit, not before he was put in it—"

"How do you know that?" she demanded. "The ME didn't, did he, Colin?"

"Well, he wasn't able to prove it with blood and tissue studies, which he said would prob'ly happen when he finally did do 'em, but I don't discount that hunch of his, which if you recall, he said he didn't think the head wound looked bad enough to kill. And Ivan isn't the type guy who has hunches, so when he does—

"Besides, there are two holes in those diving helmets," MacWhirter said heavily, "for the air hoses. And the two holes in that one were carefully plugged up—with kleenex, for godsake, so's no air could get in. Didn't see 'em till later. If John was already dead, why bother with plugs? He wasn't dead. It stands to reason.

"But I'll tell you guys something. Overlooking the way he smelled, and even if he had an easy death, not all slashed into strips like London broil with a knife, or splattered into mushy bits with a bomb or a handful of bullets—'specially through his brains—or with a rope around his neck so his eyes pop out and his face turns blue and his tongue bulges out like a big fat sausage, I'll never *ever* get used to seeing death from thisthat'ntheother no matter how long I'm in this business."

Jane put her hand over her mouth.

"I can appreciate that," Ben said, paling a bit. "This one was only my sixth—two of 'em murders—but it was as bad as the first. But with all this chitchat, where the hell are we?

"Oh—and then there's this small matter, which for some reason nobody seems to have mentioned, not even you, Colin. A sort of alibi in reverse, if you want to call it that. Nora said John was expecting someone to take that diving suit away sometime that day or night. Then John's found dead in it. If she and George did the deed, why did they leave him in the storeroom? After all, they could have loaded up George's van, and who would know what he had in it? He could have dumped the body anywhere. Or why didn't they at least lock the storeroom door? It was pure chance made me open it. It's a powerful argument in their favor. Have you thought about that, Colin?"

"You think we didn't? What do you think we've been doing? Listen, we've gone through John's papers with a fine-tooth comb and haven't found one damn thing that leads to the individual who was going to buy that suit—supposed to be going to. We dialed every scribbled phone number. We contacted every swimming equipment store, every college or other swimmers' club, the Boston harbormaster, every marina from Newport to Cohasset for starters, everything and every place and everybody you can think of with the smallest connection to diving and diving suits of any description. Sports magazine ads, newspaper ads, you name it.

"We've had an army on this and we're not finished yet. And what've we come up with so far? Zilch. The only thing we haven't tried is one of those Ee-Ess-Pee-ers, for crissake!

"And what're the alibis? Nora's sick and asleep, and her

kids are asleep. George came but went home and stayed there, according to his wife and kids—well, Connie didn't say anything, and the boy said he guessed so. And Everett couldn't've done it no matter how mad he was. Because if he actually did manage it, Clarkson says, he'd undoubtedly have dropped down dead right beside John when he was finished, and then you'd've found two bodies in that storeroom, Ben. Which would've given you a real rush, right?

"So even *if* Nora and George put John in that suit, leaving him in the storeroom and leaving it unlocked was a pure stroke of genius, assuming they did it deliberately. And if for some goddam reason they were prevented from stowing it in George's van to be driven away—another question being who else came that night and interrupted them?—the same thing applies. Because the main question still is, who the hell would be so stupid as to kill someone and dress him up in like a goddam Halloween costume and then leave him there! All Nora has to do is keep on saying she was asleep and doesn't know anything about anything!"

"But you don't think leaving him was deliberate, do you," Ben said.

"Course I don't, and I think that sooner or later those alibis're gonna break down altogether. Way I see it, something had to've interrupted them! Let's say there were lights on downstairs, and someone wanted something from the shop—who knows, it could even have been the buyer for the diving rig! Which if it was, all Nora had to say to him—the buyer—was gee whiz, sorry, it was just sold to someone else. It's possible, isn't it? So what I think is, they were in the act of carrying him out of there when somebody came to the door or one of the kids came downstairs—something!—so George dragged the body into the storeroom, and Nora answered the door and said sorry she was sick and had to go back up to bed, and George scooted out the back to his van and waited a few minutes to see if it was okay to drive away, and then he went home, hopefully before anybody there noticed he was out. And to put the cherry on top—I mean make it impossible for them to shift John out first thing in the morning—you got there too early, Ben, and for some goddam reason you open that storeroom door and see the body on the floor and like a good neighbor you tell Nora and handle everything for her. So then it's too late, and both of them are locked up tight in those cockamamie alibis!

"Which I admit I haven't been able to crack. Don't think I didn't try. I've had them all down the station, the kids too, and—zilch! But as sure as God made little apples I know I'm gonna crack 'em! Maybe all Nora has to do is keep saying she don't know anything about anything, and maybe even Perry Mason couldn't nail her. But that don't worry me. As I see it, George is the one to go after. Through his family. That's his weak spot. That and that temper of his. Yeah, I think we'll get him by that route. Take some doing, though."

Jane poured him more coffee and moved the cake the least bit nearer. "Well, I'm sure you'll pull it off, Colin. Find out who interrupted the out-take, so to say, and that'll do it."

"Yeah, where do I look? Where do I start looking?"

"And if you come up empty again, then where are we?" Ben said.

"I know where I am right this minute—late!" MacWhirter eschewed more cake but slurped down the coffee and heaved himself up, sighing. "Used to be dead easy solving homicides and so on, but now . . . I don't know . . ."

"It used to be dead easy in my racket," Ben said with an echoing sigh. "I used to think so, anyway. Now everything seems shot to hell. What really gets me is how many victims there've been because of some lousy wiring. Maybe not victims per se, but casualties, so to speak. There's Blair, and John. There's Everett, campaign-wise. And Val Elliot. And Merran, job-wise, shed-wise, and head-wise. And, well, there's me."

MacWhirter set his cap squarely on his big head. "What're *you* griping about, Ben? Everybody knows you got one hell of a good job coming up, if you want it."

"Now how did you know about that!"

"You kidding me? In this town everybody knows everything about everybody. You know how people talk. And personally I think you'd be a damn fool to pass it up."

"Thanks for the advice, and I'm relieved for your sake that you won't miss me. But a good job doesn't seem so good when you get it by default."

MacWhirter marched to the back door. "I don't see that. You were thinking of quitting the ed biz anyway, and you didn't get that offer because your committee gave you the boot. It's just coincidence it came when it did. Which fits in with everything else that's been happening around here, just about. It's one more thing that matches. If you can call it that. And anyway, if you'd kept quiet and not bothered with any smartmouth lecture and let Merran take his lumps and fight his own battles just like everybody else has to—not that I think people shouldn't help each other—you'd still be in your office. Now. *If* you think of anything else about this case, I'm not sure I want to know about it till a week from November thirty-first! That way I can at least enjoy my Thanksgiving dinner."

He went out the kitchen door and slammed it irritably, opened it, said, "Thanks for the treat, Jane—and the news about Ben's job and all," and, with a grin at Ben's astounded face, closed himself out with enormous care.

In the middle of the night Ben sat up with a start.

Years of conditioning brought Jane instantly and completely awake. "Darling, what's wrong? What's the matter?"

"Nothing. I mean, it's those keys, Merran's dreams about keys. I keep forgetting to mention this to Colin, and I don't know if Merran did. Because here's another pair of happenings. Someone takes Val Elliot's key and burgles her apartment. And someone must have gotten a key to Merran's office building so as to steal in in the dead of night and open Jo Miles's desk drawer, or how would he—or she—have known who Merran's clients are, so as to call each one and warn them away? Was it the same person?"

"We should have remembered to tell Colin. Oh, Ben, it's just so crazy. Because who'd be out to get Merran—George? John or Nora? Val? Anyone in school bucking for his job or his practice? Because the thing is, whoever it was, that person put Merran at liberty with all kinds of time at his disposal. Is that what the poison pen calls and letters were supposed to accomplish? Or maybe the ultimate intention was to drive Merran out of town altogether. Now, who'd want to do that?

"Ben?

"Benjamin!"

He answered with a gentle snore.

Jane clucked in annoyance.

Presently all was still.

▽

TWENTY-ONE

"BEN, I THOUGHT OF something, after you woke me up in the middle of the night," Jane said at breakfast. "Which is, if you look at Merran's situation another way, he hasn't lost a job so much as gotten a lot of free time on his hands."

Ben laughed. "The distinction's too refined for me."

"No it isn't. Think. Who'd want him to be free as a bird?"

"I give up. Look, how about we give crime a rest for today and throw a party."

"Mmmm, yes, it would make a nice change. And talking of Merran, I wish it'd make a change for that poor jerk, or to him. He's flat as a pancake again, the way he was before Blair Bush died. What is it going to take to smarten him up, Ben? And when?"

"Well, he's got all that free time to work at—"

"No fooling, Ben. All those preparations Bec's making to go to New York, putting the house on the market and all—it's killing him—her too, but she keeps it pretty well hidden—and he's too stupid or too stubborn to know why."

"One good jolt and he will, sooner or later, you'll see, darling. Okay, we don't have to make this big. Just Merran, Bec, and Guy. Mind if I call Everett too?"

"Of course call him. Why do you ask? He hasn't been

proved guilty of anything. Besides, we all care about him. And I'd kind of like to invite Colin MacWhirter. I've gotten rather fond of that old monster. Now, what should I serve?"

"Oh, anything. Keep it simple. You could make marinated newspapers and Colin would think it was a feast. And it would be, now I come to think about it. You make out a shopping list, I'll do the calling." He kissed her and reached for the phone.

Guy McKay answered immediately and accepted the invitation immediately and hung up immediately.

Ben shook his head in disbelief. "I've never known anyone else in the world who spends less time on the phone."

"I bet he doesn't go to any meetings either. Oh boy, would he be a miserable flop in the ed biz!"

Police Chief Colin MacWhirter said he would have to come alone, if Jane didn't mind, being as his wife was following a program on the tube.

Everett's phone was busy.

Becca did not answer her phone; she answered Merran's. "I was just making him breakfast, Ben. For almost the last time." She cleared her throat, as though something had stuck there. "He still feels a bit tired. A party? Oh, lovely. Of course I'll come. . . . Yes, my last with you too for a long long time." She cleared her throat again. "I don't know. He may have other plans. He can speak for himself. I have an omelet going for him. I've, uh, I made good coffee, Ben," she added.

"Hi," Merran said dispiritedly. "Sure. I suppose. Everett coming too, no doubt? Well, why not. Every party needs a wet blanket, right?"

"But not two," Ben said, hanging up. "Oh boy. A good jolt wouldn't do it for that guy. More scope is needed—something in the nature of an earthquake. Soon as I sign Everett up, I'll drop over there and see if I can modify the lad."

"Mark Twain said the only way you can modify some people is with an ax," Jane said darkly.

"If that's what it takes, then that's what I'll do. I don't

want him spoiling our evening, and if it looks like he might, I'll cut him out. So to say."

"Ben!"

Everett's phone was busy. Busy. Busy. Busy.

"Guess I'll have to go over and ask him in person. Think I'll stop by and check on Merran first. The way Bec sounded, I almost think she was asking me to."

"Go now if you like. I'll call Everett."

"Something tells me you'd waste half the day at it. No, I better go, since I'm going out anyway. He could be on his way to Timbuktu right now, and he'd still be terribly hurt if I hadn't at least left a note on his door. Want me to shop on the way back?"

"Thank you, darling. I really don't need much. Here's the list."

But he only sat staring at nothing.

"Ben? Ben, are you there?"

He turned to her. "Sorry, what?"

"The list. As in shopping. Here."

"Oh. I was just thinking of something. Something Garth told me . . ."

He looked up presently. "Just reviewing the permutations and combinations. And the complications. I forgot to tell you. With all that excitement over the trip to see Rob and so forth, something else Garth said slipped through the cracks. I don't know why it just popped back out, but anyway, know who Everett's house belonged to? You'll never guess."

"I don't know. I can't guess. Well . . . want a way-out guess? Gardiner Holdridge. Bec's great-uncle."

"Give the little lady ten silver dollars. Bec's great-uncle. Doubling as Everett's father. Oh, undoubtedly his father."

"Ah. That may be why he didn't come back to Manton till fairly recently, Ben. Remember we wondered why he stayed away so long after he retired? He must have waited till he could get exactly what he wanted. His father's house. For starters. And from there he could work on his status. His place, as he calls it."

"Could be. Just shows what lengths single-mindedness can go to, doesn't it."

"I'm saying his single-mindedness is very sad. Are you saying his single-mindedness goes all the way to murder?"

"No, I'm not saying that. I don't think his does, in fact. I thought we'd agreed on that."

"Then what's this all about?"

"Nothing. I just find it interesting, is all."

Ben found Becca and Merran breakfasting in a most peculiar atmosphere. Merran, with an elbow on the table and a hand propping up his head, morosely pushed dry yellow lumps around his plate, mashed them flat, pushed them around some more. Becca, her manner desperately brittle, was making a determined assault on a bowl of corn flakes whose level remained magically the same.

Ben bent to kiss her cheek, which was very thin now, and very pale. "Where's Joy Taylor, Bec? I seem to have lost track."

"Sorry, Ben, but with all my packing and everything, I forgot to tell you. She's with an aunt in Pennsylvania. We had to get the court's permission to put her on a plane while you were in Michigan. It's best, really. George came around, and of course I wouldn't let him in. He was pretty fierce, demanded to see his girl, yelled that we had no right, and so on. I even expected him to break the door down—he banged on it a couple of times. And called. Those people have a lot to learn before their daughter's willing to go home again, if she ever is. She's a sweet child to have around, Ben. Poor kid."

Merran said harshly, "Save it. Joy's a survivor, much stronger than you think. George Junior won't suffer as long as somebody does some talented cooking for him, and Connie won't as long as she can watch her father squirm."

"As long as she can handle her guilt, she'll be even happier if the chief can put him away," Ben said. "I never saw anybody want to do anything so much."

"Why? What for?" Becca said.

"Breaking and entering. And probably more of the latter than the former, what else?"

(I didn't hear that, Jane would have said.)

Becca, having heard nothing about George Taylor's handling of house calls, looked puzzled, but Merran smiled a little at the mischievous expression on Ben's face. It even roused him enough to get up and clear the table.

"Everett's phone's been busy," Ben said, "so I'm going over to invite him in person. Why not come with me? It's a gorgeous day. A little outing might do you both good."

"Well, sure, why not?" Merran said. "And it'll do Everett good to see our happy faces."

"He's never glad to see my face," Becca said. "You go. I'll just clean up here and then get on with my packing and sorting. It's enough that he'll have to see me tonight."

"No way, my girl," Merran said. "We're in this together. You'll wear him down eventually, because I'm going to help." But his voice was dull, the way it had been early in the fall. So was his wit, or he would not have missed the rich color that flooded her cheeks and as quickly drained away.

How can anyone who's supposed to be so smart be so dumb? Ben asked himself.

The silence grew awkward.

Ben said, "Garth told me a few things about Everett, just before I left for Detroit. What with one thing and another, I haven't had a chance to fill you in. Apparently he was a real itch as a kid, and a snob of the first water. Picked fights with everybody, had a real quick temper. Garth still can't understand why Everett attached himself to him, he wasn't nicer to the kid than anybody else was. Called him his albatross, said it was a relief when he and Honora left town. I said if he ever comes home, he'll be pleased by the adult Everett. Okay, I'm going out and start the car. Which'll give you enough time to wash the dishes and clean the house."

After some persuasion the old Ford started, its doors *scrawawked* open, and Merran and Becca got in. Immediately the car seemed terribly crowded, and all at once Ben sensed that Merran's anger, smoldering, bitter, and confused, was taking an inordinate amount of space. He sighed and addressed the clutch, which gave in ungraciously after a brief argument.

Everett's car was in the driveway.

"Good. He's home," Ben said, and honked the Ford's horn, which blatted like a cow with diarrhea.

Everett came out smiling. "I hope you weren't trying to call me? I always take the phone off the hook when I'm baking. Come in, come in, gentlemen, and I'll give you the royal tour and some tea. This particular cake is best when it's warm."

Merran stopped and whispered angrily in Ben's ear, "He's still doing it—leaving Bec out!" But with Gifford herding him in with nips at his ankles, he obediently joined the others in admiring the rooms and the fine old pieces Everett had collected.

Everett served tea and the fresh cake in the dining room. "It's a good thing you came when you did. I'd only just taken this cake out of the pan. Another few minutes, and Gifford and I would have been out for our walk."

"Glad I thought to come, then," Ben said. "Because Jane and I feel a little party is indicated. No special reason, just on general principles. Come at five, and bring Gifford, if he has nothing else to do. Also, I am the bearer of best wishes from Garth Shaw. Spoke to him the other day. He knows this house and said you were very lucky to get it."

"Thank you, Ben. Thank you for telling me. Garth was my best friend, you know. I'd be even more pleased if you told me he was coming home."

"Well, he's thinking about it. He's feeling a lot better about everything. Been playing a lot of golf lately—said he's looking forward to playing with you, Ev—and he's working as a bank messenger, getting about, meeting people, and enjoying life."

Only Everett was startled, then angry. "But—but that's a

menial's job. He's an engineer, a professor. An eminently successful man by any standard. It's hardly suitable for someone in his position. How can he even think of such a thing!"

"Everett," Merran said softly, "what exactly is his position?"

"Well—well—it's like mine! We have a certain standing. One can't run around with a manila envelope under one's arm. It's demeaning!"

Ben's laugh was kind and spacious. "Garth hated engineering, Ev, and he despised academia. But one of his two main principles of mental health is that work is man's saving grace, any kind of work. The other one he lives by is *Illegitimati non carborundum,* and he never ever lets them. Maybe it's taken him longer than we would wish to pull his socks up and get cracking—he and Philippa had a good marriage—but I'd say he's just about done it. I predict he'll be home by New Year's at the latest."

He turned away from Everett's white, angry face to look out of the window. The trees cast no shadows now, a reminder that the day was advancing. "It was a fine treat, Ev, and thank you, but we better get going. Promised Jane I'd do the shopping on the way home. But would you mind if I tour the grounds first? This place is like a park."

"Thank you for the compliment. Go right ahead," Everett said, opening the door for him. "Stay, Giff."

But Gifford shot out and flew around rapturously in the noon perfection like a four-footed bird hardly knowing where to light. A little rabbit unwisely left a sheltering forsythia to seek safety in the wood, and he charged after it along the path leading to the Chester ruin.

Ben stood laughing in the doorway, but Everett said anxiously, "Oh dear. I don't like him going over there. He knows he's supposed to stay in his own yard. Actually he never goes far without me."

"We'll get him back, Ev, don't worry."

"Well, all right. I'll just clear away, then, and join you in a few minutes?"

Ben nodded and started across the lawn, Merran and Becca following spiritlessly.

"He can say what he likes about Gifford obeying the rules," Merran said when they were some distance from the house, "but it's obvious that dog goes pretty much where he pleases when he gets the chance. This may surprise you, but the day Blair Bush died, I think John was telling the truth when he said he hadn't let Gifford into the pool area. Because, remember at the beginning of the campaign when Ev put a tie or whatever around his neck after he lost his collar? Well, I found it. Half burned in John's yard."

"But John's dog—"

"Is small. Or was. Nora should spend a few months living in the same way she treats him. Wonder if the poor little bugger's still alive." He described what he had seen, the afternoon of his dinner party, and why he had not invited Nora after all. "Guess I should've checked on him . . . meant to . . . Oh hell, he's probably dead by now. If Nora doesn't care about him, why the hell should I? What difference does it make anyway?"

No longer amused by Gifford, Ben cajoled, commanded, threatened, but to no avail. Gifford ranged ahead, now on one side of them, now the other, complaining at the rabbit's unwillingness to come forth and meet its doom.

"The hell with him, he knows how to get home," Merran said. "Let's go back. This place is too depressing, it's spoiling the whole goddam day."

So are you, Ben thought, completely out of temper now.

They emerged from the wood to see Everett brushing dust and debris off Gifford and himself.

"For all his training, that animal still jumps all over everybody," Merran grumbled.

"Lighten up and say good-bye nicely," Ben said, "or you can walk back."

He sensed almost at once an indefinable wrongness in the

way the car handled. You haven't been very cooperative, he told it soundlessly, but this is ridiculous.

Manton's picturesque country roads were domed in the middle, shoulderless, and narrow, and they undulated vertically through steeply cut hillsides: good fun for thrill-seekers but hell to negotiate even cautiously in foul weather or when church services were beginning or ending. A wedding party was dispersing from the Episcopal Church now, and Ben's lips thinned in concentration in the bumper-to-bumper traffic. He began to notice that each time he braked, the pedal softened a little more under his foot.

Willing the cars ahead to turn into side roads *now,* he shifted into second gear, which slowed the Ford perceptibly, and mentally crossed his fingers. The last leg of the ride back to the Shaw house, where he would rid himself gladly if only temporarily of the shared misery in the back seat, was steeply downhill—a long hill—into a right turn.

The road leveled somewhat for a short stretch, and he down-shifted to first, which helped some more. The road dipped again; turned sharply. The brake pedal, which had lately shown a tendency to stick, stuck. The speedometer needle moved steadily upward.

Ben tried twice, fleetingly, to gauge time, speed, mass, and distance.

Head across the road into the side of the hill? That oncoming car'll hit us amidships halfway over.

Pull up on the hand brake? Might go ass over teakettle and hit the car in front.

"Sit tight and hang on," he said coolly, very much the school administrator—one of the few people in the world who never panic in a crisis—but inside his head he was shouting, Turn off, damn you! Turn off, you swine, turn off!

As if they had heard him, the oncoming car and then two of those ahead of him turned into a lane decorated at its entrance with multicolored balloons. The wedding party, he thought, belatedly switching on the hazard lights and pressing hard on the horn. It gave a bleat of despair and expired.

At the same instant the lights flickered and dimmed.

The agile compact in front of him accelerated perilously around the curves as the old Ford hurtled toward it.

The Shaw house was now less than three hundred feet away. Between its two stone pillars safety lay.

He'll keep going and I'll turn in, Ben thought. Something'll stop us—face it when you get there.

The driver of the compact whipped in between the pillars and stopped abruptly, possibly to get his breath and count his blessings.

"Oh no!" Ben yelled as the Ford, a vehicular toreador, twirled in behind him on two wheels and, with a thundering crash, shot the small car forward and shoved its trunk into the rear seat.

(Right in the side pocket, but no score—you didn't call it, Jane would have said.)

"Mmmf!" Dr. Clarkson said to Merran, as who should say, What else can be expected of you! To Becca he gave painkillers, a bath towel to wrap around her neck, and an order to lie down on the couch. "Been looking like hell lately, Rebecca," he added, going out the door. "Do something about it. Benjamin, get a good car."

"I think this deserves a brandy," Ben said and went for it.

"Ben, I'm sorry but I don't think I can make it this evening," Becca quavered. "Will you apologize to Jane for me? Merran, help me up, please. I'll go home. Then you can rest."

Merran knelt beside her and took her hand. "No. Stay where you are. How do you feel?"

She smiled shakily. "Better than I expected to for a few minutes there. I was beginning to hear the harps. Oh, this thing itches." She tugged at the towel around her neck and moved her head from side to side, grimacing with pain.

"I know, I know, but leave it, don't take it off. Now look, you've made the end come loose. Here, let me fix it." Taking more time than was necessary, he gently adjusted, tucked, pinned. "You're tired," he said, brushing her hair back. Caressingly, lingeringly, his fingertips outlined the shape of her gracious forehead. "It should have been me," he murmured. "It should have been me." He covered her hand with his free one.

Her hand was warm and firm, the nails well-shaped, the fingertips blunt from years of playing. A competent hand, which might so easily have been mashed to useless pulp. He put his other hand over it and felt the strong steady pulse. "You're thinner. Since before you went to New York. You've lost a lot of weight."

"That sounds like an indictment."

"Yes," he said thoughtfully. "Yes, I guess it is."

"You feel you prefer me overweight." Her lapis eyes gleamed. "You feel it's—"

"Come off it, Bec. And anyway, you were never overweight, you were always just right."

"Thank you." She regarded him calmly.

Ben sipped his brandy: a difficult thing to do since he was grinning broadly.

Merran groaned and put a hand to his head, as if the room had begun to spin. He tightened his hold on Becca's hand. "I'm a fool," he said bitterly. "A blind stupid fool."

"That's true." Her tone was entirely neutral. "It's the first worst thing about you, Merran. Worse even than your moodiness. But that I should hear a tautology from you? Shame."

"You're right. But I'll stay with it."

"If you like. But what brought all this on?"

He shook his head as if there were no point in telling her.

Oh yes there is, if you're going to build a relationship, Ben warned him soundlessly, tiptoeing to the door. For all the two noticed him, he could have stampeded out like a herd of buffalo, but all he got for his care were cramps in his calf muscles (which is what you get for not exercising, Jane would have said).

"What is it, Merran?" Becca said. "Tell me. Have we ever had secrets from each other?"

"Well," he said slowly (and Ben lingered at the door—to

ease his legs, he told himself), "for thirty-two years we've been like brother and sister, good buddies, and then all of a sudden . . . and I never realized . . ." He let go of her hand as though he didn't deserve to hold it.

"Never realized what?" she said conversationally.

But he did not hear that. "Time. God! You know? I mean, thirty-two years, Bec. Such a gift. And gone in a flash. And I wasted damn near a year of it. A year I can never get back. I can't say, 'Hey, I did that one wrong, used it badly, screwed it up, didn't understand its value, please can I do it over.' "

"You're in good company, I'd say."

An equable response just a step beyond the nondirective. Very good, Ben told her silently.

Merran shook his head slowly, heavily, as if it weighed a ton. "Oh . . . I guess. But what good's knowing it! What'd really help is somebody to dole out time to us poor stupid mortals. And monitor our use of it. Our improved use of it. In stages. Otherwise we can't be graduated to the next stage. And learning too late shouldn't count. I mean, there ought to be a time limit, or we lose, being too blind to see what we've done with such a gift. Know what I mean?"

"Frankly, no. I never found philosophy therapeutic after a car accident, Merran. I'm not sure I can follow you. What would learning too late disqualify you from—living any longer? And which year did you waste? And why do you say it was wasted? Seems to me you've been accomplishing a lot right along."

(Oh, Bec, Bec, careful you don't outfox yourself, Jane would have said.)

"Oh . . . professionally." He shrugged off professional growth as though nothing in the world could matter less, then or ever. "That's the easy part, Bec. That's not what I'm talking about."

"Well, what are you talking about, then? In fact, why don't you just take me home, Merran," she said kindly, "and we'll talk some other time. Maybe you can come down to New York in a few months when I'm all settled in, and you can tell me just what you wasted—and with whom—and what it was you didn't realize till too late, okay?" She made to get up. "But right now I think you're losing me."

(Very *good!* You're on Ben's level with that one, Jane would have said.)

"Well, it's not that easy to explain, Bec." He groped for her hand; found it; held on as to a lifeline. "That year . . . the months with Val . . . I didn't love her. I never loved her. Maybe she was just a way of evading something I didn't think I was ready for. But I didn't even realize it until it was too late to . . . to tell you it took too long for me to . . . to get used to something else. Something more . . . much more. With you."

He kissed the back of her hand; kissed her fingers one by one; kissed the palm; closed her fingers over it; reluctantly released her: a farewell.

She seemed to be arguing with herself about how, or even whether, to respond to that.

(My god! Jane would have shrieked. What are you waiting for!)

"I did," she said at last.

"Did what?" he said absently, still involved with the enormity of his loss.

A slow blush rose out of the towel around her neck and suffused her face. "I said, I did. Got used to something more, I mean."

"You—what? You did? *When?*"

"Oh . . . a while back. A very long while back."

He stared at her, incredulous, stunned, angrier than he had ever been. "*Now* you tell me? House on the market, whiplash and collar and Juilliard and—*now* you tell me? Now that you're packing and going?" He turned away, still on his knees, heartbroken, extinguished. "Now that I love you—I mean, now that I know I've loved you all my life, that I never loved—never wanted—anybody else. You got what you really wanted and you're going . . . and it's too late . . ."

He looked at her and bounded up, aghast first at his loss,

then at another of his errors. "Oh god—I'm sorry, Bec. Forgive me. You don't deserve that. If what you want most is to go, you should go. For you it's a good decision. And it's not . . . well, New York's not all that far away."

"Oh darling, darling, I'm not going. You're only partly right. I once told Juilliard it wasn't definite yet, that I was waiting on a better offer. Don't you remember? And I just got that better offer after all." She blushed again, and as the rosy glow reached her tear-filled eyes, she burst into her rich deep laugh and held out her hands to him. "Everything else—New York—can be changed back."

In an instant he was on his knees again beside her, his arms around her, his lips on hers—an exercise that caused her neck to hurt more.

Ben opened the door and went out, the brandy glass still in his hand, its contents unfinished. Unaware of this, he put the glass into his pocket, where it promptly emptied itself, and walked happily home.

Later, when told the last details of the scene he had exited, he said, "Well, so what? Pain in a good cause never hurt anyone."

▽

TWENTY-TWO

MARTY GUINNESS, ONLY SON of Ben's chief tormentor on the School Committee, had been Ben's student and Merran's client. All three had given up in mutual disgust, and Marty had helled around for a while and then left town. Now back, he was driving a cab and studying for his High School Equivalency Exam. He no longer smoked, drank, or ate meat. His hair hung in a thick braid down his back, a peace sign from his neck. His jeans, T-shirts, and open hightops with laces trailing perilously—a universal costume—had given place to Martha's Vineyard raunch: faded Madras pants, tie-dye shirts, and sandals made of rubber tires, for which proofs of intractable failure the senior Guinness blamed Ben.

"Good to see you, Marty," Ben said, shaking hands and going around to the passenger seat. "How do you like the taxi business?"

"Keeps me off the streets." The lad grinned, and Ben thought, Maybe we've done him some good after all.

"You're the only important guy in this town with one car, Dr. Louis. My old man naturally thinks you're sick. So what're you gonna get this time?"

"Any suggestions?"

"Something bigger and tougher than that Ford. If you could find another Marathon like this old war horse—they're cheap too—you'd be doing yourself a favor. Course, what with that new job you're taking up, you won't have to think about cost. Okay, where to?"

"You ought to know without my telling you. You seem to know about everything else."

"No offense, Dr. Louis, but this town knows what you had for breakfast."

Ben couldn't help laughing. "Oh, no offense. But for your information I'm not sure I'm going anywhere, and I'm not sure I want to. Nothing's settled. Or is it?"

"As soon as I hear, you'll be the first one I call. Okay, meter time. Where to?"

"Whit's. My car was towed there. Maybe he has a car I can borrow awhile. Besides . . ." But the rest of his thought he decided to keep to himself.

Still tired from yesterday's accident, he was asleep when Marty pulled up at a dirty sagging shed on the outskirts of town where worked a man with golden hands. One of these articles pressed a cold Coke bottle against his cheek. He opened his eyes and blinked.

Jim Whitman was grimy all over except for a head of puckish curls that gleamed red and gold in the cold sunlight. A cigarette dangled, as always, from his lower lip. He inhaled; drained one of his own countless daily Coke bottles; exhaled. "Go on," he said. "Drink it. Good for what ails yuh."

Ben drank. Refreshed by the mild stimulant, he paid Marty and thanked him, and climbed out. He moved upwind of Whit's cigarette smoke as obtrusively as possible.

"Yeah yeah," Whit said, mashing the butt under his heel. His bloodshot eyes regarded Ben as they did everything else in the world, with a weary, not ill-tempered irony. "I like to suffer. Just don't tell me you got no vices."

"I don't. I don't have a car either. But first—listen, Whit, take a look at those brakes, will you? You only just did them."

"Yeah. But brake shoes're one thing. The lines can always rupture from wear, all that pressure they hold. They looked okay two months ago, I remember that. I was gonna look 'em over when she was hauled in here yesterday night, but I been busy. What—you got one a those hot flashes a yours? Yeah, I can see you do."

Standing in like company behind the shed was the Ford, to Ben's fond eye oddly unconquerable still.

Whit's T-shirt hiked up over his bellybutton as he inched under the Ford's front end, and inched out again, and under the rear wheels. He emerged with a strange expression on his face. "None a them lines were *ruptured,* Ben, that's for sure."

"But?"

"But one line on the front was, shall we say, improved on. No way I coulda done it—or missed it. Neat little cut. Not all the way through, a course. Dead easy to do—do it with a hacksaw, take four, five seconds if you know where to look. Fluid bled right out. All that stop-and-go yesterday, it wouldn't take long. Looks like someone don't like you all that much. I was you, I'd sit with my back to the wall from now on."

Ben stood in thought, and something fell into place with a solid *thunk,* leaving him tireder than before, and sadder. "Whit, keep this under your hat. The adjuster probably won't come for a week or more anyway—they never do—which'll give me time . . ."

"To do a little sleuthing, huh? Yeah, well, you're pretty good at that, as I remember. Hey look, I just got a Camry in. Old lady drove it to the store 'n' back real slow, five thousand miles 'n clean as a whistle. Nice taupe-y gray too—real professional. You can loan it, or I'll give you a price. Not that you can't afford a bran'-new one, that job you're gonna get. You sure are one lucky guy, Ben. What's your secret?"

"I stopped smoking," Ben said, and burst out laughing.

If he had known that it was the last laugh he would have for the next several days, he would have choked on it.

"That Camry sounds too good to pass up, Whit. Let's do business."

He told himself that Chester's Swim Shop was on the way home or he wouldn't have bothered stopping. Still, he hoped he wasn't too late.

He went apprehensively around the trash bin enclosure to the lonely place where Merran said Nora kept the little mutt, swearing under his breath as he ran the last few steps.

The dog was panting feebly at the end of the rope, which was so twisted and taut that it held his head and shoulders off the ground. His eyes were dull, his coat filthy. The excrement in which he had struggled to free himself was white, evidence that he had been given nothing to eat or drink for several days. He was shuddering with cold.

Ben took out his old Boy Scout knife, knelt, and cut the rope. The collar was almost buried in the loose skin around the emaciated little neck. His throat tight with outrage, he took off his warm jacket, laid it on the ground, and with infinite gentleness wrapped the dog in it. He carried his little burden into the pool building.

"Just what are you doing! What do you think you're doing, Ben Louis!" Nora shouted. "How dare you interfere!"

Ben went into the dressing room, wet his fingertips under the washbasin faucet, and moistened the dog's parched tongue. He soaked his handkerchief in the bowl and wiped the gummy eyes and cracked nostrils and the inside of the mouth. No answering twitch of tail, no flicker of eyelid, but the panting continued. Without a word or glance at Nora, Ben carried him out to the Camry.

Veterinarian Len Kenney clip-clopped into the examining room in his wooden clogs, his lunch napkin tucked under his chin.

"Jesus Christ and God Almighty," he whispered as Ben uncovered the dog on the table. "I know this little tyke. Oh boy, he's in bad shape. I don't know, Ben. He's about as far gone as you can get. I just don't know."

"What can you do?"

"Rehydrate him first, real slow. Kidneys may be shot, and who knows what else. And pray he doesn't have heartworm into the bargain, he'd never make it through the treatment. Well, I'll get started. No time like the present." He pulled off the dangling napkin and stuffed it into his pocket.

"Do whatever it takes, Len. I'll keep him, of course. Fee can help nanny him. Guess our house is big enough for two dogs."

"That castle you'll be living in'll be plenty big enough, what I hear. Okay, Ben, let me get to it. I'll call you when I see how things go. I'm also calling the SPCA. You may not want to press charges, but I'm sure as hell going to."

How does it happen, Ben yelled inwardly as he got into the Camry, How in hell does something I said to someone over the phone in the privacy of my own house or halfway across the country get around—drums? And yet a woman gets herself murdered in a more or less public place and there isn't a whisper about it, and not one person heard or saw one goddam thing!

The murderer did.

Ah yes. The murderer. And all I have to do is find him. But first back to Nora Chester.

In the Chester driveway stood George Taylor's van, its flames leaping and lunging around and around it.

A phallic metaphor if ever there was one, Ben thought, and opened the shop's front door. The bells hanging on the inside jingled like coins. Naturally—what else!

The shop was empty but the office door stood ajar, and he heard a scuffling inside, then Nora's voice.

She was sitting back in the chair carelessly twiddling a pencil and making talk about estimates. George Taylor stood by the desk in a casual pose. But the sheaf of invoices he held like a screen before his crotch might as well have been a piece of glass.

Faintly revolted, not by carnality, of which he was ordinarily a fervent advocate, but by the corrupt atmosphere of the room, Ben gazed at them.

His silence gave him the advantage. He looked terrifyingly omniscient, as does every school principal to wrongdoers, and these two were shrinking from him. They're scared! he thought, obscurely ashamed, and as swiftly thought, What do I do now?

"Well," he said, playing for time. "Well well. I wondered, and now I know."

"I don't know what you think you know," Nora said, "and I don't care. What *I* want to know is, what did you do with my dog, Ben Louis?"

He could have told her, but another thought had struck him, a theory of murder, a possibility that Jane had offered a few days ago, and he would not be sidetracked from it by a suburban housewife who was as shrewd and dirty a streetfighter as any he had ever known.

"Where were your kids when I found John in that diving suit?" he said, pressing his advantage in a cold judicial voice suggesting that he knew not only the answer to his question but the reason behind the answer.

Did he only imagine that she blanched? that George tightened up a little more? Had he really seen, or only wished to see, the pure panic terror that arced between them for a fraction of an instant?

Nora said coolly, "Upstairs getting dressed for school. Where do you think they'd be before breakfast on a weekday, Ben?"

He would have been surprised if she had said anything else. "I asked almost out of courtesy," he said with a grim little smile. "I didn't have to. Ask *you,* that is."

He waited just long enough to measure the effect of that shot. Satisfied, he reached for the *mot juste.*

"Catch you later," he said and left them.

Even in the clean sanity of his kitchen he was too preoccupied to detail the Camry's virtues to Jane but went straight to the phone and called Bill Tempesta. "Bill, do me a favor. Check the Chester kids' attendance the Friday I found John. Were they in school? Were they okay? Yes, it's urgent, and Bill, don't mention me to the teachers, right? Thanks."

The principal called back in twenty minutes. Ben snatched up the phone; listened; said thanks; was about to hang up when Bill said, "Hey, Ben? Maybe it's just coincidence—been meaning to tell you, but things're so damn busy around here, you know how it is.

"Listen, come over and see Connie Taylor's work in the art exhibit in the lobby. Merran too—she goes to his office now. All black paint and red paint and parts of bodies—wow!

"And speaking of Merran, it'll be lonesome as hell around here when he and Becca leave too. You pirate, you ought to be jailed, snatching two of Manton's best for that new job of yours! Hey, great news about their marriage! Look, let's do lunch soon and you can fill me in, okay? Also, give me first refusal on your house, okay? I always wanted to live in the historic district."

"That's the *fourth* time today I've heard what I'm going to do with my life! And Bill just told me what Merran and Bec are going to do with theirs! I give up," Ben said.

"I wouldn't give this town the satisfaction, darling. Okay, what was all that about the Chester kids?"

"I walked in on Nora and George having a bit of slap and tickle, and several items flashed in front of my eyes. First, whether the Chester kids were in school the morning I found John. Nora said of course they were, and they were—Bill just checked—but they were late and seemed logy, sleepy. It hadn't happened before and hasn't since, which is why their teachers remembered, because generally they're antsy little pests who always get to school before it opens and have to be dealt with before they wreak havoc. So one question is, *why?*"

"We'll work it out later. I have another question. What's bothering you, darling? You're pretty antsy yourself. Did something else happen? I'd have expected that gorgeous car to really set you up, but maybe after the Ford it's just too rich for your blood. We don't have to keep it. You can find another old wreck to love and cherish. Besides me."

He didn't even smile. "It's what Whit found out about the brakes," he said, and told her.

And added something that had after all not been jolted out of his memory by a runaway car.

Such a small detail—emerging from the woods with Becca and Merran and seeing Everett standing by the Ford and brushing himself and the returned Gifford off.

Brushing himself off not because Gifford had joyfully jumped all over him but because he had been lying under the car and destroying a brake line with a hacksaw or other sharp instrument.

"Oh. Oh my god. What do you say about his single-mindedness *now?* Ben, do you know what he did? Just after you left this morning, he called to ask how you were! Are you going to call the chief?"

Ben shook his head as he picked up the phone again.

"Sure, Ben," Merran said, "I'll go with you. Bill's right. I've been seeing some unsettling changes in that fat little kid too, lately. Pick me up in the Camry, it should be a nice change—"

"Jesus Christ!" Ben exploded. "What is this—black magic? I only just drove the thing home!"

"And would you stop off at Pete Swiggett's afterward?" Merran said with a laugh. "That cold water hose on the washing machine blew again. Thanks. I'll be out front."

The school was emptying noisily, but Ben and Merran stood absorbed by two paintings in the exhibit.

"This kid's work used to be just like what she was when you last saw her, Ben—it didn't give anything away except maybe the fact that it damn well wasn't giving anything away. You know, regulation blue sky, yellow ball with lines sticking out all over it, house with door and path, smoking chimney, green lawn with maybe a stick figure on it, though usually there aren't any people in a mute's isolated world. Not that she's all that isolated. She does have friends here.

"But these are dynamic statements of hatred and murder and bloody violence. Could be just a safety valve. Could be a warning. Before Ricky Priest killed himself he was writing nice bland happy sophomoric poetry for English class."

"Oh? Well, whichever it is, what happens to a kid like her if it comes to the last straw?" Ben said as they went back to the new car.

"There's no rule. Usually a selective mute gets even more so, maybe even goes all the way into a catatonic state. Implodes, as it were. Or he does the other thing—explodes, blasts forth—"

"Attacks someone physically, you mean?"

"Maybe. Or verbally. But there's no way to predict, and we won't know till it happens. Either way, it'll be a real wow addition to that article I did on Connie. How relevant it'll be to the topic other than as a colorful aside is another matter."

"You haven't gotten anywhere with Doris and George?"

"Not even off the ground. And Connie went from bad to worse when Joy left, but I didn't—don't—have the authority to send Connie with her. Wish I did. I told Doris and George I'm giving them one more chance before I take them to court, but they don't seem to believe me."

"They'll believe Colin. There's nothing he'd like better than to haul them in, and I think I can give him the muscle to do it. I've got news," Ben said, and told him.

Merran sighed gustily. "Oh boy. I thought I was worried before. But I'm really worried now."

"I'm glad," Ben said seriously. "It's a good sign. Bodes well for your future."

"Bettelheim, may he rest in peace, said love was not enough, but in this instance he was wrong. And so was I." Merran stretched his long legs luxuriously. "Boy, was I wrong! How could I have been so dumb?" he said dreamily.

* * *

Leaving Ben to rest and to try out the Camry's radio, Merran went into Pete Swiggett's shop and found the showroom empty. He called out but got no answer.

His van's here so he's here. Probably he and his big fierce watchdog are sleeping off a Weight Watchers in the sitting room, Merran thought, and headed for it.

The key cabinet over the desk was an open mouth trying to tell him something.

Bingo! he said to himself. My dream. My dream about keys. There's the key to my building. Right there for anyone who's out to get me. But who'd want to, and why?

The sitting room door was open, too, and dog and master were asleep on the couch. He shook them awake.

Sam Houston blinked peaceably at him. Pete sat up yawning and rubbed his eyes. "Sorry, Doc. Guess I nodded off. Hope you weren't waiting long. I been flat out for three days now. You'd think it was the middle of winter, way boilers're quittin' and pipes're burstin'. What can I do you for?"

"That new cold water hose blew too, Pete—"

His breath caught in his throat as if someone had hit him hard in the solar plexus.

On the table at one end of the couch was a small white television set with a gray sticky patch on the top of the case. Merran touched it with a fingertip. A little mouse photographer had sat there, glued into place. Had Val taken it off? Or had she left it there for old times' sake—if she thought of it at all—and her murderer removed it?

"The wife tried damn near every kinda scrubbin' powder on that sticky stuff."

"What channels can you get?" Merran said, his heart beating fast. You could get two local channels on a good day on that set and that was it. He took his hand away and put it in his pocket as if he had burned it.

"Don't get much, Doc, and that's a fact, but I'm too busy most of the time so it don't matter. I don't think Mr. Upham knew the condition it's in, but what the hell, it's company for the wife when she covers for me sometimes. He knows I don't need company, what with Sam here." With the slow care of someone taking inventory of complicated stock, he gathered his long loose frame carefully off the bed and set it upright. "Sorry about that hose, Doc, they come in defective sometimes, what can I tell you? I'll go get you another one, and no charge."

"Seems to me we have a two-pronged problem here, Ben," Merran said as they drove away. "Or rather, two independent problems that somehow got joined at the hip. What do you think?"

Ben told him.

"What are you planning to do about it?"

Ben told him that too.

"Need any help?"

"I'll let you know."

"*Now* are you going to tell the chief?" Jane demanded.

Ben shook his head and went to the phone and dialed.

"Everett," he said, "I think we have to talk."

▽

TWENTY-THREE

"PLEASE SIT DOWN, BEN. Make yourself comfortable." Everett inclined his head regally toward a chair and took his place in the middle of the couch opposite, a disquieting stillness about him. Gifford, who lay at his feet, rolled his big round eyes from master to visitor, his ears twitching as if monitoring the beginning of something to do with that stillness. "May I offer you coffee? A brandy?"

"Thanks, Ev, I just had supper," Ben said, but thought distractedly, This is crazy! He's crazy!

He said smoothly, "It was nice of you to see me, Everett"—Everett inclined his head again—"but I expect you're disappointed that only my car was totaled. Disappointed and very angry."

Everett crossed his legs, folded his hands in his lap. "Angry? Do I look angry?"

"No, you don't. It's just that, well, in your place, I think I would be. But Ev, I don't get it. Why would you want to hurt your best friend by hurting his son? And me—I know you like Jane and me. And Bec—your cousin, Ev—your blood relative! And why'd you want to hurt Merran anyway? You tried twice—"

"Oh no. Three times, Ben. The night I burned his shed

down. I think he must have an unusually hard skull, don't you think so?"

"Looks like it. Funny—I don't think anyone thought you were the one in his yard that night."

"Who did you think it was!"

"You know, somehow or other, Ev, I lost track of that incident. But the first time was on the golf course, I know that. It wasn't your fault you didn't hit him hard enough."

"Of course it wasn't my fault! It was that drunken fool slicing right into the rough. That's what gave me the idea, you know. But Merran turned his head at the last second when he heard it. It was *not* my fault. I would have had him if he hadn't turned his head."

"You're right, it wasn't your fault. I didn't mean that, Ev. In fact it was clever of you to grasp the opportunity and act as fast as you did."

"I've always been able to do that. It was one of my greatest strengths, to see or hear something and know immediately how to apply it to something else, or someone else. For instance, I knew you'd had your brakes done," he said triumphantly. Then his face fell. "I thought yesterday I'd have him—have all of you—but I was cheated again. You cheated me, all of you!" His voice rode the first small ripple of hysteria, and Gifford popped up, alarmed.

"Sit, Giff, it's all right, boy," he said lovingly.

"But you came close, Ev," Ben said, marveling that this lovely gracious room should be the scene of such lunatic conversation. "I'm really impressed. Always have been, you know, with everything you do. But I don't understand *why.* We're your friends."

"Friends! Do friends laugh at you the way Garth did, calling me a dreadful name when he talked to you on the phone? Do friends insist on making public fools of themselves, as Garth is doing with his ridiculous manila envelopes? I'd have given him advice, excellent advice. I gave Merran excellent advice—said I'd back the boy—and what did he do? He turned me away, said he didn't need anything. Well, I know better. Better than any of you, and I don't like people ignoring me as if I'm nothing anymore. As if I never was anything or anybody. I *will not stand* for that."

"I don't blame you, Ev. And Merran of all people understands how you feel."

"He understands nothing. And he calls himself a psychologist. Always so superior—knew everything, swam a mile every day, worked day and night. He was always so busy that he never had any time for me. He fit me in now and then, when it occurred to him to give me a crumb. You call that being a psychologist—or a friend?"

"Well, you certainly fixed it so he'd have enough time, Ev. Plenty of free time, as Jane said. It was quite a scheme, ruining his career. How in the world did you manage to do that?"

"You won't know unless I choose to tell you. And you don't know, do you!"

"Well, I—no. Please tell me, Everett. I'd really like to know."

"Very well. I was at Pete Swiggett's one day to order a new timer for the clothes dryer he sold me. It hadn't ever worked properly, and I decided to put in another one. Oh yes, I do tasks like that myself. Dead easy to fix all that sort of thing, you know. I always could."

He stopped and looked sharply at Ben, who said hastily, "I'm not surprised."

"Quite . . . Where was I?"

"At Swiggett's."

"Ah yes. A nice boy, excellent manners. He'd asked for a house key when I moved in here, and I'd given him one. Seeing all those keys in his cupboard gave me the idea, naturally? ["Naturally," Ben echoed.] I took Merran's building key and let myself in one night. I returned it the next day, of course. The rest is simple."

"Posing as a client of his and calling the others, you mean? You certainly scared them all off, Ev. And of course you called the schools. You did an excellent job—just look at how the

School Committee reacted. And the Superintendent."

"I wish you'd let me tell it," sulkily. "But you're right, I did. And before Merran and I went over to the Y to swim—at my suggestion—I called there too. Naturally they wouldn't let him in."

"Naturally."

"Yes. I don't miss a trick, Ben. But I said that, didn't I? Yes. Yes. There it was, a perfectly good idea, and I snapped it right up! But he came out of it very well, and that made me furious. It. *Made. Me. FURIOUS!*" gritting his teeth. "And then he had the incredible gall to tell me he'd find the paranoid b-b-b—the swine who was doing it to him! Ha ha! He never guessed, did he? Neither did you."

"No, Ev. You were very controlled, very clever. None of us guessed."

"He did everything he could to hurt me, you know. He had a dinner party for you and—and *her* and the McKay fellow, but did he think of inviting *me?* I was terribly hurt. So before going over there I told the police a high school girl was staying with him. For immoral purposes."

He's all mixed up, Ben thought. Now what? "Yes, but it didn't stick, Ev. There *was* a girl, and she *did* go in, but only after all of us had left. But she was just one more runaway child, nothing else. Bec took her home."

"That—that"—Everett's lips formed a forbidden word. "And what did I get out of all this? Time with Merran? A scrap of land in the cemetery? Did I win the election, which I was well on the way to winning? No! What I got was the most dreadful calumny. A hideous vicious slander that cost this town a better man than John Chester!

"That was why I killed him, you know. I was very put out when they lowered the flag for him. Imagine—for someone like him!" He said this casually in an astonishing change of tone as he recrossed his legs and flicked a thread off his trousers.

"I wish you could prove the slander, Ev. It was an outrageous thing for anyone to do, and it was probably John who did it. And he should have taken your money for the land. Nora wanted him to, she needed money. After all, you'd burned his house—"

"*I* want to tell it, Ben! Yes, I got the idea from what George Taylor said about John's meanness with money. There was no penny in his fuse box, you know. I put one there." He giggled like a naughty boy. "Oh dear, it's so easy to get into those old homes. I didn't need a key for that. And I loosened the wires on that heater a little more. It really was a piece of junk to begin with." He smiled reminiscently. "That was the night Gifford lost his collar. And afterward, when I went to John again alone, he said terrible things, Ben. He said I was a b-b-b—, a b-b—

"It's one word I never can say. But I know what he meant. That my parents weren't married, you know. Which is a lie, of course. They were married in Michigan. In Michigan! My mother said so . . . she *said!* The book is *wrong!* And I was born here. *Here!* But John said I had no place anywhere, he said his whole family had always known it, that everybody had known it. He said it would be wrong for me to be buried there, no matter how much money I offered him! That was when I took a weight out of that hideous suit and hit him. He didn't even see it coming."

"It was a cruel thing he said, Ev, but you didn't kill him any more than you killed Merran and Becca and me. Surely you realize you couldn't have killed him."

"I did kill him! I hit him as hard as I could!"

"I'm sure you did your best, Ev." Ben wished he could wipe his sweaty face. "But John died in that suit, didn't you read about that? He suffocated in the suit—"

Everett put his hands over his ears and shook his head. "I'm not listening to that, I'm not listening to that!" he chanted, stamping his feet like a child in a tantrum. "*I* killed him, Ben, *I* killed him!"

"I'd say you certainly made it possible. You really hit him very hard, Ev. I know. I saw the wound. Tell me, did you hit Val Elliot the same way?"

"I don't want to talk about her, Ben. She was the only one who genuinely cared, who really extended herself for me. But someone killed her, and I was sick and couldn't go to her funeral. I felt terrible about that."

"We all did, Ev. Did George Taylor kill her?"

"No. It was someone I think I know. I'm not sure. I can't remember. George may have wanted to kill her. She despised him, of course. He was always running after her, and she just laughed at him. She was nicer to me than to anyone else in this whole town. She used to visit me even after the campaign, bring me little gifts, tell me the gossip—in fact she came over the night she was killed. Very late, it was. After the dinner party. She wouldn't have minded my giving Swiggett her television set. She didn't need it any more . . ." Again that giggle, sly, mad. "Or her camera. I got rid of it. The whole thing."

"I can understand why. Those pictures she took of Becca's family tree upset you very much."

"That—that *person!* Always thinking she was better than I! I took her filthy lying tree and I burned it! I couldn't find anything else about me in her house, though."

"I can see why it all upset you, Ev. But what you say about Val really surprises me. Everybody but you said she was nasty."

"She—she liked to tease. She could be cruel. But not to me, oh never to me! Why that other man wanted to hurt her—make her bleed on my lovely Oriental—

"I don't want to talk about her, Ben. It upsets me, and you're getting me all mixed up and that isn't fair to me at all."

"I'm sorry, Ev, I didn't mean to upset you." Ben's voice was richly comforting. "Is it all right to ask you if anyone came to the shop while you were talking to John? Or was it just Nora who came downstairs?"

Everett's eyes went blank as he thought back. He nodded. "Yes, just Nora, around six. No one else came. And my word, was she mad at him! Of course she was always, this time because once again he refused to take my money. He was fussing with that diving suit, polishing the brass, can you imagine it? It infuriated me, so I simply grabbed one of those lead weights and—*bang!* She said I should go home before anybody saw me and not to tell anybody so as not to get myself into trouble, so I did as she said." Again that giggle, that of a child hugging a dreadful, wonderful secret. "I cried at his funeral, Ben. It was very sad."

"I thought so too."

"But I did tell. I just told you, Ben. Should I have told you?"

"Of course, Ev. You did the right thing. As usual." Should I chance it? he asked himself. Should I bring up the Michigan trip? He crossed his fingers.

"Ev, I don't want to upset you again, but about that trip to Michigan, I was damn glad I happened to be in the courthouse when you suddenly got sick. I was so busy taking care of you that I kept forgetting to ask if you'd done all you meant to do, or if there was anything you wanted me to attend to for you. You mentioned something about it a few minutes ago."

"No, thank you, Ben, though it's very nice of you to ask. No, I'll just have to go back again and make the names right. When this is all over. Then it will be all right, and John won't be able to say anything bad about me again."

"And then will you be sorry you killed him?"

"I would have had to kill him anyway, don't you see?"

"You had another reason? You didn't tell me that."

"Am I required to tell you everything?"

"No no, Ev, of course not."

"I will if I want to."

"That's understood, Ev."

"Very well." Another regal inclination of the head. "As long as you realize that, I'll tell you. It was that little dog, Ben. The way John kept that little dog. I couldn't bear it. A dog is a child that never grows up." He bent and stroked Gifford tenderly. "There's only one reason to have a dog, whether you hunt with it or use it as a guard or whatever, and that is to love it. And be loved by it. But to the John Chesters of the world a dog is an object that endures its life on the end of a string, day and night, until it's dead. Never to run free. Never to eat and drink from clean bowls or cuddle up in a warm room with its family or follow children back and forth in games it doesn't understand but enjoys all the same.

"Ben, they never talked to that poor little pup, never called him by name. I don't think he had one. I called him Digby—rather dignified, don't you agree?—because he dug so many holes. Do you like the name, Ben?"

"It's perfect. I expect you cut him loose before the fire, right?"

Another regal assent.

"Then you'll be glad to know, Ev, that I cut him loose yesterday and took him to the vet. He's in bad shape, Ev, he may die—"

Everett turned white with rage. "How dare you! How dare you keep on with your vicious one-upmanship! *I* cut Digby loose! Are you saying I didn't do enough? Are you insinuating that you did it better than I did it?"

He reached behind him and from the back cushions brought out Garth Shaw's mashie. Yelling something unintelligible, he flung himself at Ben.

Barking madly, Gifford flew up and bounded around—movement that Ben sensed rather than saw or even heard. He leaned forward, braced his feet on the floor, pushed hard, and tipped over backward just as Everett came at him swinging the mashie like a baseball bat. It could have cracked his skull like an eggshell but only whirred past the soles of his shoes as he went over. As he scrambled up, Everett came at him again. Silently, now. Concentrating.

Ben grabbed the end of the club and hung on with all his strength. For an instant he was outside the struggle and saw—absurd!—two kids tugging at a coveted prize. But this ageing paranoic, intolerably frustrated in the last degree, had all the advantage. He rushed Ben backward against the mantelpiece and, wrenching the club away, changed swiftly from the interlocking grip to the Vardon grip, squeezing his hands powerfully for a long straight drive.

He began his backswing, twisted on his hips, came around again, stick raised high and aiming for Ben's head—

While Ben watched, immobilized, fascinated—

While Gifford yelped and growled and darted in every direction like a referee totally confused as to what the game was and who was breaking the rules—

And then Ben clarified the matter by launching himself off the mantel, ducking under the club, and butting Everett in the chest. They went down together, and Gifford sprang, sinking his teeth into Ben's leg.

After a feeble attempt to free himself, Everett went limp.

Ben sagged against him, his leg burning like fire. When he looked up, he saw what he had seen in the Hillsdale courthouse—the contorted face, the hands tearing at the collar. He rolled off immediately, taking Gifford with him, the pain in his leg now excruciating.

Everett panted, his hands as ineffectual now as they had been murderously capable before.

At once Ben forgot everything else. "Everett, let me help . . ." he pleaded, and his tone reassured the dog, who released him and backed away.

Everett opened his eyes, and sanity came back into them as life ebbed.

"Ev, Ev, it's all right, I'll get Clarkson. Hang on—I'll get help—"

Everett shook his head. His lips moved soundlessly.

"What, Ev? What is it?"

Whining, Gifford lay down by the dying man and licked his sweating face.

Everett smiled faintly and turned his head a little, his eyes always on Ben's.

"Blink for yes," Ben said. "Is it about Gifford?"

Everett blinked urgently.

"Don't worry, Ev, I'll take care of him. You know I will. He'll get the best, I promise. Until you're well again. And you will be. We'll all help you. Now let me call Clarkson."

He felt Everett's hand close on his. It was cold now and wonderfully gentle. And then it fell away, and he died, still smiling.

▽

TWENTY-FOUR

SEVERAL THINGS, EXPECTED AND unexpected, happened over the week following Everett's death, beginning with his removal to a funeral home, hastily arranged by Becca, and Ben's before-dawn arrival at the hospital's emergency room.

"Worst kind of pain, dog bite. Right down to the bone, this one," Clarkson said with a certain satisfaction. "And I'll ask you not to flinch, Benjamin. No chance of rabies," he added regretfully.

"There has to be a way of giving that horrible old curmudgeon a bit of his own back, Ben," Jane said, wincing as he struggled out with the prescribed crutch. She drove him home smoothly, soothingly, in the Camry and settled him in his study, with the telephone and other necessaries at hand.

The instant he sank into his favorite chair, the phone rang.

"Ben? Mack. Didn't wake you up, did I? Aitch-Jay just faxed me something for you that sounds really weird. It must be important for him to have forgotten the time difference, so I thought I better call you right away—"

"Just read it, for godsake."

"Okay, *okay!* Here goes. You ready? Want to take it down? I'll wait while you get paper and pencil—"

"Mack. Read."

"*Okay!* Quoting now. 'Just the odd thought about your friend, which I was about to utter when you bashed off to Jerome. I do not think he murdered—'

"Murdered? Ben, what's this all about?"

"Just get on with it," Ben said, understandably cranky.

"You sick? I've never heard you sound like this before. Sure you're all right?"

"Mack."

"Uh, 'I do not think he murdered John because of land or even insults re illegitimacy but because of the dog—'

"Dog? What dog? What the hell is this, a script for a soap opera?"

An ominous sound came over the wire.

"Uh, right, okay, Ben, let's see, where did I leave off . . . Oh. '—the dog. I am persuaded that John's treatment of his dog was in Everett's perception not merely an outrage per se (and I concur)'—that's him concurring, Ben, not me; I don't even know what he's referring to—'but the ultimate rejection—more, the total invalidation of Everett himself, inasmuch as he and his dog are so inseparable as to be one. Poor fellow, to view a dog as the sole source in his life—indeed in anyone's, as he sees it—of utter trust, love, unconditional acceptance, items not even his mother gave him.

" 'Time presses and I'm off, as usual, hence uncertain whether I've said precisely what I wished to say. The thought struck clear enough at the Detroit air terminal, God knows, but had I been required to discourse upon it during the morning meeting here (something said there reminded me of it), I should have made a right cock-up of the matter.

" 'A further thought re Everett's tardy return to Manton following retirement. Had he been waiting for that particular house to become available for purchase that it might wield, for him, the magic of a dead lamb's skin wrapped round an orphaned newborn? I rather suspect this to be the case. Best to Jane.'

"That's it, Ben. Want to reply?"

"No. Wait. Yes. Say, '*I* take your meaning, all right, but if He doesn't, suggest He ask Browning. At the same address.'

"Underline the eye, Mack. And capitalize those aitches."

"If you say so. I guess he'll know what it means, he knows just about everything else. How you doing?"

"Oh, limping along."

"Like that board of yours. Yeah, those buggers are still dithering around. That bastard Guinness is leading the opposition. Surprising in view of the lawsuit you've got going, wouldn't you say?"

Annoyed, Ben changed his position—he was about to say, "Who the hell told you about that lawsuit!"—and received a sharp suggestion from his leg to stay cool. On reflection he saw no reason why Mack of all people shouldn't know what was happening, even though it would be another two or three weeks yet before it actually did. So he said only, "Yes, and no," and felt that he had adequately covered the entire matter.

"Know what you mean. Think I do, anyway. What it is, is, they just don't take it seriously. But when Guy McKay gets through with them, they will, right?"

Ben gave up. "Right," he said, grinning.

The phone rang again a few minutes later, proving Jane's dictum that even on a vacation (of sorts) a school administrator cannot exist without a telephone at his ear.

"Ben? Bill Tempesta. You being interested in the Taylor kids, I thought you'd like to know Connie's been looking really terrible lately. She's cranky, nasty to everybody including her friends—no, not verbally—and she's *thin!* Seems to go right along with those paintings you saw. Thought I better check on Junior, see what's happening with him. Didn't think you'd mind me moving into your domain. He said his mother's abdicated—guess he's learning something in social studies, huh?—and nobody will tell him anything, and he doesn't know what's going on. Neither do I. No I don't, I don't get it at all."

Ben could see him shaking his long horsey head in his puzzlement, the straight manelike hair swaying silkily. "Have you talked with the parents?" he said, smiling.

"Missus won't come to the phone, and Mister took off. The boy said he slammed out of the house before breakfast yesterday saying something about they'd see him when they saw him, that he had something to do."

MacWhirter will have a fit, Ben thought. If it were up to him, he wouldn't give George permission to go from his house to that van of his unless it was to drive to the station and confess to murder in the first. I wonder where Nora is. "Say, Bill, are the Chester kids in school?"

"Yes. Why? There a connection between those two families? God, Ben, way things're going lately, I don't know where I am anymore."

"Tell me about it. Okay, Bill, thanks for the word."

He yawned on the last word and dozed off even as he was telling himself to call MacWhirter.

The phone rang again.

"Ben? Len Kenney. Hope I didn't disturb you. Just wanted to say the pup's nicely rehydrated and seems fractionally better but—"

"His name is Digby. Digby. Put it on his card, okay?"

"Sure. Good name. I hope he'll have a chance to get used to it. I give him a fifty-fifty chance, Ben. And that's very optimistic. Maybe I just better put him down?"

"No. Don't. As long as he isn't in pain."

"Well, but what he really needs, and needs now, I can't give him. A home, voices, a lap to lie on. Otherwise I don't know as anything I do will take. But it means toting him back and forth for treatment as needed—"

"Then that's what we'll do. Jane'll be right over. And

thanks, Len. Oh hey, another problem. What do we do about Everett's dog?"

"Ah, that's a tough one. I've known older dogs pine away like that. A younger one generally mopes around a bit and then attaches himself to another family and does fine. And Gifford's what—five? I can't say it isn't possible, though. After all, it's *hap*pening! Tell Jane to meet me there at six, after I close up. I'll look him over and decide what to do. I take it you want him too."

Becca and Merran came for lunch, by which time the wretched canine scrap that Everett had named Digby was lying on a clean blanket in a warm corner, closely guarded by Jane's immense Fee.

Ben crutched grunting out to join them.

He doubted his ability to do justice to the perfect lunch Jane was setting forth. A high school principal is rarely required to outsmart a runaway Ford and shortly thereafter deal intelligently with paranoid insanity full-blown while a terrified dog is hanging onto his leg with all of his teeth; let alone roll off a man's body so as to watch him die in agony: a man Ben had, grudgingly at times, liked and respected. Exhausted and stunned by the time MacWhirter and the ME arrived, he had said only that in the middle of a social call Everett had a coronary, and that Ben's rush to help him looked to Gifford like an attack.

Perhaps the most astonishing thing was that not even Jane knew what had happened. Well, maybe after lunch I'll tell them. If I have the strength, he thought, picking up his fork. It seemed to weigh a ton.

"This may sound silly," Becca was saying, "but Everett looked so peaceful. But what am I going to do, Ben? I mean, he didn't want to be cremated, so where am I supposed to bury him? There's just no room for him in our cemetery."

The first mouthful of Jane's superb beef stew transformed Ben into the Compleat Administrator. "Yes there is, Bec. In his mother's grave," he said coolly.

"Look, Ben, I've had a horrible night too, so don't start with any of your awful jokes."

"But he's right, darling!" Merran said. "That grave's empty, remember? *Why didn't we think of it before!* We won't have to check the death records here or anyplace else, because Dad said Honora was buried somewhere in the Midwest, right, Ben? And that Dorothy, Ev's mother's sister went through a sentimental if not face-saving charade, stone and all. So we *can* bury him there, full length, as he wanted, and add his name to the stone. Tomorrow okay for the dig, don't you think?"

She nodded, tears rolling down her white cheeks. "Guy can arrange it. But—then why didn't Everett—it would have saved so much trouble if he had said something!"

"To whom—us?" Ben said. "No way. I'm not all that sure anyhow that he acknowledged—that he could acknowledge that it'd been a only mock interment. And here's more input on his frame of mind," and he told them about the fax he'd had from Rob Hartley-Jones in London, England.

"He's probably right on both counts," Merran said. "I could check out the land records—when the house was put on the market, when Everett bought it—but I bet it isn't necessary.

"Which reminds me. I remembered to look up the library's microfiches about George Taylor, and you were right, Ben. Eight years ago an unnamed housewife's complaint appeared on the Police Blotter citing sexual advances by George Taylor, whom she had removed from her—uh—premises, would you say? A later article said she refused to press charges, so George got out of a nasty mess by the skin of his teeth. His mute daughter was mentioned—you know how those bastards like to pad articles, to insure that a family gets all the attention it deserves—so I'm virtually certain he'd already begun making use of her so as to relieve some of his sexual tension. So that's one thing disposed of. Tentatively, anyway.

"Okay, next is Gifford. I can't get him to eat or drink or

even go out and pee. He lies by Ev's chair and just looks at me. If I come near him, he snarls. I sit on the floor and talk to him, but it's not helping. Neither is Len Kenney. Never thought I'd be afraid of a dog."

Jane giggled. "Probably Ben poisoned him."

She's definitely not in the right mood to hear what really happened, Ben decided, and I'm too whacked to tell her. Claiming the patient's right to rest and privacy, he went back to his study and closed the door.

Later in the afternoon a brisk upcountry voice woke him out of a pleasant snooze and introduced itself solemnly as Percival Jessiman, Everett Upham's attorney.

"We haven't met, Dr. Louis, but I have some rather startling news for you." He hesitated, possibly to rethink the non sequitur.

Ben, whose sense of the ridiculous may have been enhanced by pain and enforced rest, said lightly, "I'll take the bad news first, sir. Often best that way."

"I am not sure that any of it is bad, Dr. Louis, if we except the reason for my imparting it," Jessiman said reprovingly. "In any case"—Ben covered a laugh with a cough—"it is short. My client Mr. Upham made you his heir. The inheritance—including the house and its contents—will prove to be considerable. *Extremely* so."

"But—but—but *me?*" Ben sputtered, choking on the levity that had been bubbling up in his throat. "Why me?"

"Mr. Upham's own words will tell you why," and Jessiman read from the will a moving passage about an illustrious gentleman whom Ben was sure he had never met.

He was too whacked to blush (Jane would have been angry—torn him off a strip, Aitch-Jay would have said—if he had). The pain in his leg leaped like a flame. "I don't—I'm at a complete loss, Mr. Jessiman. When," he said carefully, "when did he draw up this will?"

"I am not sure your question doesn't do you credit, Dr. Louis," the lawyer said with equally impeccable discretion.

"I knew him for many years, and it is my conviction that he was never more sound in his life than when he drew up this will two months ago. He knew that he was very ill. May we meet at your convenience some time next week? Meanwhile, I have some simple instructions for you regarding the funeral, which my secretary will deliver to you by dinnertime.

"All things considered, I am by no means displeased, not at all. Nor do I expect that anyone—anyone at all—will challenge you for all or part of the estate."

He means Becca, of course, Ben thought, his brain reeling. "Well, yes, I—one wonders, naturally . . ." He mustered his forces and said in a voice as brisk as the other's, "If you would be good enough to contact Guy McKay, my attorney, I should be very grateful." He sank back into his deep chair feeling that he had been on his feet all this time and had just caved in.

He curled his tongue in or around his teeth in some mysterious way that Jane had never been able to master and summoned her with an ear-shattering whistle to give her the news. He was in no condition to say more. My circuits, he thought, are on overload.

"Oh, darling," she said, "don't worry about the money, you don't have to keep it if you don't want it. We've always managed. People learn to, in the ed biz." She kissed him and tiptoed away.

He reached for the phone. "Colin, I have news about the Taylors plus a lot else you need to hear."

"You sound pooped. What'll tire you more, talking on the phone, or should I come by? It's time to quit, anyway. I could be over in a coupla minutes." And was, spurred on by the prospect of a snack at Jane's table.

Ben got up when MacWhirter came for the snack, but accepted only a cup of tea with milk and honey, an incomparable specific for bone-crushing fatigue. "I've got a lot to tell, so nobody interrupt. For starters, you can close one case of murder, Colin. A good going-over of Everett's living room carpet will confirm this. He killed Val Elliot there, drove her in her car to the old station, left her there and went into his burglary mode . . ." and so on to the end of that part of the tale, his four listeners too stunned to do more than gasp.

Then he recounted Everett's part in John Chester's death. "Guess you'll have your wish, Colin. Everett didn't kill John, but he made it possible for Nora or George to. Take your pick."

"Why pick? I can just see it. Everett hits John after an argument and leaves when Nora tells him to save himself. She gives John another poke to keep him in the mood, then calls George for help. He and Connie come over at seven with a bill but hear a vulgar argument and go home. He sneaks out later and goes back, and both of 'em put John in the diving suit to suffocate. By Christ, how's that for cold-blooded Murder One!

"You didn't know he'd been hit twice? Yeah, well, the ME did some more fitting and measuring with one of those lead weights 'cause that dent in John's scalp looked too big, too wide, to be just from one blow.

"The onliest thing is, what Everett told you isn't worth diddley as evidence. On top of being nuts, he's dead, and even if he wasn't, it'd be his word against theirs—and *he'd* prob'ly be the one to get charged with murder. Hm. So that randy sonofabitch Taylor took off, hey? Prob'ly to where his daughter Joy is staying."

"But he's been ordered by the court to stay away from her," Becca said, stroking the sleeping Digby, who was recovering visibly under her loving hand. "Do you think he's going 'round the bend too?"

"In his state of mind," Ben said, "a court order may well become irrelevant. I'll make a bet that fantastic meals and the near presence of that girl of his kept him going, if strung out to near breaking point. Ridiculous as it may sound, without her and the crazy hope of winning her, food wasn't enough, and it could very well be that his wires have finally snapped. [No one said *"Ben!"* because he was so clearly in earnest.] I remember wondering once when they would."

"So what do we do about it?" MacWhirter looked so disconsolately at the last crumbs of chocolate cake (left there for good manners) on his plate that Jane cut him another piece and refilled his cup.

"He said he was coming back, and I think he will, to try readjusting his life to the status quo ante," Ben said, "so it's probably safe to sit tight and wait till he does."

"Yeah, right. We don't want to scare him off by telling Mrs. Taylor to call when he pulls in, and/or putting a watch on that house of his. Same goes for Nora." Cake crumbs scattered out of his mouth as he spoke. With a ruthless fork he chased down each fugitive crumb and swallowed it up.

Merran got up, took Digby from Becca, and deposited him lovingly in Jane's lap. "Let's go see Gifford, darling. He'll listen to you."

She smiled sadly. "I'm no Pied Piper, you know."

"Oh, I don't know about that." He held out his hand to her.

Smiling, she took it and followed him. There was a kiss-long pause, during which Ben, Jane, and MacWhirter sat beaming benignly. Then the front door closed softly.

Percival Jessiman's secretary delivered two envelopes to Ben at 6:30, her manner as grave and discreet as her employer's. "You are to read the contents of this one only at the graveside. The other contains instructions about the interment, which you may read now. Mr. Upham was precise about his arrangements, so you should have no trouble following them."

In accordance with one of Everett's wishes, Jane was removing a silk paisley scarf from his dresser when Len Kenney arrived with a needleful of sleep. He administered it so deftly that Gifford was unconscious and safe in the Louises' kitchen before he knew what had happened.

All that night and the next day he lay in his basket showered with attention, not least from Fee and the ever stronger Digby, but he ignored them all. From time to time his ears pricked up as if he were listening to a lost voice; then he lay his head down with a deep quivering sigh.

"Len, can't you force-feed him? Intravenously? He's drying up before our eyes," Jane said at dusk.

"Sure, but I'd have to have him, and then the whole purpose would be defeated. Let's wait a bit. Tomorrow's the funeral, right? Well, okay, bring him over after that. But don't expect anything. He may be a dumb animal, but he's telling us what he wants. We should respect that."

All that second night Jane sat on the floor beside him, stroking his head, coaxing him with bits of food, talking to him, but such attention was an irrelevancy; he did not even move his head away.

Jane handed Ben the paisley scarf Gifford had worn in place of his lost collar during Everett's campaign. It slipped out of his hand and fell to the floor, a little heap of colors, softly gleaming.

"It smells so nice, just like Everett," she said, bending to pick it up.

Gifford looked up. His nose twitched. He came out of his basket and, somewhat unsteadily, went over to Jane and sniffed at the scarf.

"He remembers it. After all this time," she said, folding it.

Ben put it into his jacket pocket. "Okay then, are we ready? No, Giff, you can't come. Stay here with Fee and Digby. You stay, boy."

Gifford stood his ground.

"We'll be taking him over to the hospital afterward," Jane said tearfully. "Might as well save ourselves a trip back here to get him."

Everett's will directed that no minister attend his interment, that the undertakers withdraw after lowering him into his grave, wherever it might be, that Ben then read the contents of the second envelope that Jessiman's secretary had given him, and throw first his paisley scarf—Gifford's scarf, he called it, in his instructions—and then one shovelful of dirt onto the coffin. There were no directions regarding the presence of anyone else, so Ben, Jane, and Gifford (who had jumped out of the Camry before they could stop him), Merran and Becca, Guy McKay, and Pete Swiggett and his dog Sam stood in a circle and watched the coffin slowly descend.

Gifford whined once, softly, and Jane kept firm hold of his lead. But he never moved, nor did he seem to hear the delicious crunching of leaves under the undertakers' departing feet, which at another time would have called him to a joyous romp.

Ben adjusted his crutch; took a sealed envelope out of his breast pocket and opened it; removed the sheet of fine stiff bond; read and recognized the single line that was its contents: a line from Exodus.

His breath caught in his throat. His eyes stung with tears. He blinked and swallowed. " 'I have been,' " he read huskily, " 'a stranger in a strange land.' "

He took the scarf out of his pocket and released it over the deep hole. As it floated down out of sight, Gifford whined again and strained toward it.

Ben picked up the shovel and spilled dirt onto the coffin, the sound terrible, unforgettable, appalling. The shovel slipped out of his hands and he turned away.

"Come, Giff," Jane said, but the dog bared his teeth, snarling, then sank to the ground. She knelt, coaxing him softly. He neither moved nor looked at her.

"Leave 'm lay awhile, Mrs. Louis," Pete said.

"But Pete, we're supposed to take him to the vet."

"He don't want to go anywhere now. Maybe never. I'll keep a eye on him. I pass this way often enough."

"I'll call Len," Jane said. "He can give him a shot and take him back to the hospital—"

"No, darling," Ben said, putting a loving arm around her. "Gifford's *in extremis*. The only difference between his wishes and ours is that we wrote them in our living wills. He can't write, but he can speak."

"That's right, Dr. Louis," Swiggett said. "I wouldn't want it any other way for Sammy. Okay then, I'll be off."

He went home, but only to fetch back bowls of food and water.

Jane found the food untouched. A leaf floated in the water bowl. She took it out and offered the bowl to Gifford, who lay still, his head on the canvas-covered mound. Only shivering sighs from time to time showed that he was breathing.

They came together and by turns, Merran and Becca, Jane and Ben, Pete Swiggett and Sam, to see him and keep him silent company. He gave no sign of recognition but lay in the same place, his head on the slowly settling mound. Each day he shrank a little more. His eyeballs dried in his skull. His once beautiful tan coat was only a dull thin bag that held his bones together.

Five days later Ben found him dead, his docked ears perky as ever, as though he were at last hearing what he had waited so long and faithfully to hear.

They buried him next to Everett, with a small stone to mark his place.

It was the least, and the most, that they could do.

▽

TWENTY-FIVE

MACWHIRTER WAS LIKE A child testing a loose tooth. He meant to leave the Taylor and Chester homes strictly alone until George returned, but he could not resist driving by both on his way to and from work—a circuitous route, but never mind—and he had his men do the same.

They were not to linger, and didn't—they did slow down: police are only human, Jane would have said—and therefore could not see the effect on the neighborhood of this unusual traffic. Which was nothing more than Nora Chester, perhaps a trifle more self-possessed and relentlessly brisk than usual, going about her business, which included reasonable care of her children, and Doris Taylor, grown slovenly and pasty-faced, spending most of the days and nights peering through her bedroom window sheer-on-sheers, watching for George while the resident offspring managed as best they could and the proud house grayed with dust.

"*Mmf!* Leg's about mended, Benjamin," Dr. Clarkson pronounced sourly, the day George Taylor came home. "Stay with the crutch or a cane another day or two. Don't come back."

"In your whole life did you ever see a man more disappointed? I ask you!" Jane yelled as Ben, once again in the driver's seat and with a casual hand on the wheel, deftly steered the Camry out of the parking lot.

There was a lot to be said, he was thinking, for a luxurious almost-new automobile, but—and here was a conceit Jane would not have appreciated in her present mood or possibly at any other time—this Camry was a dog, sweet-tempered and obedient, whereas the Ford was a belligerent old alley cat, always to be wooed but rarely won. He rather missed her.

He patted Jane's thigh. "Darling, he's impossible. Still, he's one of Life's verities, and we ought to be grateful for continuity or stability of any kind in a world gone mad."

Gentle snow obligingly covered everything but the roads, making the historic district, the town's most beautiful area, more beautiful than ever. (Sometimes a lily can be gilded, Ben said to himself.) They drove home without haste, enjoying it, talking inconsequentially, avoiding weighty matters like school boards and jobs and inheritances and crime, and so missed seeing George's van enter the road they were just leaving.

It jerked and swayed along as if its brilliant flames had burned through to the interior and were consuming the frantic occupants. Presently it swung crazily into the Taylor driveway and rocked to a stop near the side door of the house. Curtains twitched at an upstairs window as George emerged from the van, one hand clamped like a vise on his eldest child's arm. She struggled to free herself, then collapsed like a demonstrator resisting arrest, forcing the loving father to drag his only joy screaming through the snow and into the house. The door slammed shut.

The shadowy form at the upstairs window withdrew.

Not one inhabitant of this generously zoned neighborhood saw or heard a thing, nor did any of MacWhirter's men happen to be cruising purposefully by.

But because Frances Hartmann neé Taylor, long and ruefully married into a religious community, cordially despised her brother, she walked out of a caustic dispute with the elders about the need to protect a girl they ruled too beautiful to be pure *anyway,* and trudged cold snowy miles to town to report the violent violation, the night before, of a court order. The police gave her a gray damp towel, stale doughnuts and bitter coffee, wholehearted admiration for her marathon walk, approval for her courage, the courtesy of a prompt call to Massachusetts, and a ride home. (All of which resulted in heartburn and another barrage of pietistic claptrap, she later wrote to the Louises and the Shaws from Washington State. But all things considered, she added in a reassuring postscript, everything's worked out just fine, now that there's a continent between us, and here's some pictures of the kids.)

"Huh!" MacWhirter said to Sergeant Dave Bates after thanking Pennsylvania and hanging up. "Now we got something to be going on with. George left Lancaster last night so he oughta be back by now, driving hell for leather like always. 'Cording to his sister, he said he was taking his kid home where she belongs. Go make sure. And take the little pickup this time, I don't want to alert the sonofabitch, in case. And call in the minute you see that van of his, and I'll give Merran Shaw a jingle, he's still seeing that family. Boy, I don't envy him. Then get back here. Well, what're you standing around for with your head up and locked? Pop off!"

A few minutes later Dave Bates called in. "Van's in the driveway, Chief. Nothing happening that I can see."

So MacWhirter called Merran, thus shooting all to hell his and Becca's plans for the afternoon.

"I've had the feeling George was working himself up to something, for all he's been trying to play it cool," Merran said. "You think a little crisis intervention's indicated?"

"Yeah. Miz Becca around? Good, 'cause George's kid's gonna need some TLC and seems to me the best kind comes from her. Okay then, meet us over there. I'm gonna give George a lesson in what it means to flout the law. Think he might get nasty?"

"Possibly. Why? Do you need reinforcements?" Merran

said, and thought, the more the merrier, and called Ben.

"Sure, Merran," Ben said. "But I don't know what I can do—fell George with my trusty crutch, maybe? Okay, pick me up, I'll be out front."

The temperature had plummeted, treacherously glazing the roads before the snow began accumulating in earnest, and the car began to slide and fishtail. "Oh no!" Merran groaned, "not again!" But they reached the Taylor house without incident and came to a stop behind George's van.

MacWhirter's cruiser should have been standing solid and menacing on the white shell driveway, but Dave Bates had flouted inexorable laws regarding speed and ice, and the cruiser was in a ditch, Bates nursing a twisted wrist, the furious MacWhirter trying to make contact with the station. This took all his energy and concentration, or he would have maimed his sergeant permanently in one way or another.

"Where the hell is he?" Merran muttered. "What's keeping him? If George is feeling playful, we may need the Marines!"

"Guess it's up to us, for now. You two take the side door, we'll divide and conquer," Ben said, not because the front door was closer—it wasn't—but because there was something he wanted to do. He watched them hurry up the drive, heads bent against the snow. Then he opened the back door of the van.

Supplies neatly lined its walls from ceiling to floor, but the large equipment George usually carried had been replaced by a blanket-covered, battle-torn mattress, an insulated food carrier, a storm of crumpled kleenex tissues, and an open suitcase, its contents a-jumble.

Ben's nose crinkled. The odor in the rapidly chilling interior was unmistakably that of semen and related body fluids.

He poked among the tissues with his crutch and saw more blood than he had expected or was prepared to see. With his crutch he lifted out a scrap of silk with a dainty flowered pattern. It was the sleeve of a blouse.

You swine, he thought, and outrage swept over him in dizzying waves. Breathing deeply, he lifted his hot face to the snow. There's always a reason for behavior, he cautioned himself as he shut the door. Remember, there's always a reason to explain it, even justify it.

But he knew what George's reason was, and it simply was not reason enough to explain away his violent crime against his child. The gratifying of lust, the easing of frustration, never could be reason enough. Neither could greed, nor the stupid carelessness that ends in disaster to the innocent, nor the cold deliberateness of war waged in the name of God, king, and country.

All of those things could be subsumed into a single word—"ignorance," Ben thought, and ignorance could never justify violent crimes against children, or indeed against any other helpless creatures—animals, or the aged, or the infirm.

He wanted to go for George's throat with his bare hands, break his face with the crutch, tear off his genitals.

Sick with misgiving, and with a certain anger that not even this once could he ignore the canons that had shaped him, he crossed the snowy lawn, which gave him secure footing and soaked his shoes through, and went up the fussy brick and fieldstone steps. As he grasped the big brass knocker, Merran and Becca hastened up behind him.

"He wouldn't let us in, Ben," Merran said, brushing off his pants. "Actually shoved me off the step."

"Oh?" Ben said and banged thunderously on the door.

George opened it. He was thinner than ever and seemed to have aged overnight, so that he looked more pathetic than ridiculous in his hairdye and unsuitable clothes. His Western-styled shirt with its tabs and pockets and mother-of-pearl snaps bloused sloppily over his waist, covering the big belt buckle. His movements were oddly economical and jerky.

Any minute now, thought Ben, his fancy always alive to possibilities, any minute now this guy's going to explode right out of his skin into millions and millions of bits. Why in hell did I get myself into this? Then he saw George's punishing grip on Joy's arm and knew why he had come and what he must do.

There were shocking bruises on the girl's face and neck, terror in her swollen eyes, but Ben nodded as if this were a pleasant encounter in the school corridor. Her lovely head drooped like a spent flower.

"What do you want?" George said through stiff lips.

"To talk with you and Mrs. Taylor for a few minutes, George. It's important."

"Sorry. The wife and I're having a little tea party for my best girl here. Now we're together again, way a family should be. Well, Junior's still at hockey practice, but I expect he'll be back before too long. Whatever you want'll have to wait'll tomorrow."

"Sorry, George, it can't wait. We can't wait. The police will be along shortly, and they won't wait either. You're in deep trouble, as I'm sure you realize. I suggest you don't make things worse than they already are. Let go of your daughter. Now!"

Unwillingly George did so and with anguish in his eyes watched her back away from him and stumble out of the room. If she had been anybody else, or if he had, his pain would have melted a stone.

"Well?" Ben said, the snow swirling around his head.

"Guess you better come in" was the mumbled answer, and George led the way into the kitchen, where his wife stood watching a kettle on the boil. The trestle table in the dining alcove, big enough to seat ten, was set for five with cups and saucers, gleaming silverware, damask napkins, perfectly cut lemon slices, a milk pitcher, a sugar bowl: all the necessaries for a tea party.

"Come on, come on, get with it," George snarled at Doris. "About time you did something around here. Place is a mess. Connie! Where the hell is that—*Connie!* Get in here and help. Rotten kid. Never does a goddam thing but eat." And in a sudden, dreadful travesty of Welcoming Host, "Siddown, folks, siddown, make yourselves comfortable."

Merran and Becca shrugged at each other and sat down on a long bench. Ben stood behind them, leaning casually against the wall.

The child came into the room. Bill Tempesta was right. She was so thin that her clothes hung on her like sacks.

"Finally!" George said. "Now help!"

She glared at him and pointed to the table, meaning that everything on it she had put there.

Her mother handed her a plate of bread and butter and another of commercial cookies.

"*Tchah!* That junk all you got for a homecoming?" George sneered. He turned menacingly to Ben. "I said siddown."

"I'd rather stand," Ben said. "I've been sitting for too long. Hard on the leg." Funny, I've never seen him messy before, he thought. Does he have something inside his shirt? If he tries anything, I'll tie this crutch around his neck. Damn it, where's the chief?

"Ready!" Doris said cheerfully, pouring boiling water into the teapot. She was expanding, beginning to bustle.

George sat down, slipped his hand inside the bulge of his shirt, brought out a snub-nosed little gun. "Siddown, I said. This is a party, a celebration. People sit at a party."

"Hey, come on, lighten up," Ben said good-naturedly, firmly, automatically. Thus simply had the high school principal stopped many a thoughtless troublemaker in his tracks.

But George was at this moment a half-demented mind reader, not a thoughtless high school lad. "Put that crutch down. Slide it over to me. Now *sit.*" Tense though he was, the gun did not waver.

I'll throw my jacket at him, Ben thought, slipping it off. The gun butt rapped a sharp warning on the table. Ben dropped the jacket on the floor and sat down on the end of the bench, next to Merran and opposite George.

"Now," George said to Doris, "we're ready for that tea. And we're going to have a pleasant time. My girl's back, and it's gonna be all right." And to Connie, "Siddown, you."

She slumped down on the other end of his bench.

"No, it isn't going to be all right," Ben said. "You two are facing multiple charges, George. This is a police matter. Don't make it any worse. Put that gun away."

"Connie, where's your sister?"

The child pointed to the ceiling.

George whistled shrilly, and the six of them sat like stones until Joy appeared, trembling, lips bloodless.

Brightening at the sight of her, George transferred the gun to his other hand and ordered her to sit between him and Connie.

Doris took her place at the end of the table, Ben on her left, George on her right. Ignoring the gun so close to her hand, she presided over the teapot like the president of the Ladies' Aid. "Joy, pass your father the sandwiches. I'm sorry I don't have anything fancier, dear, but I didn't know when you'd be back."

"So I'm back, okay? *Dear?* So you can start making some decent meals for a change."

"Cooking's not where it's at anymore, George," Merran said. "Or where it's going to be for a long long time. You know that. Thanks," as Ben passed him a steaming cup. This is grotesque, he thought. My god. That article of mine is going to have a socko finish. Glad I didn't get around to submitting it. "Look, George. We both understand where you're coming from—"

"None a that now, Doc, we're celebrating. Connie, pass the doc the milk and sugar."

Becca said, "Then I insist that Joy change her clothes and wash her face and hands. I'll go with her." And call the police, she thought. Her intention plain on her open face, she swung her legs over the bench and squeezed along the narrow space between it and the wall.

George said, "Siddown. I'll see she does what she has to," and got up, yanking the girl out with him.

She was deathly pale. Her knees buckled, and she held

onto the table, wincing in pain. She said in a strangled whisper, "I'll go alone!"

"Oh no you won't!"

"Let go of her, George," Ben said sternly and found himself looking into the eye of the gun. "I said put that away. And let her go. It is not fitting. Do you understand me? It is *not fitting.*"

The gun wavered, fell away. "Awright, you can come," George told Becca. "I'll just take care a the phones upstairs so you can't try any tricks."

Connie shrank away behind him, grabbed something from the counter, and vanished.

Joy moved around to her mother's other side, where Becca was standing. Suddenly she cried out as blood ran down her leg. She stared, and collapsed. Becca bent and whispered. She nodded and began to cry softly.

"Oh dear, just look at that mess!" Doris said and jumped up.

"Mrs. Taylor, get me some towels and then call your doctor or the Emergency Room," Becca said.

George said, "Stay where you are, Dorrie. And you siddown, Miz Holdridge. I'll take care a my own kid." He bent over his daughter.

"Mama! Help me!" she moaned, twisting away, but Doris Taylor said "Not now" and fetched a bucket from under the sink. Over the splash of the water came the sound of her humming.

"Just keep away," Becca told George and began searching for towels. Finding them in one of the many drawers, she took out several and handed them to the girl. "Merran, I think we'd better get her out of here. This isn't ordinary bleeding. I don't know, there might be internal injuries. But even if it's just stress, if this keeps up she could easily go into shock."

"Stay where you are, Doc, or I'll—"

Merran got up and began to edge past Ben. "Or you'll what, shoot us? And when? Before or after your child bleeds to death? You stupid bastard, don't you realize that if you keep this up, you may never see her again! Never! Is that what you want?"

"God damn you, I told you to stay outa my business—"

A noxious odor and a deafening noise filled the room, the noise bouncing off the metal cabinets, swirling around, enlarging in the dining alcove, enclosing them. Only tardily did Ben realize that Merran had fallen behind him and was sliding down the wall to the floor.

Connie was nowhere to be seen.

"Merran! Darling!" Becca cried, trying to reach him but blocked by Doris sponging the floor in wide sweeps and by Joy lying in her blood.

Whimpering, the girl crept away on hands and knees like a wounded animal seeking cover, leaving a bloody trail.

Ben stretched out a long leg and retrieved his crutch. Between him and George was nothing taller than the teapot. He raised the crutch and launched it like a lance just as Becca, trying to reach Merran, stumbled over his jacket and knocked him off balance. His only weapon clattered impotently onto the table. His hand shot out to it.

George was faster. He knocked it off, stood up, and kicked, and a horrified Ben saw it slide the length of the room toward the back door. Almost simultaneously George gave Ben's forearm a numbing crack with the heel of his gun hand.

Once again deafening reverberations filled the room. This time the bullet lodged in the ceiling, and George sat down in a daze as if the noise had pushed him down. Plaster dust misted onto the bread and butter.

"Oh god!" Becca said over the unconscious Merran.

Doris got up from the floor; poured tea; said, "Here, dear."

Slowly awareness came back into his eyes. He regarded his wife with hatred and disgust and backhanded the cup off the table. "There, you bitch. There's something else to clean up! Bitch. You ruined my life. From the beginning you lied. All these years you cheated me. You—"

Ben watched index finger curl trembling around trigger, and stopped breathing.

The back door opened, and from the little vestibule the junior George said, "Hey, Pop, you're back! Cool, man. What's with the crutch? Somebody break a leg? Hey, Pop, guess what! Coach put me on the first team."

Sound of wet shoes being kicked off.

"We play Mansfield tomorrow, Pop, and maybe you can—"

The boy came eagerly into the kitchen, snow-wet jacket hanging from one shoulder, crutch in one meaty hand. He stopped short at the sight of his father leveling a gun at his mother's chest.

"Gee, Pop, where'd you get the gun? Hi, Mama, what's for snack—tea? Nah, better have milk, gotta build myself up for the team. We got 'ny milk? Oh, hi, Dr. Louis. This yours?"

He was so dense, so stupid, so utterly self-involved that even George gaped at him and the gun turned its eye to the floor.

Ben took back his crutch (Once more unto the breach, my hero! Jane would have said) and swung up and over, aiming for the side of George's head. But he swung too wide, and the crutch tip caught under the boy's jacket.

"What the hell—!" Ben shouted as George grabbed the crutch tip and yanked hard.

But despite his surprise Ben had a two-handed grip and, just as he had done several days ago with another lunatic, yanked harder. Very suddenly he won.

Once again certain immutable laws of physics prevailed, causing two skulls to hit two walls simultaneously. In accordance with those laws, Ben's wall provided the greater impact. But George's wall sent him sliding forward off the bench, whereby the bones below his knees received such a tremendous shock from the knife-sharp edge of the table's stretcher that his arms flew up over his head.

Another ear-splitting noise, and another bullet into the ceiling.

Doris Taylor flapped her napkin at the plaster dust powdering down. "Oh dear," she said, "oh my, just look at that mess!" She got up and began clearing the table.

Ben, only slightly disoriented, was on his feet now. "Out," he said to the boy, who had just taken in the fact of Becca and Merran. "Out!" he said again. The boy looked at him dully. "You hear me? I said *out!* Take your mother upstairs—you have a phone in your room?—and call the police emergency number. Nine-one-one. You understand? Take your mother upstairs, she's very upset and tired, and call nine-one-one and report a gunshot wound and say we need an ambulance. Got that? *Now.*"

As he spoke he kept his eye on George and waited, looking entirely poised, for George to collect himself and crawl out from under the table.

Ben smiled. It was going to be much easier, more accurate, certainly more discreditable, and infinitely more satisfying to render the bastard *hors de combat* with a kick to the jaw while he was still down.

For once ignoring the canons, Ben did.

It was George's turn to look into the barrel of the gun.

Ben said, "We have to talk," and remembered when he had last said this, and to whom, and the outpouring it had occasioned.

Neither he nor George noticed Connie emerge from the broom closet near the back door, one hand behind her back.

"I don't have to talk to you or anybody else," George snarled.

"I have news for you." Ben braced himself against the noise and put a bullet into the fine vinyl floor, one inch away from George's right boot heel, and outside. "I can get closer than that," he said (Better cross your fingers that you don't, Jane would have said) when the noise had died away. "And claim self-defense or defense of my friends without even trying. Now, talk."

"About what?" George said, less confidently.

"About murder. About John Chester." No answer being forthcoming, he put a bullet well above the left foot and perilously close to the inseam.

George's hand went to his crotch. He licked his lips. His

eyes darted. "Can't tell you a thing about John. I went over after supper to get the money he owed me. Took my kid. He and somebody else were arguing. I never went in. We went home. That was that. I told MacWhirter a hundred times."

"If you told him the truth, you'd only have to tell him once."

"It was the truth! Connie'd tell you if she could talk. It is the truth!"

"It's a lie," Connie whispered, coming up behind her father. "A lie. You went out again, but you stayed home till you thought we were all asleep. I heard you talking to Mrs. Chester *before* we went out. I heard what she said. 'He's on the floor, he's knocked out cold. Now's the time to finish him,' she said. 'I'll do some yelling when you and Connie come. The kids won't hear anything tonight,' she said. You said, 'Okay, sweets, I'll be right there. With my witness. Hold the fort.' That's what you said. I listen to you all the time. I just pick up the extension. I can do it real quiet."

Ben said gently, "You must have been very unhappy, knowing all that. Why didn't you tell Dr. Shaw? Or Miss Holdridge? They're your friends, Connie. You know that."

"Yes. I know."

What was the next question? What would Merran ask her, if he could? What would anyone ask her now? What did the police want to know?

The answer to one more question: Why was John's body left in the storeroom?

It was a dreadful question to ask a ten-year-old. Ben had to ask it.

"Because somebody came to the shop late. I don't know who," the child said. "After work. To buy something. *He* got scared and came home. I heard them talking about her later on the phone. Mrs. Chester said she could've killed her for interrupting."

"And then it was too late to move him? Because your father didn't go back before I found Mr. Chester, I mean?"

She nodded.

"Still, why did you wait? It must have been harder and harder for you, Connie. What were you waiting for?"

"For the right time," she said hoarsely, tears spilling down her cheeks. "When I could help Joy some way. I waited too long. She went away, and then he went after her, and he hurt her, he hurt her real bad, like he hurt me a long time ago and made me stop talking if I told. Now she'll die or she'll never come back, and they won't let me go with her, and my throat hurts and I hate him!"

Crying, "Hatehimhatehim*hatehim!*" she sprang at George with the small lemon-cutting knife in her hand and stabbed him in the chest two or three times before Ben could stop her.

And then MacWhirter arrived, puffing and purple-faced, with a shamefaced Sergeant Dave Bates in tow holding his gun in his left hand because his right wrist hurt. Should he have had to shoot somebody, he couldn't have hit the side of a barn.

Later MacWhirter said to Ben, "Making provision for Nora Chester's kids after we took her in was rotten enough, or I'd've had a field day watching her squirm after she'd played it cute for so long—and boy! did she ever crack fast when we brought in that late shopper Gerry Carr who had to buy a jogging suit after suffering through a night of PTA. Nice lady. My older kid had her when she taught in your school, Ben, remember? But anyway, at least Nora had some concern for her kids, including who's gonna have them for the next few years.

"But the rottenest part of this whole dirty business was after Jane drove you and Miz Bec home in your snazzy car. We had to tell Doris Taylor what the kid said and did—and incidentally George was only scratched through that denim he's so crazy about, those pearly snaps saved the bastard's skin—and you know what the Missus did? Hauled off and planted a haymaker on that poor little kid like you wouldn't believe. Knocked her right off her feet. For talking. For telling the truth. For upsetting her big beautiful applecart. I ask you!

"Then she took off her apron and went around dusting with it and humming. But when the DA lays a charge on her for a few things like suppressing evidence—oh yeah, she knew all about George! And mind you! It was the strain of trying to overlook murder that unstrung her, not the rape of her daughter—both daughters, ackshally! Well, when she has to go into court, she'll snap to fast enough."

"Or not," Ben said presciently.

When Merran emerged from that delicious preoccupation with self that most recovering patients relinquish almost unwillingly, he supported Ben's recommendation that the three Taylor children, who were presently staying with Becca, live permanently with their paternal aunt in the State of Washington.

Because events had proved, of course, that Ben was right.

▽

TWENTY-SIX

"SHOULDN'T WANT TO DO this again," the doctor said, applying the finishing touches to the bandaging of Merran's chest, the tinge of satisfaction in his dry voice suggesting that Merran had achieved something since being born that was worth bothering him about. "Wants mending. Restraint in"—with a flickering glance in Becca's direction—"everything for a while. See Sydney for physical therapy. She's a third your size but three times stronger. Then go somewhere else."

His stern thin Yankee lips moving in the faintest suggestion of a smile, he nodded and was gone. As were, magically, all the bits and pieces he had used to dress the wound.

Becca laughed as she helped Merran with his shirt.

"There's nobody else like him. And nobody works the way he docs. I bet you didn't bleed one drop when he operated." She paused, a hand on his shoulder. "He's right, you know, Merran. It is time to go. I won't approach Juilliard again, of course—I'll find something around here, preferably in Boston—but my resignation stands even if the committee is taking you back unconditionally."

"And may name the middle school after me."

"That's what I mean! With all due respect, darling, who

wants to work for people as stupid as they are? It isn't Ben they've made a hero of, it's you."

"Well, sure. He was here only once. It's the third time for me. Nothing like a shooting, my girl. Drama's what counts. Now kiss the hero. It speeds recovery."

"Poison ivy is hardly heroic."

"I suppose a dog bite is? Name me one person who doesn't think a dog bite is due to somebody harassing the animal."

"Well, I—"

"You're saying you don't want me to get better."

"But—"

"You enjoy seeing me weak and in pain."

"Well, hardly that, darling, but—"

"You feel that our heroic supersleuth is worthier of kissing."

"Yes I do," she said, "but not by me," and laughed richly as her lips touched his.

Ben would probably have agreed with her. Jane would not. At that very moment she was saying, "Ben, do you realize what an idiot you were, messing with an armed lunatic with a temper like a rocket? My god, even Doris might have jumped you in defense of her turf. Now I'm telling you something. If you ever pull a damfool stunt like that again, I'll destroy you."

"Hey, what kind of guy do you think you're married to?" Disarming her with a smile, he grabbed her wrists. "Now hear this, it's peculiarly apposite. 'Cowards die many times before their deaths; the valiant never taste of death but once.' That's part of how Uncle Bill lets Julius Caesar straighten out Calpurnia's thinking. Have I made my point? Fine. I'm ready to accept a statement, a token, whatever, of your trust and goodwill."

She prodded his shin with the tip of her shoe. "How would you like a swift kick right about there?"

"It'd be authentic, at least. Fire away."

"Ben, really! I mean really! I could—!"

He grinned and backed off, hands up in surrender. Laughing, she put her arms around his neck.

The front doorbell rang.

"Hell with 'em," she said and kissed him soundly. "That's my statement. Go see who's at the door and then we'll have some cake and coffee."

The caller was Marty Guinness, his hair modishly trimmed, his earring gone. He was wearing gray flannel slacks under a short camel's hair coat, and he had swept snow off the steps with the edge of a pricey RocSport.

"Hi, Marty. What's up? You've undergone quite a sea change," Ben said.

"Yeah, well, I just might not get to cast off, if you don't mind me getting into your act, Dr. Louis. I was at BU, checking out that CBE program—you know, for dropouts with promise, which I've come to believe I have. Would you be willing to write me a reference? Great! This is why . . .

"No, thanks, I won't come in. Gotta lot to do. My father kicked me out when I told him I was going to get my BA and then study law. Gonna bunk in with Whit awhile. See yuh!"

Ben said, around a piece of Jane's chocolate cake, "It was his father's treatment of Merran and me. He's been reading law with Guy, both of which he characterized as noble. Guy'll be a great mentor." He laughed. "The kid heard his father say to his mother that if they didn't do something real quick, McKay was gonna sue their asses off just like in East Lyme, Connecticut. He's smart, Jane. He'll do well. He informed me that the law's very plain about the duties of school committees re executive sessions and due process, so what are these jokers trying to pull off?"

"Think Garth would take him in when he comes home after New Year's? It'd be good for both of them." She stirred restlessly; put down her cup. "But it'll be hard, Ben, on his own through undergraduate school and law school."

She was saying that even if Ben paid for all of it out of the property he was soon to receive, he would still have an appalling amount left: appalling, because most school people are uneasy about money in large amounts. They are not used to it, and they have anyway come to suspect that what the enemies of public education keep drumming into them and everybody else may be true: that only three kinds of people merit a professional wage—people who can, and do; really *useful* people; and people who are too proud to batten—like teachers and other parasites—on the public treasury.

"I hear you, darling," he said. "And we'll work something out."

With this his conscience shook off some of its burden. Which was helpful, since it was still wrestling with the infinitely more difficult question, to be or not to be a public school administrator for the duration.

He was filling the Camry's gas tank in preparation for next day's trip when a superb maroon Mercedes 600 glided up behind him. Its horn tooted the equivalent of a rude tap on his shoulder.

"Glad I happened to catch you, Louis," Martin Guinness Senior said. He interrupted himself to scrutinize the Camry. "Heard about your accident. Too bad you got yourself stuck with another used car. Kind of a washed-out color, wouldn't you say? Ought to have it repainted.

"Well now, guess you're anxious to hear what the Committee voted last night—naturally you'll have a confirming letter in a day or so with all the details spelled out. You were voted in as superintendent—which means you can drop the suit now, right?—as of the first of July, by six to one. I was the dissenting vote, but you can't win 'em all. With a one-year contract, a reasonable increase in salary though not as much as we're paying the Super now, of course, a review twice yearly the first year, and no more history lectures unless I review the script first.

"Doubt you'll have time for any of that stuff anyway, we'll be keeping you plenty busy. I may say I was against the lectures *period*, but since I'll be the watchdog around here, I'm not too worried, although it'll be a lot more work for me."

He looked not at all worried but rather like a carnivore eyeing with grim glee the victim in its talons.

Ben took his time seating himself behind the wheel, and in that little interval a few things became crystal clear.

He lowered the window and smiled pleasantly. "I don't want you to worry at all, Mr. Guinness, or have all that extra work, so I'm resigning at the end of the school year and taking a job elsewhere. You'll have my confirming letter in the mail. Naturally. And Dr. Shaw and I aren't dropping our suits, the matter's much too serious for a good citizen to walk away from. You and your colleagues are about to be impeached, Mr. Guinness.

"Okay then? Glad I bumped into you. Have a good one!"

He rolled up the window, switched on the ignition, and left Guinness gaping, baffled, furious, and very worried indeed.

Ben's conscience remained serene, or perhaps it was only unconscious, until the following morning when he and Jane and Digby, Becca and Merran and Fee, headed for the other side of the commonwealth to the estate that would be permanently called Thornwood, no one having come up with anything better.

During their rare times away, the Louises went to Maine, whose grim aspects their vacationing eye either viewed as quaint or simply overlooked (because only social scientists can afford to pay to be depressed, Jane would have said). The Berkshire hill country, where twenty-odd years ago they had spent their last vacation alone, they remembered as gentler, richer, slower-paced, its beauty more continuous if more enclosed than Maine's, in fact rather like Manton's historic district spread over many more square miles. So Ben wondered uneasily, as he paid the toll at Lee and left the Pike, whether anything had changed.

But despite the garlands of Christmas lights, the red ribbon bows, the festoons of laurel, the sparkling snow that covered the green lawns of summer and narrowed the roads, everything seemed the same, giving him the odd certainty that somewhere among the holiday crowd the young Ben was holding a not yet pregnant Jane by her slim strong eager hand. The Camry steered of itself through a haze of nostalgia that was piercingly sweet, acutely painful; in short, indescribable.

"Ben," Jane said, "would you kindly pay attention to the road? You look like an owl the way your head's swiveling around and around. We aren't there yet. We still have about four miles to go. Trust me."

"There's a driveway on the right," she said several minutes later. "Just past—oh there! The stone pillar with the lion! What do you bet Rob exchanges it for a nice round sphere signifying integrity, wholeness."

"Oh I don't know," Merran said lazily. "Nothing wrong with a symbol of strength and aggressiveness for the kids who're going to come here."

A sign saying Thornwood hung like a bib from the neck of the tranquil creature resting head on paws and looking as if it never did anything more aggressive than eat itself stuporous.

Smiling, Ben turned in around it and drove slowly along a road that wound suspensefully, promisingly, between fine old oaks and ended at a snow-covered island encircled by a sweeping driveway. In the middle of the island stood a snowman wearing a jauntily tipped bowler and leaning on a gold-headed cane (its tip carefully protected by a plastic baggie). Beyond this stood a replica of a Tudor manor house, a massive yet graceful pile of sandstone blocks and red brick.

Do I deserve this? Ben thought.

As if in answer the great paneled oak door swung in, and Robertson Hartley-Jones emerged smiling, arms outstretched.

"Welcome," he called out, coming down the steps. "And well done! You're just in time for tea."